S J Burnham lives in a rural area called Ballygrangee, in County Down, Northern Ireland. He lives there with his wife, Lorna, and their three children, Reuben, Bradley and Tolole. At present, he is the Ireland Coordinator for an international charity as well as a lecturer in a local college. Together, Burnham and his family enjoy getting involved in the life of the Church they attend as well as exploring and enjoying as much of Ireland and Great Britain as they can.

For the love of my life, Lorna.

S J Burnham

SEND THE HEALER

AUSTIN MACAULEY PUBLISHERS

LONDON * CAMBRIDGE * NEW YORK * SHARJAH

A CIP catalogue record for this title is available from the British Library.

ISBN 9781398437296 (Paperback)
ISBN 9781398437302 (ePub e-book)

www.austinmacauley.com

First Published 2022
Austin Macauley Publishers Ltd®
1 Canada Square
Canary Wharf
London
E14 5AA

Thank you to my closest friends, my dad, Thomas, Dorothy, Paul, David and Evan, who have never failed to encourage me during my writing.

A special thank you to Scott, who helped me with some research.

Finally, a big thank you to the fantastic team at Austin Macauley Publishers.

Chapter 1
The Beginning

The door was in front of him. It was time. He could feel his fingertips tingling with the anticipation of what was about to begin. He opened the door and stepped out into the street. The door crashed closed behind him as it normally did, and just for a few seconds he paused to adjust his senses to the city noise. The traffic that never stopped was moving slowly in front of him and the smell of the exhaust fumes filled his nose. So many people in this big city of London, but only he knew what was coming. The time for contemplation was over and he started walking along the pavement. It wasn't far to the bus stop and thankfully not far to his destination. He hopped off the bus with his usual sense of optimism and strode purposefully through the big front doors of the huge city centre building, known as St Mary's. As soon as he entered the main foyer he was met with a different kind of traffic. People walking in straight lines, this way and that, all of them clearly with a specific job in mind. Some had the usual stethoscopes hung around their necks, just to make sure people knew who they were, while others wore all kinds of different tops. The nurses in their familiar blue uniforms, the porters in their maroon shirts and everyone else in a different shirt or blouse to denote their role in this branch of the National Health Service.

He had only just taken stock of this busyness in the foyer when there was a familiar pat on his back. 'Come on, Ben, look lively, this place doesn't run itself ya know!' He had barely taken the words of exhortation in when the giant frame of Eddie blew past him. Eddie looked over his shoulder at him with his playful grin and kept walking. It was just the invitation that he needed, and without a moment's hesitation he smiled at the bald head that had now turned away and started after him. He had known Eddie for a couple of years now. When he started working at St Mary's, it was Eddie who showed him the ropes, just as he had done for many others before him. He knew so much about the hospital and the staff; it was almost as if the place did depend on Eddie to run it!

It took a while to catch up with his friend, due to his much larger strides, but when he did, they were both going through the door into the staff room at the same time. After the busy streets and busy foyer, the staff room was a change of pace. All of a sudden, life slowed down as he entered a familiar space. The polished concrete of the foyer became the cheap laminate of the mini kitchen part of the room. At the other end of the room was a red carpeted area with a big TV in the corner. The glow from the screen was exerting its hypnotic power over a dozen or more people who were slumped in their seats, waiting for the caffeine to kick in!

At the kitchen end of the room there were a few lockers on the left and on the right, there was a small sink with some bench space; enough room for a kettle, a microwave and a coffee machine. Standing at the bench was a familiar blue uniform. It was the unmistakable maternal presence of Enid, more commonly known as 'mama' because of her mothering nature. As usual she was busy slicing and buttering some homemade scones that had been freshly baked earlier in the morning. This was a daily source of delight for Eddie who never failed to make his pleasure known!

'Oh, Mama, that smells delicious!' he declared as he opened his locker and flung in his bag! Enid's back straightened a little as she put the last lick of butter on the scones. She didn't do it for the praise, but Eddie's compliments clearly raised a smile on her face. She swung round with plate in hand, licking some butter off her thumb. As she set the plate in the middle of the small kitchen table, she gave the usual instruction; 'now eat them quickly before they get cold! They always taste better when they are still warm!'

Ben automatically made a beeline for the table and grabbed the first one. As soon as he had his prize in hand, he collapsed backwards into the soft seat in the corner and grabbed one of his books that were piled up on the ground beside him. He opened up the book that he had lifted and looked into it, as if to start reading. But reading the next chapter of his many loans from the library was not on his mind that day. Instead, he was consumed with the thoughts of his new purpose; a purpose that would change his life and the life of those around him forever. Today was the day! He was looking forward to getting started! But as the excitement of this new venture started to get his heart pumping, he couldn't help but look up at the familiar faces around him. How would the coming events affect

Enid; now busy gathering cups from the cupboard? What would Eddie think of this new aspect of his character. Would he be the same friend that he had been in the past? Everything would change, that was for sure! But he could not let the unknown hold him back from his mission. He was committed to the path ahead of him and he had to follow it to the end!

As his hand automatically lifted the scone to his mouth for another bite, his thoughts settled on the open book in front of him. It was a book that was simply entitled, *The Heart*, an introductory text book that was designed to give first year medical students a good grounding in all things cardiac. It was a hobby of his to get an insight into the conditions that were being treated in whatever ward he was assigned to. At the moment, he was working in the cardiac wards, and therefore it was the workings and pathology of the heart that he was interested in.

He had barely found his place, when, all of a sudden, the door swung open and in rushed Mo! Wearing his familiar green Pakistan cricket zip hoodie, he breezed across the kitchen space to the table, whipped out a chair and plonked himself and his bag down. The beads of sweat were dotted all over his light brown skin and he sighed with the relief of a man who had just finished a race. 'Well, well, look what the cat dragged in! exclaimed Eddie with his hands on his hips and a wry grin on his face. 'Mo, my friend, you have got to get yourself going earlier in the morning! This mad rushin' of yours ain't gonna do your blood pressure any good, mate!'

'I know, I know!' sighed Mo. 'But what can I do? This baby won't stop crying all night and then in the morning Ayesha wants help getting the two girls up! It's crazy!'

Eddie's deep laugh suddenly boomed around the room! 'Oh dear, oh dear, listen to the woes of the modern dad!'

'That's right!' Mo retorted quickly, seemingly with his breath back now. 'You should be showing me great sympathy! Old men like you don't know what it's like for young men like me!' Mo always liked to get a little dig in at Eddie about his age and immediately flashed a quick smirk as he finished delivering it.

'Now, now,' said Enid as she put her hand on Mo's shoulder, 'you've done very well, young man! Just catch your breath and have a scone; you need to keep your strength up, you young dads!'

Mo instinctively put his hand on top of the hand on his shoulder and looked round at Enid with a smile. 'Thanks, Mama!' he said. 'I really shouldn't, but I'll

11

just take one!' And with that, he promptly took one in each hand and started eating hungrily.

With Mo now settled at the table, Enid returned to the kitchen and started to make the coffee. 'Are there enough pods for the machine, Mama?' came the enquiry from Eddie, who was still at his locker.

'Yes, but just for the next couple of days!' Enid responded with a quick glance in Eddie's direction. Eddie was always keen to keep on top of the rota for who was due to contribute pods for the coffee machine.

'So, who's next for bringing in more?' inquired Eddie in a general address to the room?

'That'll be me!' came the voice from the corner. 'I'll have them in tomorrow, Eddie,' Ben chirped from behind his book.

'Good man, Ben! Good man!' Eddie bellowed. Satisfied with the update on the rota, Eddie went back to his locker and Enid put the two fresh cups of coffee on the table for whoever lifted them first.

Having wolfed down the scones that he had in both hands, Mo was the first to lift one of the cups and was about to take the first sip when something clearly caught his attention. 'Oh, come on, Eddie, we do not want to see that at this time of the morning; or at any time, come to think of it!' The momentarily topless Eddie turned in the direction of the protest with a laugh.

'What's the matter, Mo, feeling a little inadequate?' It was no secret that Eddie was bit of a fitness freak, and even at the age of 50 he still had a very muscular frame; something which he wasn't shy about showing off while changing into his work shirt.

'Not feeling inadequate, my friend, just a little nauseous! And why are you keeping your body all pumped up like that anyway? Shouldn't a man of your age be taking it easy?' This was the second age reference of the morning, a fact that Mo was very proud of!

Unperturbed by the second dig at his age, Eddie casually turned to the quiet corner. 'Ben, tell him!'

'Oh, here we go,' sighed Mo.

'Yes, you're absolutely right Eddie,' said Ben, lifting his head sharply from his book. 'There is no reason that older men cannot continue to maintain a high muscle mass. In fact, it has been proven to provide a wide range of health benefits that last into old age.'

'Well, thank you, professor!' said Mo sarcastically.

'You're welcome,' Ben chirped, with his head descending back into the book in his hands.

At that moment, the door into the staff room swung open and a spritely elderly lady in a grey skirt and white blouse put one foot into the room. 'OK, folks, let's get cracking!' The, soon to retire, duty manager, Madge was always on time to get the staff moving.

'Yes, Madge, we're all ready,' piped Eddie as he straightened his maroon tunic. And with that, Madge was gone like a morning mist, leaving the door purposefully open. 'OK, everyone, you heard the lady, let's go!' Eddie barked. From his slumped position, Mo gave a comical salute and dragged himself to his feet. Enid tidied up the remaining scones into a tub and put them in the cupboard; at which point, they all began to file out to their various work stations. 'Come on professor, let's go' said Eddie as he strode past Ben. With the rest of them making their way out the door, Ben put his book to one side and leaned forward in his chair. The chatter of the staff room had been a pleasant distraction, but now the time had actually come. He was about to do what he had been sent to do; to change things forever. And with that thought, he walked out of the staff room and towards the place where it was all going to happen.

Chapter 2
The First Attempt

The cardiac ward was on the second floor of the hospital and, as was his custom, Ben opened the door to the stairwell rather than take the lift. As he bounded up the stairs, he passed the usual cluster of nursing students, all huddled round their smart phones, giggling about the latest Instagram posts from the weekend. Within a few seconds, he was on the second floor and looking directly at the entrance to the ward. It had a giant blue plastic sign stuck on the wall above the double doors, stating that this was ward number 5, and below was the one-word addition, 'Cardiac.' In the opposite direction was ward number 6 which was an assessment ward, and in between the two entrances were the doors to the lifts. Without a moment's hesitation and with a bounce in his step, he walked through the doors and into the ward. Once in the ward, he was greeted with a flurry of activity. The kitchen and dining staff were busy collecting the empty plates and bowls from the patients after their breakfast, the auxiliary nurses and staff nurses were in the process of making beds and in the midst of it all, the doctors were preparing to do their rounds.

It was always interesting to observe this preparation for the ward rounds because it made the pecking order of authority very clear. In the centre of this huddle of stethoscopes was the very distinctive figure of the consultant, Dr Pujara. He was a relatively tall man, about six foot or thereabouts. He had a thick covering of black hair on his head, although there was clearly a receding hairline; and across his top lip, he was sporting the most amazing thick moustache that Ben had ever seen. This moustache never ceased to impress and had actually prompted him to make a couple of attempts at growing one himself. However, the sound of Mo laughing at it was still loud enough in his memory to prevent any attempt in the future. He said that it looked like something had crawled across his lip and died!

Shaking himself out of that painful memory, he then looked at the inner circle that surrounded the king of the jungle. These were the registrars who were one step below the level of consultant. Dr Pujara seemed to be talking mainly to them and every now and again they were nodding in agreement, assenting to the words of their master. Then on the outer edge of this gathering were the junior doctors. Much younger than the rest, they were waiting like mice to pick up any crumbs of wisdom that might fall from the master's lips. As soon as Dr Pujara said anything at all, their heads immediately went down to their notepads and they began writing furiously so that nothing was missed. In his role as porter, there wasn't much that he could do at this point apart from wait around. Until the orders of the day were passed down the chain of command, he just had to stand there and look available. It was a bit boring, but he didn't mind because it gave him an opportunity to see who was on the ward and maybe even say 'hello' to a few patients. It was mostly men, as usual, on the cardiac ward and as he looked around the bay ward in front of him, he saw a couple of familiar faces whom he had spoken to during the previous week. They looked up and waved at him and he subtly waved back so as not to draw attention to himself. These men were mostly in their sixties and seventies, although there was one much younger man on the ward who looked strangely out of place.

However, none of these men were the focus of his thoughts this morning. No, instead, he was thinking about one individual in particular who was in one of the side wards, a little further down the corridor. The side wards were individual rooms for patients who were generally weaker than the patients in the bay wards. That was certainly the case for the patient in Side Ward 1. He had been in the cardiac ward for a couple of weeks now and during that time, he had seen him get steadily weaker and weaker. He wasn't sure what exactly was wrong with this man, but given the ward that he was on, it seemed that his heart was gradually failing. He had never seen any people go into visit him, and perhaps it was for that reason that he had decided to start with him. The man who was getting the least love would now get the most.

Just as he was focussing his mind on what he was there to do that day, his concentration was interrupted by the dispersal of the doctors from their little meeting. As they dispersed in different directions, Dr Pujara remained where he was and in the absence of the cluster of staff around him, Ben could now see a slender figure fixed at his side. She was dressed in the red uniform of a ward sister, her jet-black hair was tied tightly back into a short ponytail and she was standing ram-rod straight, like a sergeant on parade. Sister Montgomery was certainly an imposing figure; however, her appearance was nothing compared to her tongue! She liked to run a tight ship and was very quick to let you know it. She would bark out orders at everyone, no matter how far away they were on the ward; and if you didn't do as you were told then you could expect the sort of tongue lashing that would reduce a grown man to tears. This threat hung over all the staff on the ward and even rubbed off on some of the patients. There was one time that a trainee nurse was taking a patient's temperature with an ear thermometer and while she was doing it, Sister Montgomery barked at her so loudly that she nearly pushed the thermometer through the poor man's head and out the other ear!

Ben was fairly new to the cardiac ward, but he already knew to keep his distance. However, as was mentioned earlier, even distance wasn't enough! 'Porter!' came the harsh voice like a gust of cold wind. He instinctively jolted himself upright, having been leaning against the wall. Sister Montgomery had her eyes firmly fixed on him with a hard stare; her bony finger pointing commandingly to the floor in front of her.

He quickly marched over to the spot that he was being summoned to. 'Yes, sister,' he said.

'I want you to take all the bloods that are being taken this morning down to the labs, and once you've done that, I want another wheel chair up here; the other one's gone missing! Are we clear? Good. Get on with it!' And with that abrupt final instruction, Sister Montgomery took a sharp intake of breath from her inhaler and then quickly turned on her heels to make her way to the sister's station. There was some element of her strong Scottish accent that made Sister Montgomery's words distinctly aggressive. Perhaps she was conscious of this effect and purposefully made use of it, but whether she did or she didn't, he knew not to hang around, and so he made his way into bay one where the nurses were already busy taking the relevant blood samples from each patient.

Safely out from under the gaze of sister sergeant major, and with a moment to wait while the blood samples were being taken, he couldn't help but notice the door to Side Ward 1 across the hall. Once again, he could feel his fingers tingling as he rubbed them against each other. The anticipation was building in his mind now and his heart began to race. It would have been wiser to wait until the ward was quieter, but there was an opportunity now! As each second passed, the pressure of excitement and anticipation kept on building to the point that it was unbearable. The door of the side ward was calling to him louder and louder and eventually he cracked! It really is time, he thought. It is time to begin the work that would turn this hospital upside down. With the decision made, he gave a quick glance around to check that the coast was clear and then he took several quick and large strides which brought him quickly to the door of the side ward. He paused one last time to look around him, and with that, he opened the door and went into the room.

Once inside, he could see the forlorn and frail figure of Mr James lying on the bed with the oxygen mask covering his nose and mouth. His breathing was laboured and, at times sudden, like a man gasping for air after being under water. It was a terrible sight and would have been very traumatic to witness for any loved ones who came to visit. Perhaps there was some small mercy in that no-one did. At least this suffering was, therefore, limited to one person. After a couple of seconds to gather his wits, Ben slowly approached the bed. He walked around to the left side of the bed until he was standing right over Mr James. The grey hairs were almost matted to his face; the grey stubble around his chin and jaw had now grown to about a couple of millimetres. It really did give him the look of a man whom the world had forgotten about; a man who no longer mattered. But now he had been sent to show that Mr James had not been forgotten; to show that his life and the lives of many others could be changed. The moment had arrived! He slowly raised his hands to perform the act. He knew what he was going to do, but for a moment, he felt a little disorientated. His hands hovered over Mr James for a second and then he chose his spot. In that moment, his hands began their slow descent onto the chest of the patient. His eyes quickly flitted between Mr James' face and his chest. Was it going to be dramatic or subdued, loud or quiet? What would the doctors say? What would the nurses say? What would…

'What do you think you are doing?' A voice like the screech of lightning suddenly struck him from the open doorway. He instinctively drew his hands sharply back to his own chest and looked to the doorway with dreaded expectancy. With her hands fixed firmly on her hips, there stood Sister Montgomery. She had a face like thunder and was already leaning forward, ready to strike lightning bolts in his direction! 'Are you a doctor? Are you a nurse? Are you a relative?' She was just getting started and he already felt the size of a mouse.

'No, no, no!'

She continued. 'You are a porter! Do you hear me? A porter! And that means that you do what you're told and you go where you're told! And you most certainly do not put your stinkin' mits on one of my patients! Do you understand me?' He paused in a moment of awkward silence. He wanted to make sure that he wasn't going to interrupt her, which could have been a fatal mistake at this point. 'Well?' she demanded aggressively!

'Yes, Sister Montgomery,' he replied sheepishly.

'Well, don't just stand there, then! Get out of this room and go and do what you were told to do!' He gingerly stepped round the bed and made his way towards the intimidating figure who was still standing in the doorway. The sense of humiliation seemed to intensify with every step he took in her direction and just when it seemed that he was going to have to stop, she took a small step back to let him past. He quickly side-stepped round her burning gaze and headed out into the hall way as quickly as he could. But just when he thought he was out of danger, one final bolt of lightning came from behind him. 'And don't let me catch you near any of my patients again!' His shoulders automatically tensed up as if he had been hit over the head from behind. Everyone in the hall way and even the patients in the bay wards momentarily stopped and looked in his direction. They all shared the same look. It was a look of shared embarrassment and pity at the same time. Quickly, they all looked away in a collective effort to bring the awkward moment to a close. As he stood there awkwardly for a couple of seconds, he urgently scanned the hallway for the pile of blood samples. As soon as he spotted them on a nearby desk, he swooped on them as quickly as he could and made a bee line out of the ward and went straight for the stairwell.

Once in the stairwell, and safely out of sight, he leaned his back against the cool concrete wall and breathed a deep sigh. He could feel the blood pumping in his face because of the embarrassment he had just endured. But after a few seconds of feeling relieved, that feeling was replaced with a sense of anger. How could he have been so foolish? Making the dash for the side ward was bad enough, but then leaving the door open behind him was just asking for trouble. He felt so stupid! Here he was, on this day of all days, trying to do something powerful, something that would change the world, and instead he ends up behaving like an impulsive school boy! And with that thought, he pushed himself off the wall and hurried down the stairs. If he was too stupid to do something powerful, then at least he could satisfy himself by doing something simple. This burning sense of self-recrimination kept him going for the rest of the morning.

He blocked out all other thoughts from his mind and simply concentrated on the portering duties that he had been given.

Chapter 3
Down to Earth

After rushing around the hospital and going up and down the stairs for about three solid hours, which included skipping his tea break at 10:30, he eventually began to slow down. His last job before lunch was to go to the children's wards to pick up more samples for the lab. Actually, he volunteered to do it because it meant that he didn't have to go back to the cardiac ward and risk another encounter with the dreaded sister. It was on his way to the children's wards when he noticed that his aggressive stride had become a casual stroll. The adrenaline that was in generous supply after his humiliation earlier that day was beginning to wear off. However, he was still angry with himself and it was because of that anger that he was still not ready to think about the main purpose of the day. The daily duties were just about all that he could cope with right now. In order to help with this mental detachment from his mission, he began to concentrate on his surroundings. He was now in the corridor that led to the children's wards. As he progressed down the corridor, there was an increasing frequency of colour and decoration on the walls. The usual pasty shade of grey became a bright sunny yellow and on top of that bright yellow were a number of cartoon animals and Disney characters. He wasn't sure how much this decor helped the sick children who came to these wards, but just for the moment, that little bit of bright colour was helping to lift his mood.

He pushed his way through the heavy yellow swing doors and into the paediatric department. Once through the doors, he was faced with a choice. He could follow on through the doors in front of him which led to the critical care unit or he could go up one flight of stairs to another paediatric unit and up another flight of stairs to yet another. Thankfully for his legs, which were beginning to tire now, all the samples for testing were left at the nurses' station in the critical care ward. Thankful for this small mercy, he pressed the security buzzer on the wall which was followed by a small click and as if by magic, the doors automatically opened up in front of him. He walked through the open doorway and expected to walk straight over to the nurses' station when something caught his eye. There was a familiar hat being worn by a man sitting on a chair outside one of the side wards. It was one of those American football team caps that had become very popular in recent times. However, this particular cap was even more familiar to him because he had seen it on a regular basis in his apartment building. As he paused for a closer look, he suddenly realised that the head that was bowed beneath this cap was that of his neighbour Jeff. Jeff had come over from America to live in London after getting married to a local girl called Sharon. They had lived in his building for about a year now and had recently had a little boy called Thomas or 'little Tommy' as he had come to be known.

'Is that you, Jeff?' he said softly, almost in a whisper. Jeff suddenly lifted his head as though coming out of a long day dream.

'Oh, Ben, how's it goin', man?' said Jeff as he immediately got up from his chair and put his big arms round him and pulled him close. It wasn't a very British thing to do but this hug was deeply welcome. After a couple of seconds of a very firm squeeze, Jeff released him, which actually had the effect of leaving him feeling a little lighter. 'So, what are you doing here?' he said. A stupid question to ask someone in a hospital ward, but it was the customary thing to say.

'Oh man!' sighed Jeff. 'We have had a bad night, dude! Little Tommy got a fever and he was throwing up everywhere and we just didn't know what to do! Sharon was freakin' out and so we just decided to get straight down here; and as soon as they saw him, they brought him up here. So, me and Shaz are just waiting for the doctors to find out what's goin' on!' Jeff was usually a very easy-going sort of character, but he could see that there was a lot of worry in this big man.

'Oh, hi Ben!' came a voice from further up the corridor. It was Sharon in her usual jeans and T-shirt. She had the elfish sort of short haircut that was common for many first-time mums who couldn't be bothered looking after a baby and big hair. But more importantly she had a couple of cups of hot coffee for her and Jeff to keep them going.

'Hi, Sharon! Sorry to hear about little Tommy. Is he OK?'

'Yeah,' she said casually as she handed one of the steaming cups to her husband. 'He's just got some kind of fever or something, so I reckon he just needs some fluids and that should perk him up. The nurse is in there right now checking him over.' It seemed like Sharon had calmed down from the state Jeff had described during the night. Jeff and Sharon shared the same laid-back attitude to life and that was probably why they were so perfectly matched as a couple.

'Well, I hope you get him home soon! See you later!' he said as he waved and turned away.

'Thanks, man,' piped up Jeff as he took his first sip.

'Yeah, see you back at the building, Ben,' called Sharon from behind him. It obviously wasn't a good thing that little Tommy was on this ward, but despite the circumstances, Jeff and Sharon were so positive that he really did believe that he would see them all back at the building very soon.

On that positive note, he soon reached the nurses' station where the samples were sitting out ready for him to collect. However, no sooner had he put his hand on them than a terrible alarm began to ring in the ward. Immediately he swung around to see the red light flashing above the side ward door. It was the door to little Tommy's room. Jeff and Sharon barely had time to turn their heads when a nurse, with a look of alarm on her face, swung the door open violently and leaned out into the hallway. 'Get the crash team now!' she yelled at the top of her voice and rushed back into the room. After a second of stunned silence, the whole ward was thrown into fast forward! Jeff and Sharon both simultaneously threw their cups of coffee on the floor and dashed inside with Sharon screaming her son's name at the top of her lungs. The sister and another nurse sprinted from the nurses' station down to the sideward and ran inside. Ben was frozen to the spot with sheer panic. All he could do was watch. As the next few seconds passed and as Sharon screamed hysterically for someone to save her son, there was a sudden buzzing at the door to the ward. It had barely sounded when the door flung open and a couple of young male doctors burst into the ward. They ran for the sideward across the floor that was covered in spilt coffee. The first one slipped a bit on his way in, but the second doctor managed to grab him and they both bundled themselves into the sideward and slammed the door behind them. With the muffled sound of Sharon wailing behind the closed door, Ben felt a shiver going up his neck. Without thinking, he put his hand back down on the samples that had been left for him and he started carrying them past the noise of doctors and nurses yelling instructions around the room. Suddenly a nurse emerged from the room and ran to the nurses' station to get something with the instruction of 'hurry' following loudly behind her. Stepping through the coffee on the floor, he left the ward and let the doors close behind him. The sound of the crisis was muffled yet again, but it was no less loud in his mind. He could only imagine what his friends were going through. He should have been able to do something; especially on this particular day. But he didn't. He felt weak, he felt helpless. From a position of being ready to change the world at the start of the day, he now felt like the most useless person on the planet. With his spirit feeling as though it had been completely crushed, Ben finished off his run to the lab and made his way to the staff room for lunch. As he entered the room, it felt like he had gone for lunch at the wrong time. The place was completely subdued. There was no Enid bustling around the kitchen. There was no sign of Mo. Apart from a few zombies slumped in their chairs around the TV, there was only Eddie, who was leaning back on one of the chairs at the table, with one of his legs up on a chair in front of him. Eddie looked to be in a bit of pain and he could see that the foot that he had on the chair had no shoe on it.

'Oh dear, what happened to you?' he said, making a gently inquiry.

'Oh, Ben,' Eddie growled in a distinctly frustrated manner. 'I can do a vigorous work out in a gym for an hour, but I can't get up and down a flight of stairs without injurin' meself! I can hardly put this foot to the floor!' As if to prove his point, Eddie then leaned forward and gave his ankle a rub, which immediately made him wince with the pain. 'So, what do I do, Ben?' Eddie continued. 'I can't afford to be taking time off. I need to keep working this week.' Strictly speaking that wasn't the case, but Eddie was of a generation that felt the responsibility to be at their place of work, no matter what. 'Come on, Ben, give us a clue about how to get this foot working again,' said Eddie with another grimace. It was odd that after a morning of dismal failure, his friend Eddie would still put his faith in him. He may have had a reputation for reading a lot and knowing a few things about medical practice, but after the day he just had, all of that seemed pretty worthless. However, Eddie was still looking at him, and even though he was feeling inadequate, he went over to the chair that Eddie's foot was resting on and had a look.

Gently, he started to roll Eddie's sock down his ankle. Eddie stiffened a little. 'Easy does it, Ben, easy does it!' said the big man in a rather unmanly way.

Upon rolling down the sock to the heel, he could see some purple bruising beginning to form around the lower part of Eddie's ankle. He put both of his hands gently around the ankle and lifted it a little off the chair. 'Can you move it at all?' he asked Eddie, whose eyes were strangely widened. Without speaking,

Eddie wriggled his toes and bent his foot slightly up and down. He set Eddies' foot gently back down on the chair and Eddie let out a little sigh as though he had been holding his breath slightly during the examination. 'Well, it doesn't feel like anything is broken,' he said with a slight air of authority. 'But you should probably get it X-rayed anyway, just in case. Probably just a bad sprain though.'

'No, no,' said Eddie, gingerly rolling his sock back up. 'No need for an x-ray, Dr Ben, I'll be fine.' And with that consultation finished, they both sat and finished their lunch in relative silence. After finishing his cheese sandwiches, which always afforded him some comfort, since he loved cheese, he leaned back in his soft chair with book in hand. He opened the cardiac text book at the place where the book mark had been left and within a couple of paragraphs, his mind had already started to wander. The day had started with a promise of great things! He had felt so much potential and power within himself that he thought he just needed to show up and good things would start to happen. But the opposite happened! He had failed at every turn! There was the fiasco on ward 5 which still left a burning sense of humiliation in his gut. Then there was the feeling of helplessness as he stood by and watched his neighbours fall into panic and despair as their little boy toppled over the line between life and death. And now, even as he was sitting here in the refuge of the staff room, there was the sight of the formidable figure of his friend Eddie, now reduced to a hobbling clown, limping from one part of the staff room to the other. Almost with a sense of shame, he dipped his eyes down further into his book. He wasn't powerful; he wasn't special; he was a weak little fool with ideas above his station. Even reading these medical textbooks was a pretence! He wasn't clever; he didn't get good grades at school; he was a fraud! The experience of this morning had proven that very clearly. He was wrong to believe anything other than what he could see with his own two eyes. And what he could see was a man who should stop pretending to be something that he was not!

He could feel his fingers gripping the book a little bit firmer than before. The level of self-recrimination was rising with every minute and it was making his blood boil. If he wasn't going to do anything special, then he had better just content himself with doing what was normal. He was just a normal person and he should simply get on with living a normal life. At that point, the argument in his mind suddenly ceased. There was a calm that flowed through his body as if he had just let go of something that was pulling against him. He lifted his head, closed the book and got up from his chair. Without saying a word, he walked to the door and left the room; and that was pretty much the manner in which he conducted himself the rest of the day. He presented himself at the cardiac ward for further instructions, he snapped back with clear affirmatives for every instruction that he was given and marched from point to point without looking to the left or right or talking to anyone on the way. He shut himself off from every personal encounter because he wanted to be completely self-contained. It was all that he could cope with right now. It was all that he wanted. He wanted nothing! He wanted no-one!

Chapter 4
The Moment of Doubt

When the end of the day eventually arrived, it felt like he had been walking constantly all day. Normally he would have gone back to the staff room for a few minutes to catch up with everyone before they clocked off, but this time, he was so tired that he just wanted to get home as fast as he could. Thankfully he didn't have a bag or coat with him that day and so there was no need for him to stop by. With the big clock in the foyer now showing that 5 o'clock was a good few minutes in the past, he slowly ambled across the floor and out through the big doors. No sooner had he stepped outside than the cool evening air wafted over him. Just for a moment, it seemed to calm his nerves, but it didn't slow him down. He kept walking and didn't stop until he got to his bus stop which was only a few hundred yards along the pavement. There weren't many people waiting at the bus stop, and by kind fortune the familiar red bus arrived within a minute of him being there. He got on the bus and slumped into the first available seat. With his elbow on the rim of the window, he rested his head on his hand and kept his eyes firmly fixed on the floor. The rumbling of the bus engine vibrated through his arm and into his head. It was oddly therapeutic. His mind focussed on the changing gears of the engine and little else and it was in this kind of trance-like state that he stayed for the rest of the journey.

Almost by chance, he realised that he had arrived at his stop. He lifted his head from his hand and got to his feet. After letting a couple of people past without looking at them, he filed out of the bus and walked quickly to the door of his apartment block. He punched in the code for the front door and after hearing the click in the lock, he pushed it open and closed it behind him. As soon as it closed, he walked down the hall to the flight of steps on the left. He skipped up the steps to the first floor and turned to the right. Thankfully there was no-one around and he was able to get his key in the door, get into his flat and close the door behind him. As soon as the door closed, he leaned against it and let out a long sigh. He felt absolutely drained! All he wanted to do was sit on the sofa and put the TV on and that was exactly what he did. He walked over to the old leather sofa and laid himself out across it. As soon as he was horizontal, he pulled the large blanket off the back of the sofa and covered himself with it. With the blanket pulled round him, he was about to reach for the remote control when found himself looking out the window. He could see the branches at the top of a tree and the branches were now swaying in the wind. There was only a small breeze when he had arrived home but it had obviously picked up a little since he had got in. As the branches swayed this way and that, the leaves that had long since changed colour were just about hanging on. It was a comforting feeling to be in the calm silence of his apartment while the wind was blowing leaves around outside. The weather could not touch him and it could not speak to him. But that wasn't always the case. It had been a few days ago now that the Sender had come to him; and it had been the strangest experience of his life. He had been lying on the sofa, much as he was now, when a thick fog had begun to develop outside. This heavy fog was nothing new in London and so he thought nothing of it. But then the fog began to pour through the open window and before he knew it the apartment was full of it. He had got up to close the window but by that stage he could hardly see his hand in front of his face. He had tried to grope his way to the window; but unfortunately, his shin found the edge of the coffee table first and he found himself sitting on the floor, rubbing his shin bone to try and dull the pain. It was at that moment that he got the strangest feeling that someone else was in the room. It was a feeling that he had never had before, and it was as if this person was filling the whole room. His nerves were tingling as if there was some kind of energy all around him. He wondered if he should say something. Should he say, 'hello'? Should he ask who was there? And what would the answer be? This situation persisted for what seemed like at least five minutes and then something changed. Having been still and quiet for quite some time, he was about to speak when the level of energy in the room seemed to go up a level. The fog, or whatever it was, seemed to take on a life of its own. It was thicker and it was more highly charged than before. It almost seemed to be emitting a light of its own and this light was so bright that he had to close his eyes. And then came the message. It started as a brightness in his mind. He had his eyes firmly closed but it was as if he still had them wide open and he was looking into a white space. Then people started to appear in front of him. He didn't really recognise them, but they all had one thing in common; they were all wearing hospital clothes. However, far from looking ill, they were all looking very happy indeed. In fact, they seemed to be overjoyed! They were looking at their own bodies and at each other's bodies in a shared sense of celebration as if some great transformation had occurred. Then, all of a sudden, they looked at him! It was a look of gratitude. He could feel their appreciation as if he was the cause of their happy state. It was a great feeling; and that feeling began to grow. It was as if the power that was in the apartment was filling his own body and giving him extraordinary strength. The power from the fog was surging through his whole body, but he could feel it most in his hands. He looked at his hands to see what was happening to them and when he looked down at them, they were glowing, as if white hot. Then he noticed that the people in the hospital clothes were walking towards him, their faces still shining with happiness. But it wasn't just the people who were moving towards him because now he noticed that he was moving towards them. It was as if his hands were pulling him towards them; as if the power that had filled his apartment and his body was now leading him in their direction. As he got closer to the people, he saw his hands getting brighter and brighter, to the point that the light actually became too bright and he had to turn his head away. Then, suddenly, as soon as he turned his head, everything went dark.

He opened his eyes and he found himself lying face down on the floor beside the table. It took him a good few minutes to get up from the floor. The fog had gone, the light had gone, but it felt like the presence that he had sensed was still inside him; and with that lingering presence there was also a sense of purpose. It was as if he had been programmed for a mission that he had yet to accomplish. He couldn't put it into words, but in his deepest thoughts it was the clearest sense of purpose that he had ever felt; and that was why he had begun the day the way that he had. He was so sure of himself! He had absolute clarity in his mind about what he was going to do and what was going to happen. But then it all went sideways! It was a complete and utter disaster!

With these thoughts in his mind, he turned away from the window and faced the back of the couch; pulling the blanket closer around him. The light of the day was fading fast and the room was noticeably darker. The fading light somehow suited his mood. Then with the darker room came the darker thoughts. Perhaps he had completely misread this encounter with the Sender! Maybe there was no Sender at all! It was very real at the time, but now he wasn't feeling quite so sure.

He could feel the pain of his faith shrivelling within his chest and it made him bury himself even deeper in the blanket; blocking out what remained of the evening light. All of a sudden, he felt a profound sense of being lost. Where his faith had been so strong that morning, there was now only doubt. He didn't know whether to hold on to the memory of this encounter or simply let go of what he thought was real. At this moment, he decided it was too painful to decide one way or the other and therefore he consciously shut down the conversation in his head. At once he fell asleep, giving in to the deep exhaustion that the day had left him with.

Chapter 5
Back to Faith

When he awoke the next morning, the first thing that grabbed his attention was the terrible pain on one side of his neck. He had obviously not given his head enough support during the night and the resulting pain made him get up very slowly. When he was eventually sitting upright with the blanket still around him, he stared out through the window again. The wind from last night was still blowing and now there was heavy rain falling with it. He shivered at the thought of the journey to work, which prompted him to go and jump into the shower straight away. After a hot shower restored the warmth in his body, he quickly got dressed. He grabbed a breakfast bar from one of the cupboards in his small kitchen and as he was eating it, he put on his big black winter coat. He had picked it up as a bargain at the end of last winter and as he walked towards the bus stop with his hood up, he felt the satisfaction of his sound investment coming to fruition.

After getting on the bus and taking the first available seat near the front, his thoughts began to turn to the events of the day before, and in a very short space of time any feeling of satisfaction disappeared. His confidence had been rocked and his faith had been shattered. Therefore, he quickly concluded, if he was going to act on his sending in the future then he was going to require fresh instruction. At this moment he doubted everything, especially himself, and therefore it was up to the Sender to make the next move, that's if he even existed anyway. Having detached himself from the responsibility of his sending, he could feel himself relaxing a little more into his seat. There was also a certain sense that he had taken back control of his life. The last few days had taken him way out of his comfort zone, and therefore, making this little decision made him feel a little more comfortable about his life, or at least, the day that lay ahead.

However, no sooner had this sense of control over his day emerged than it was quickly extinguished. Without warning, the bus slammed its breaks on hard! Ben's whole body was thrown forward. Unfortunately, his hands were still in his pockets and he hit the seat in front with his head and upper body. Thankfully, he had instinctively turned his body at the same time and this saved his face from hitting the back of the seat full on. However, as he was getting acquainted with the plastic backing of the seat in front, he was also conscious that everything else on the bus was thrown forward as well. A number of bags that other passengers had been holding came tumbling down the aisle towards the front. There were shrieks and squeals from some of the other passengers, including some men. But worst of all was the noise from the front. At the point of hitting the brakes, there was a terrible shout from the driver and at the same time a terrible thud from something that the bus had collided with. As the bus came to a halt, everyone was thrown back into their seats and at that point, the doors of the bus opened and the driver bolted from his seat and jumped through the open door.

Everyone on the bus gradually began to gather themselves. There were a few whispers of concern and inquiry further up the bus and added to that murmuring there were the noises of a gathering crowd around the spot immediately in front of the bus. A couple of people shouted for an ambulance; a few more wanted to know if he was alright. Eventually the reality of what had just happened began to dawn on those who were in the bus and there was then a steady stream of passengers who began walking to the front. As they went, the women picked up their bags that had slid down the aisle. 'Are you coming?' said one older lady who was wrapped up in a thick green coat. All he could do was look at her as she picked up the leather bag that had stopped just beside him. It was as if she was already on her way to the funeral to pay her respects. Without making any conscious decision, his body got itself up on its feet and he began to file off the bus with the rest of the passengers. As soon as he stepped onto the wet tarmac of the road, he found himself staring at the backs of a crowd of people who were all gathered around one point on the ground. There was a chorus of murmuring from those on the periphery and from within there was the sound of a man sobbing. The cold winter rain kept falling over the whole scene. Every drop was like a cold dose of reality crashing down on his head. He should have put his hood up but that didn't seem to matter right now.

Eventually a few people began to move away from the centre of the gathering. They shook their heads as they went; some going back to the pavement to continue their journey to work and some returning to their vehicles. In their absence. He could see a man's leg protruding from the small cluster of people that remained. The foot was wearing a smart black shoe and above the shoe there was a trouser leg that had been fastened with a black bicycle clip. There was no movement. Cautiously, he made his way over to the body on the ground. As he did so, the lady in the green coat passed him in the opposite direction with a grim look on her face. She put her hand on his shoulder and gave it a gentle tap. She had paid her respects and was now leaving the graveside, as a professional mourner would. After a short pause, he continued walking closer to the tragic scene. The bus driver, who was still sobbing, was kneeling over the body. Another man who was wearing old jeans and a jumper was standing over him with his arm around him. To the right of the scene there was a bicycle with a mangled back wheel lying on the ground. Eventually, he got to the place where the body lay and as he peered over the head of the driver, whose sobbing was now a little more muffled, he could see a watery pool of blood. He stepped a little closer and there was the man's head. The first thing that struck him about this man was how smart he looked. He had thick black hair, a clean shave and a smart white shirt. He looked like a young professional who was just starting out in his career, but now that career had come to an abrupt end. His face was pale and there was blood around his mouth, but there was no sign of life in him whatsoever.

For a moment, he couldn't move. His eyes were fixed on this young man's face. A sense of helplessness returned to him; the same feeling that he had when little Tommy had become severely ill in the children's ward. Except this time, there really was nothing that could be done. This man's life was gone! It was over! The time for healing was over and now the finality of death had settled in. All that anyone could do now was mourn the passing of this stranger. With that thought, he noticed the sniffing of the driver who was still kneeling over the body. The man who had his arm round him was giving him all the comfort that he could. 'It wasn't your fault, mate! There was nothing you could have done! Look, he didn't even have a helmet on or nothin'!' While the man had a point about the helmet, there didn't seem to be much acceptance from the driver. This man would always wonder if there had been more that he could have done. Could he have seen the cyclist earlier? Could he have jumped on the brakes sooner? Forever, this man would be haunted by the thought of what more he could have done.

But, no sooner had this thought crossed his mind, than a powerful impulse took hold of his whole body. He took a sharp intake of breath as if suddenly awoken from a daze. It felt like the bus that had killed this man on the ground had just hit him where he stood. Except this was no physical impact, it was an impact that came from within; a conviction that came like a bolt of lightning from the clouds above. Never mind what the poor driver could have done; what could he have done? What if he really did have the ability that his sending suggested? He could have been out of the bus faster and got to him before his last breath! He could have helped that man in the cardiac ward! Was it too late to help him now? He could have helped little Tommy? He could have helped everyone in that hospital! Who knows how many people were now in the morgue because he didn't do what he could have done! All of a sudden, it felt as though he was backed into a corner. He had tried to run from his sending but now it appeared that events had conspired to reel him back. It was as if the Sender would not let him go until he had done what he had been sent to do. There was no mist or fog or any sign of the Sender's presence but his hand was unmistakably present in this moment of tragedy. With senses that were now heightened due to the adrenaline that was rushing through his whole body, he became aware of the blue flashing lights that were heading quickly in his direction. It was an ambulance that had come from the hospital which was just a few blocks down from he was. The big yellow and green vehicle came to a halt just a few metres away and the two paramedics ran over to the man on the ground with a couple of bags in their hands. Everyone who was still there was ushered back, including the poor driver who was still being supported by the man in the jeans and jumper. It was clear now that the bus wasn't going to be moving any time soon and so although he felt guilty leaving the scene, he decided to start walking to the hospital. He could feel the rain starting to run down his neck and even down his back and so he now pulled his hood up over his head. As he made his way along the pavement, dodging other pedestrians and stepping over puddles, he began to feel that same sense of purpose that he had started out with the previous morning. Yes, yesterday had been tough, and he had felt like giving up, he said to himself. But in a way, this difficult experience was now a confirmation of his sending! Surely, there was going to be some element of push back when trying to do something amazing and life-changing; that was to be expected! But it was no reason to give up. In fact, it was a positive sign that he needed to keep going and persevere. And besides, he reasoned, life was too short to hold back. If the events of this morning had taught him anything, it was that he needed to step out in faith. What exactly it was that he was putting his faith in, he still wasn't sure, but if it was real, then there were many people he could help; and there was no way that he was going to let anyone down from here on in!

This renewed sense of purpose quickened his steps and in no time at all he was walking through the foyer of the hospital entrance and reaching for the door of the staff room. As soon as he entered the room, he got his second shock of the morning. Instead of slouching at the table as usual, Mo was actually at the kitchen making the tea. As he closed the door behind him, he couldn't help but stare at Mo, standing there in his Essex cricket shirt with a teapot in his hand. He was about to look around the room for an explanation for this strange phenomenon when a loud and familiar voice grabbed his attention. 'Oh, there he is! There he is! The man with the magic hands!' He looked towards the lockers and there was Eddie walking towards him with no sign of a limp at all. In fact, he was positively bouncing across the room and in no time at all he had gathered him up in a bear hug which almost lifted him off the ground.

'Thank you, thank you, thank you!' Eddie sang as he dropped him back down to the ground. Eddie now gripped his shoulders and held him at arms' length. 'I don't know what you did when you looked at my ankle the other day, but as soon as I woke up this morning, all that pain and swelling and bruising, it was all gone! You're a genius mate! I don't know how you did it, but my ankle feels better than ever!' With that statement, Eddie gave him a solid slap on the shoulder and turned away to go back to the locker which still had some of his casual clothes hanging out of it! It didn't seem to matter that Eddie had absorbed some of the rain from Ben's coat onto his porter uniform, he was just happy to be healthy.

As he watched Eddie walking away, the adrenaline that was still coursing through his body was now complemented with a thrill of excitement. What other explanation could there be? He had seen how bad Eddie's ankle had been the day before. There was no way that he should walking around the way that he was! In fact, he probably shouldn't even have been in work at all. But there he was; fully fit, fully restored; it was nothing short of a miracle! Was this the confirmation that he had been looking for? Surely it must be! What a contrast a day had made! Yesterday his heart had been in his boots, but now he felt a renewed confidence surging through him. It was like a warm glow coming from his chest and it wasn't long before that warm glow resulted in a big smile across his face; like a child on Christmas morning.

'Well, well, Ben! It looks like all that book reading has paid off after all!' said Mo with a wry smile as he carried two cups of tea over to the table from the kitchen. He set one down in front of Enid who was already sitting at the table knitting and then proceeded to sit down at the table himself. 'Look at the big smile on his face,' laughed Mo, pointing a finger in his direction, 'he's all pleased with himself! He's a proper doctor now!' Ben couldn't help but laugh at himself too. He was all too aware that he was now standing in front of everyone with a big goofy grin on his face and when Mo and Eddie laughed, he couldn't help but laugh with them. As he was still chuckling, he proceeded to unzip his coat and take it off. He then walked over to the side of the lockers where there were a few hooks to hang wet coats.

Not to be outdone, he turned to Mo as he was hanging the coat, 'Never mind me having something to be proud of, what about you making the tea? I didn't think you had it in you, Mo!' he said with a healthy dose of sarcasm.

'Oh, ha ha!' came the response from the table. 'Well, doctor Ben, let me tell you something about me. I am just like the great Essex cricket team...' Mo paused briefly for effect, 'I am full of surprises!'

'Oh, you are definitely that!' said Eddie with a big laugh as he closed his locker door; 'you are definitely that!'

It was a relief to get his heavy coat off and wipe some of the dampness off his head and neck. Now that he felt a bit drier and warmer, he sat down in his soft chair in the corner and looked instinctively down at the left-hand side of the chair where his books were. While he was still trying to get the big cardiac text book into his hand, the door into the staff room swung open. The ever-fresh Madge put her head through the door as she always did and looked straight at Mo, who was just finishing off his cup of tea. 'Mo, thanks for helping me out yesterday,' she said and then she nodded in Enid's direction as she added, 'you know.' The subdued figure of Enid raised her head slightly to acknowledge what was being said and then looked at Mo with a timid smile.

'No problem, Madge. My pleasure; any time,' said Mo and he reached over to Enid and touched her gently on the arm. Clearly something had happened with Enid yesterday. He had noticed she wasn't around at lunch and neither was Mo. It seemed that Mo taken her home for some reason. He presumed it must have been because of some illness that Enid was suffering with, but whatever it was, she seemed to be better now and was putting her knitting away, getting ready to get back to work.

'OK, folks!' said Madge switching her attention to the room in general. 'Look lively, let's get out there!' Madge then did her disappearing act with the door left open.

It was then Eddie's turn to be the motivator. He clapped his hands together loudly a couple of times, 'OK, lads and ladies, let's get moving!' There was no hiding it, Eddie was even more pumped than usual. His miraculous recovery had, literally put a spring in his step. But Eddie wasn't the only one with extra spring in his step today. As he watched Eddie walk quickly across the room, he shifted himself forward onto the edge of his seat. This really was the day that it was going to happen! He was going to do what he had been sent to do; and nothing, not even Sister Montgomery was going to stop him. With that thought in his mind, he slapped his hands on his thighs and got to his feet and strode purposefully off to the cardiac ward.

Chapter 6
The First One

He bounded up the steps to the first floor, passing the same group of student nurses who were huddled around their phones in the usual place. In no time at all, he was walking through the doors into the cardiac ward and was faced with a familiar scene of activity. The catering staff and the auxiliary nurses were gathering up the breakfast dishes and the junior doctors were already doing their rounds. As he surveyed the people wearing stethoscopes, two of the doctors, in particular, caught his attention; Dr Black and Dr Kanu. Although relationships between staff were frowned upon, it was pretty obvious that these two were standing a little closer together than the rest. As for the nurses, they were gathered around the nursing station with nurse Montgomery making her sharp, jabbing gestures to indicate what she expected to be done that day. With the other staff occupied for the moment, he made a beeline for the sideward that he had been in the day before. As soon as he was in the room, he went straight round to the other side of the bed near the window and with a quick deep breath to steady himself he reached his hands out over the elderly man's chest. The patient's old grey head was sunken deep into his pillow; his mouth was open and his breathing was shallow. He began to lower his hands down towards the man's chest and as he did so he could feel a certain glow of warmth entering his fingers; and then there was contact. As soon as his hands pressed down on the man's chest, the whole of his hands began to buzz with a feeling that could only be likened to pins and needles. It felt as though something was being transferred from himself to the patient; perhaps some kind of energy. This feeling went on for a few seconds, during which he felt rooted to the spot. The whole of the room seemed to be electrified; the air seemed thicker as if the Sender Himself was in the room. Then, as quickly as this feeling had come, it disappeared. He instinctively lifted his hands from the man's chest and with a sense of anti-climax stood back from the bed. He waited for a moment in silence, not sure what was supposed to happen next; and then it all happened at once! Without warning, the man's eyes opened as if he had just got the shock of his life! At the same time, his chest seemed to shoot up about a foot up into the air. The patient then took an enormous gasp of air, as if he had been holding his breath all morning. The movements of the patient were so violent and sudden that Ben fell backwards with shock. Thankfully there was a chair just behind him that caught him, but as soon as his back hit the chair he bounced back to his feet. By this stage the patient had started to grip both of the side rails on the bed and was rocking himself from side to side while still lifting his chest up and down. The old man began to groan loudly, as he was clearly in pain and in an effort to comfort him, Ben put his hands on one of the patient's hands that was firmly fixed on the side rail.

It was at this point that someone ran into the room. Thankfully, it was not Sister Montgomery, but one of the younger nurses, a guy called Mark. 'What's going on? What have you done?' Mark ran over to the monitors to get some idea of what was happening. 'What on earth is happening here?' Mark exclaimed as he looked at the screen. Then he looked across the bed, 'Ben!' he barked! All of a sudden, Ben came to his senses and looked back at Mark. 'Ben, you need to go now! If Montgomery finds you here, you are toast, mate! Go, go, go!' The urgency in Mark's Liverpool accent had its effect and with a couple of steps round the bed, he was soon cantering out through the door. He had barely cleared the entrance when the tall figure of Dr Black was rushing past him with Dr Kanu following behind, kicking her long skirt out in front of her. He crossed over to the other side of the corridor and stood opposite the sideward to see what happened next, but it wasn't to be.

'Hey you, stop standing around and get that guy down to X-ray!' She might have been running towards the side ward, but Sister Montgomery never missed an opportunity to give out the orders. He turned to see an elderly gentleman with wispy hair sitting on a wheelchair looking at him with wide eyes. The elderly man looked away quickly as soon as he caught his eye. The poor man was clearly a little embarrassed by the stern reference to his destination, but that was of no concern to the Sister. The feelings of the patients were not her priority.

'OK, sir, looks like you and I are going to the X-ray department,' he said as he grabbed the handles at the back of the wheelchair. Reluctantly he set off down the corridor, pushing the wheelchair in front of him. He took a glance back at the doorway of the sideward as he was leaving. There was a flurry of activity as nurses were running in and out carrying various bits of equipment with their blue gloves on. What on earth had just happened? He wondered to himself. Had he healed the man, had he killed him? His mind was rushing with questions, but at the same time there was a thrill of excitement in his body now. Whatever he had done to this patient, something had definitely happened! Perhaps something wonderful; something that would prove that his sending was not some mistake, but that it was real! Then something else real happened. He had spent so much time looking back at the sideward that he hit the corner of the entrance to the ward with the front wheel of the wheelchair. He quickly turned his head the right way to find the poor patient falling forward off the chair. He quickly grabbed the collar of the elderly gentleman and ungently pulled him back onto the chair. The man wheezed loudly as he changed direction and landed backward on the seat again. 'Oh, I am so sorry sir!' he said, apologetically! 'Are you alright?'

The elderly man looked round at him with a rather stern look on his face. 'Where did you get your driving licence from, young fella?'

The man sighed and looked forward again, waiting to move on. 'Very sorry, sir!' he apologized again and moved the wheelchair towards the lift where he stopped very gently and pressed the button.

After dropping the man off at the X-ray department and apologising yet again, he started his journey back to the cardiac ward. His curiosity was killing him! He couldn't wait to see what had happened to the patient in the sideward. Would he be walking around? Would all the staff be amazed at this transformation? His imagination was beginning to run away with him! He couldn't help but smile as he thought about the scene that awaited him on ward 5. But then something caught his eye that brought his mind right back to where he was. He was just passing the entrance to the intensive care unit on his left when he noticed a couple of familiar faces who were sitting at the doors. It was Jeff and Sharon. They were holding each other on the few seats that were always there for visitors to the ICU. He stopped in his tracks and then walked gently towards them as if to soften his approach. He got within a few feet of where they were when Jeff eventually looked up. 'Oh, hey, man,' came the greeting with its light American tone.

'Oh, how's it goin', Ben?' said Sharon as she lifted her head from Jeff's chest and added her own greeting. Jeff got up and walked towards him as Sharon pulled her cardigan around her and fastened it. Jeff put his arms out wide and drew him into a big tight hug which smothered his much smaller frame. Jeff released his grip after a couple of seconds and as he did so, held him by the shoulders.

'Thanks for coming over, man!' he said. He had done absolutely nothing but pass by and stop, but Jeff made him feel like he had done something wonderful. He was just that sort of person who made you feel good about yourself.

'Never mind me,' he replied, 'what about little Tommy?' They both instinctively looked over at Sharon who quickly lowered her head and raised a tissue to her face. Jeff looked back at him.

'I'm afraid it's not good,' he said with his eyes filling up. 'The infection that he had turned out to be meningitis, and it was really bad.' The big man's voice quivered as he spoke. 'It really hurt him…' He paused to look at the ground. 'We're just waiting to see what the damage is.' From feeling so buoyant before, he now felt heartbroken for these two lovely people. Of all the people in the world who deserved to be happy, it was these two.

He put his hand on Jeff's arm. 'Jeff, if there's anything I can do to help then you only have to ask!' he said with a real sense on sincerity.

'Thanks, man!' Jeff said and walked back to put his big arms back around his wife again.

As he watched Jeff sit down beside Sharon, he got that familiar sense of helplessness once more. What an empty phrase it was to say that, 'you were ready to do anything to help them.' It was a platitude that people just blurted out when they had nothing else to say. How many times had that phrase actually been acted on? Pretty much never! But that was not going to be the case this time, he reasoned to himself. He now had a power that he never had before and he was not going to stop until he had used it to help as many people as he possibly could! With this self-motivation ringing in his ears, he took a few steps closer to Jeff and Sharon. This time they did not look up.

'Excuse me, Jeff and Sharon,' he whispered. 'I hope you don't mind me asking, but would it be OK for me to see little Tommy?'

Jeff didn't move his body away from Sharon but simply turned his head slightly as if to indicate that he was a bit busy to talk. 'Well, that's real nice of you, Ben, but there's no visitors allowed at the minute!' With that, he turned his head away again and pulled Sharon close. He could see that this wasn't the time to push things further.

'I completely understand. Listen, I'll be back soon,' he said as he backed away slowly.

He could hear a muffled 'OK' from Jeff and with that he turned and walked away. After the euphoria of his experience in the cardiac ward, seeing Jeff and Sharon like this brought his emotions back down to earth. He was heartbroken for them. They were just such a lovely couple and they had always been so kind to him; and therefore, to see them in so much pain was a very sobering experience. However, the difference this time was that he didn't feel powerless anymore; no instead he felt even more determined. He was sure that he could help little Tommy and as soon as he could get near him, he would do exactly that! This defiant confidence made him walk a little more upright and he strode back to the cardiac ward with renewed determination.

Chapter 7
The Real Thing

Just as he reached the stairwell, a voice suddenly stopped him in his tracks. 'Oh, hey, Ben!' said a jolly looking Mo as he appeared around the corner. He was wearing his purple sterilizing scrubs that he wore during work hours. The chest hairs that were highly visible above the v-line of his top gave him a very masculine look; a fact that Mo was probably aware of, given the way that he strutted around the hospital.

'Hi, Mo!' he replied, putting his hand on the door to the stairwell to push it open.

'Where are you going mate?' Mo inquired in a rather quizzical manner. 'It's time for a cuppa! Come on let's go!' Mo patted him on the shoulder as if to turn him in the opposite direction. Mo paused for a second, waiting to see if his friend would follow his lead. Ben was still keen to get back to the cardiac ward and kept his hand on the door momentarily, but then with a nod of his head turned to follow Mo to the staff room.

'Oh, alright then,' Ben replied with a smile and they started walking in the same direction. As they walked briskly along the corridor, dodging the clerical staff who were darting here and there in their white shirts and blouses, Ben became curious about Mo and Enid disappearing the previous day. 'So, what happened with Enid the other day?' he inquired casually. Mo turned his head quickly towards him as he walked.

'Oh, mate, she was in a terrible old state. Madge called me round to her office and there she was, sitting on the chair having some kind of a panic attack or something. So, Madge just said to me, 'can you take her home?' and I said 'sure, no problem' and that was it really.' For a second, Ben marvelled at Mo's ability to describe events as if he was a London cabbie talking to a passenger, but then

Mo finished the story. 'She didn't say much on the way home, just something about something that happened back in the Philippines before she came here.'

'Oh dear,' Ben replied with genuine concern. 'It must have been pretty bad, whatever it was!'

'Yeah, no doubt, Ben, no doubt!' Mo agreed, shaking his head from side to side. 'But whatever it was, I got her home and got her a cuppa tea and she said she would be fine! Not much more I could do really!' Thus ended Mo's concise description of yesterday's drama.

'Yeah, I suppose,' Ben replied, while wondering what terrible thing Enid had suffered. 'But it was good that you were there to help,' he added quickly, wanting to congratulate Mo for the help he had given.

'Well, she's worth it, ain't she! Mo stated firmly.

'Definitely,' he replied with equal firmness.

By the time that he had been updated on the events of the previous day, they arrived at the staff room and walked through the door, one behind the other. Eddie was sitting at the table reading a fitness magazine. 'Well, old man, how's the fitness today?' asked Mo playfully as he grabbed a chair and pulled it out from the table and stretched himself over it. Noticing that Enid wasn't there, Ben made himself busy at the kitchen and started to make some tea.

Eddie put his magazine down and looked intently at Mo. 'Well, Mo, let me tell you exactly how I am! I am great! In fact, I am feeling like a new man!' Eddie was quite animated and with a quick glance round his shoulder, Ben could see that Eddie was still very excited about his recovery. Eddie continued, 'and do you know why I feel like a new man, Mo? It's because of the magic fingers of our man Ben here! He's a genius!' Eddie gestured towards him as he lifted the kettle to pour the water into the teapot.

'Really, Ben?' exclaimed Mo with raised eyebrows! 'And tell me, Dr Ben, what exactly have you been doing to Eddie with your magic fingers?' he asked with a playful grin!

He was about to answer as he brought the teapot over to the table when Eddie jumped back into the conversation. 'I'll tell you what he did Mo; he took my banged-up ankle in his hands and he made it like new! Look!' Eddie stuck his leg out and pulled his trouser leg up, revealing a healthy, if somewhat hairy lower leg.

'Ok, ok!' exclaimed Mo. 'Put it away will you! Nobody wants to see that; even if it is like new!' Mo turned his face away, as if in disgust. As Eddie was putting his leg down again,

Ben had returned from the kitchen with a few cups and set them down in front of each of the men. He was pouring tea into Mo's cup when he noticed Mo looking at him inquisitively. 'So, tell me, Dr Ben, how exactly did you get the old man back on his feet?' he asked.

'Well,' Ben began, not sure how much to reveal. 'I didn't do a lot really; I just had a look at the ankle and that was pretty much it!' Mo looked at Eddie and Eddie looked at Mo, both with faces that spoke of being short-changed in the explanation they had just received.

'Well, there has to be a bit more to it than that, Ben!' said Eddie rather abruptly. 'I mean, you must have done something to the muscles or the ligaments or something!'

'Ah…well, I suppose I must have.' Ben said, rather tentatively, looking away from Eddie as he poured the tea into Eddie's cup and then his own.

'Yeah, of course you did!' Eddie stated firmly, determined to develop his own understanding. 'Ben, you read all those books about medicine; you're bound to have learned something about joints and how to fix them! That's how you did it, mate!' Eddie seemed pleased to have reached this understanding about his healing all by himself.

'Well, I suppose that's it!' Ben agreed, almost relieved that Eddie had no more questions for him. However, Mo was not as content with this explanation.

'Oh, I don't know,' Mo said, putting his cup to his mouth. After hastily taking a sip, he continued, 'I think there may be magic in Dr Ben's fingers, after all. Maybe he's a witchdoctor!' Mo chuckled to himself and kept sipping his tea.

'Oh, don't listen to him,' said Eddie, swiping his hand in Mo's direction. 'I believe you have a great talent and you should use it!' Eddie said with a real enthusiasm in his face. 'And I know exactly who you should use that talent on next!' Eddie's eyes were getting wider and he was leaning over the table in his direction. 'My wife has had a bad shoulder for years. She got badly hurt in a rugby tackle and has only had limited movement in it ever since.' He had never met Eddie's wife before, but knowing Eddie as he did, it was no surprise that he married a woman who played rugby. 'And what I'm thinking,' Eddie continued, 'is that you could come around and have a look at her shoulder and see what you can do!' At this point Eddie was nearly off his seat with excitement. For a brief moment, he could feel the gaze of expectancy coming from both Eddie and Mo at the same time. There was no way he could refuse.

'Well, ah, that would be lovely,' he said, and took a long drink of tea.

'Great!' said Eddie. 'I'll phone Rita and let her know!' No sooner had the words left his mouth than he was up from his seat and turned away to make the call on his mobile.

Mo looked at him with a big smile! 'Well, Dr Ben, no pressure there then!' Ben smiled back, but rather nervously.

Just then, the door opened and in walked Enid. 'Hello boys,' she said softly, lifting her head briefly. It was lovely to hear Enid's voice again.

Ben got up from his seat and pulled out the seat next to him. 'Come and sit down, Enid, and I'll get you a cuppa,' he said and went to the kitchen to get her a cup. Enid walked over to the table, straightened her light blue tunic a little and then sat down with a sigh. She put her hand on the table and Mo quickly put his hand out to meet it.

'How are you feeling, mama?' Mo asked gently.

'Oh, a lot better thank you,' she replied. 'And thank you again for taking me home the other day. I'm sorry for troubling you.'

'Oh, don't worry about that,' replied Mo with a grin, 'I'm always looking for an excuse to get out of this place.' Enid smiled a little and then took the cup of tea that had just been placed in front of her. Ben stood back with the teapot in his hand for a moment. It was great to see Enid looking better. She really was a lovely lady and it was so sad, the idea that anything bad might have happened to her that would have made her feel so terrible; even all this time later. Then he looked at Eddie walking up and down with the phone to his ear, talking to his wife. It was great to see him looking better too. There really was nothing more satisfying than helping others; and with this gift that he had been given, he could do that even more. With that thought, the memory of what had happened earlier in the morning suddenly came back to him. He had finally used his power on an actual patient and the reaction had been amazing, but he didn't know what the outcome had been. All of a sudden, his mind was seized with a raging curiosity. He had to know what had happened to the man he had touched!

Coming to his senses again, he quickly set the teapot back down on the table and made his excuse to leave. 'Sorry guys, have to go! Something I forgot to do earlier!' he said and with that he swept out of the room and made his way to the cardiac ward.

He arrived at the ward a little out of breath after jogging up the stairs. Taking a second to compose himself, he walked into the ward with a sense of expectancy. Things were fairly quiet by this late morning stage of the day. Doctors' rounds had been completed, the pharmacist had been in to check on people's medicines and most of the nurses were now sitting at computers or doing paperwork. The only real activity was a couple of auxiliary nurses making patients comfortable and changing bedclothes. As he paused at the entrance, he could see that there was no-one around the doorway to the sideward that he had been in earlier. There was no better time to get in to see the patient unnoticed and so, he walked straight over to the sideward and went inside. As soon as he entered, the sight of the bed stopped him in his tracks. It was empty! A chill ran down his spine. Was this another disappointment? Had he misread another situation? All these thoughts of self-doubt began to run through his mind. After seeing the big change in Eddie's ankle, surely, he could not have got it wrong again! He turned towards the door with a heavy heart and head bowed when he suddenly ran into Mark for the second time that day. As he looked up at the rather diminutive figure in his white nurses' top, he was expecting to see a rather cross face, but instead the expression could not have been more different. It was an expression of surprise and delight. His blue eyes were literally dancing with excitement. 'Oh, it's you!' said Mark as he swept his curly fair hair away from his face.

'Come on,' said the enthusiastic nurse as he bundled him back into the sideward.

'Do you realise what you've done?' he said, still with a lot of excitement in his face. 'You turned this place upside down this morning! The whole place was buzzing!'

Ben couldn't bear the suspense any longer and so, he just blurted out the simplest question. 'Is he alright? Is he dead?'

Mark leaned back a little and the grin on his face turned to one of bemusement. 'Dead?' he said quizzically! 'Listen, mate! Does that look like dead to you?' Mark put his arm rather forcefully around him and directed his attention to the bay ward across the hall. Ben looked a little closer, not sure at first what he was supposed to be looking at. But there in the bed closest to the window was the same man sitting up in bed with a cup of tea in his hand, talking to Dr Black and Dr Kanu, who were both sitting on the end of his bed.

'Look, Ben!' Mark spoke again, after giving him a couple of seconds to take it in. 'As soon as you left the room, this whole place went boogaloo!' Ben was still looking at the patient in the ward across the hall, but this didn't slow the nurse's breathless description of the drama. 'The doctors were in here, the nurses were in here, Montgomery was barking like a Scottish terrier! It was mad! But then the strangest thing happened. Mr James' vitals all came back up. His ECG went back to normal! His breathing went back to normal! He was even able to start talking to people as if there was nothing wrong with him! No pain or anything!' Mark was getting more excited as he was telling the story, even to the point of nearly laughing. Ben turned to the excitable nurse with a smile of his own now on his face. 'So, what did you do?' Mark inquired with real curiosity. 'You were in here! You had your hands on his chest! That was when it all kicked off! So, what was it? Was it chest compressions or what?' By this stage, Mark looked like he was about to burst. With the eyes of this young nurse bearing down on him, his mind went completely blank. He hadn't a clue what to say in the face of this inquisitive mind.

'Ah…well…' he began, without any clue about what he was going to say next. But then in an instant, there was no pressure for him to say anything.

'And what do you pair of layabouts think you are doing in here?' They both turned around and stood up straight as if called to attention by the sergeant major. The grim figure of Sister Montgomery appeared at the entrance to the sideward. She had her hands on her hips as she often did; her bony fingers pressing firmly into the red cloth of her tunic. Moving her hand like a whip, she pointed directly at Mark. 'You are not paid to stand around chatting with your boyfriend here! Get out of here and get back to your work.' Mark instantly moved towards the door and stepped nervously around the Sister who did not move an inch. Mark glanced back at him with a sense of concern for his safety and then disappeared around the corner. Mark's concern for his safety was well founded. Sister Montgomery whipped her inhaler to her mouth, took a sharp draw on it and took a couple of steps towards him. Shen then pointed her bony, nail-polished finger right up to his nose. 'And you!' she growled in a lower tone. 'I have my eye on you! You are the worst excuse for a porter I have ever seen. You are not a doctor! You are not a nurse! In fact, you probably don't even have the brains to be a porter from what I've seen.' She leaned in for the final blow. 'If you step out of line in my ward one more time, I will make sure that you are carried out of this hospital and that you are never allowed back in!' Each word of the last sentence came like a bullet. She held his gaze for a moment, making him feel very uncomfortable. Then after a couple of very awkward seconds she stepped back and to the side and with the other arm pointed in the direction of the door, she barked out one last order. 'Now, get out!' He quickly obliged and walked out of the door with some haste. He stopped briefly in the corridor and quickly noticed that the whole of the ward was looking at him, including Mr James and the two doctors who were sitting on his bed. Thankfully, he noticed that there were a cluster of blood samples sitting on the desk at the nurses' station, and so he made a quick dash to the desk to grab them and walked hurriedly out of the ward with his head down, deliberately not looking to see where the sister was. He kept walking at speed until he was safely in the stairwell, at which point, he slowed down his walking and started taking deep breaths. This was becoming a regular occurrence, being humiliated by Sister Montgomery and it was very discouraging. However, he couldn't let it distract from what was really important right now. For the second time, he had seen people get dramatically better after he had touched them. There was no doubt about it anymore; it was all real! The Sender was real, his sending was real, the ability he had been given was real; and now there was proof of that! Real tangible proof! The searing embarrassment that he had just suffered began to wane and he felt a little strength returning to his body and mind. He began walking a little faster again and as he did so he began to think about his plan of action over the next few days. If he started to draw too much attention to himself, then Sister Montgomery would make good on her threat and would remove him from the hospital altogether. He couldn't allow this to happen as it would greatly reduce his ability to help people, especially little Tommy. But how was he going to keep this balance? How was he going to help people in the dramatic way that he could and still keep his place in the hospital? It was a question that had to be answered and until it was, he couldn't risk doing anything else that would jeopardize his mission. With this thought in his mind, he decided to keep a low profile for the rest of the day. He made sure that he did all his portering duties promptly and quickly and whenever he was back in the cardiac ward, he made a point of not talking to anyone. Even in the staff room he didn't say much, not even when Eddie was telling him about the lovely lasagne that his wife Rita was going to make for him coming around for tea. It seemed that Eddie was now more excited about the lasagne than his visit. Thankfully the rest of the day passed off very quietly and before long he was standing at the front door of the hospital, waiting for Eddie to walk with him to his house for the much-anticipated feast.

Chapter 8
The First Believers

As he stood just inside the front doors of the hospital, he could see the signs of winter tightening its grip on the city. The light of the day was all but gone; the neon street lights had just come on and under their pink glow, there was the occasional gust of wind blowing leaves around the wet pavement. It looked cold, and every time the automatic doors opened and closed, there was confirmation of how cold it was as a gust of cold air swept into the hospital lobby. He was just pulling the zip of his coat up a little higher when he got the familiar pat on the shoulder from behind. 'OK, Ben, let's get going!' Eddie said as he walked out through the doors in front of him. He got himself moving with a bit a skip in his step so that he could catch up with the fast-walking Eddie who was already a few metres ahead of him. He had just caught up with his friend when Eddie got straight into the subject of dinner again. 'Oh, wait till you taste this lasagne, my friend! You are in for a right treat! And the homemade garlic bread that she makes to go with it is just absolutely amazing! Are you hungry?' he added as an afterthought. He was about to answer when Eddie continued. 'Coz if you are, then there will be plenty to eat. There are no small portions in my house my friend!' Eddie finished his statement with a guttural chuckle that came from the bottom of his lungs and left a big smile on his face. It was one of his favourite things about Eddie, that he seemed to take great joy in the simple things of life. He loved his work; he loved his family and he even made dinner sound like a great event. It occurred to him that if more people enjoyed life the way that his friend did then there would be many more happy people in the world.

Eddie kept up a fast pace and it was all he could do to keep up with him without breaking into a jog. After a few turns, they soon found themselves on a street of red brick terraced housing with small gardens at the front. As they walked along the street, Eddies' pace slowed a little. 'So how did you learn how to fix people's joints then?' The question came to him with a genuine look of curiosity.

He looked at Eddies' friendly face for a moment, wondering how much to share with him. 'Well...' he said, playing for time. 'The truth is that I haven't really learned it. It's just, sort of come to me.' It was a lame explanation, but it was the best he could do without revealing everything.

'Oh, so it's kind of a natural thing then! You just have a feel for where the body is hurting! Oh well, I can understand that alright! Yeah, I've heard about that sort of thing on some of those documentaries on telly! People who just have the touch!' He was a little relieved that Eddie had pretty much come up with his own explanation again rather than asking him to explain more. This allowed him to relax a little as they came to an abrupt stop at a bright green metal gate at one of the terraced houses near the end of the street. Eddie opened the gate and led them up to the front door past a tidy front lawn on the left. He closed the gate behind him and by the time he turned around, Eddie had his key in the door and opened it wide. There was a warm glow from the hallway. He made his way up the path to the doorway where Eddie was taking off his coat and shoes. 'Alright, Ben, welcome to my humble abode!' Eddie clapped his hands together with a childish glee. 'There's a coat hook for your coat and a place for your shoes,' he said as he pointed to a spot behind the door where a few other pairs of shoes were lined up against the wall. He quickly put his coat on the hook and his shoes in line with the rest. The fact that his shoes were the smallest in the row, even smaller than the ones with pink on them, was a reminder that he was probably going to be the smallest person at the dinner table.

With a big grin still on his face, Eddie led him past the bottom of the stairs on the right and into the living room. To his delight, there was a roaring open fire in the fireplace which was belting out the heat into a room that was already warm. There was also the feel of a lovely soft carpet under his feet. It was a lovely contrast to the cold feel of his own wood flooring back at his flat. 'Alright, my friend, take a seat!' Eddie said as he walked over to the dining area and through a door and into the kitchen. He took a seat on the sofa that was facing the fireplace. It was one of those sofas that was so soft that it almost sucked you into it. From his seated position, he could hear the sound of Eddie greeting his wife.

'Alright, darling! How are you?' Came the booming voice from the kitchen. The sound of a quick embrace followed, after which a strong female Caribbean voice was also heard. 'Alright you! That's enough! Now get that garlic bread on the table!'

Eddie appeared through the doorway and was immediately followed by his wife Rita. As her shoes indicated, she was quite tall and she had a glowing, cheerful face that was surrounded by loosely curled hair that was partly tied back. She had a white dress on with a floral pattern and a red apron wrapped around it.

'Hello, Ben! You're very welcome! Sorry, I look a bit of a mess, but hey, that's the Caribbean style, you know!' As soon as she had delivered her greeting, she let out a great big belly laugh and disappeared back into the kitchen.

'And that's the style we love, my darling!' Eddie shouted after his wife as she went back to get the lasagne out of the oven. Eddie then turned his attention back to his guest. 'OK, Ben, come on over and get a seat!' he said as he gestured to the seat at the end of the table closest to the living room. With a bit of a struggle he liberated himself from the clutches of the sofa and got to his feet and walked over to the dining area which had a much cooler laminate wood flooring. It was almost a bit of a relief to feel something cooler beneath his feet, such was the heat that was emanating from the roaring fire. He took his seat and as he did so Eddie strode over to the living room door into the hallway. He opened it and popped his head round and yelled up the stairs. Alright lads, come and get it!' Almost instantaneously, there was the sound of a herd of elephants thundering down the stairs and just as Eddie sat down at the other end of the table, two big young men emerged through the door. They were both in tracksuits and had similar short hairstyles. They vaulted across the living room in what seemed like two steps and took their seats to the right of their father. 'OK boys, this is our guest for the evening, my friend Ben from work. Say hello!' As Eddie gestured towards him with his outstretched arm, both boys immediately got up to their feet again and reached across the table to shake his hand.

'Hello, Ben!' They both said, almost in unison, and then they both gave his hand a very firm shake. He put his hand back down under the table and secretly flexed his fingers in and out a few times to shake off the feeling of the squeeze that both boys had left on him.

Eddie continued; 'and Ben, may I introduce to you my two sons, Dean and Carl.'

'Hi boys,' he said. Although, looking at the size of them and their father, it was he who felt like the child at the table. Just then, Rita swept into the room from the kitchen and set a huge dish of lasagne down in the middle of the table.

As she did so, he actually noticed the eyes of father and sons getting bigger and bigger. It was as if they were all imagining themselves diving straight into the middle of it. However, as Rita drew back from the table, he was suddenly reminded why he was there. She grimaced a little and felt for her left shoulder as she rolled it backwards. Eddie broke his gaze from the lasagne and turned to his wife. 'Oh darling, you should have called! I would have carried that in for you!' he said. Rita gave a sharp 'tisk' noise as she undid her apron and threw it back into the kitchen.

'Oh, stop your fussing! I'm fine! Now put your money where your mouth is and start serving!' she said firmly and then smiled in the direction of her guest.

'Are you hungry, Ben?' she inquired politely.

'Oh yes!' he said immediately. 'And this looks great, Rita! You shouldn't have gone to so much trouble!' he added.

'Oh, it's no trouble at all Ben! Just hold out your plate there and Eddie will see you right!' she said. In compliance with Rita's instruction, he held out his plate and Eddie reached across from the other end of the table with what was possibly the biggest piece of lasagne that he had ever seen. It slid off the serving spoon and he could immediately feel the plate get much heavier. Eddie repeated the serving action for all at the table and as soon as he distributed the garlic bread, Rita invited them all to tuck in.

After taking one bite of the lasagne, he soon realised why Eddie had been so excited about that night's dinner. The lasagne was perhaps the most tasty thing that he had ever eaten. This was further evidenced by the fact that both Dean and Carl practically breathed in everything that was on their plates. Based on their appetites, it was little wonder they had grown to the size they were! The rest of them ate at a much slower pace and while they did so, the boys had finished two glasses of water and were ready to leave the table. They both looked at their father for his attention. In a rather reluctant way, he silently acknowledged their attention with a sigh. 'Alright boys, you may be excused from the table!'

They both got up from the table. 'Thanks mum!' said Dean.

'Nice to meet you Ben,' said Carl. After pushing their chairs back in, they walked quickly out through the living room and back up the stairs with the same sound of thunder.

'And don't forget to finish your homework!' Rita hollered after them.

'Yes mum!' came the muffled voices from the top of the stairs. Rita turned her attention back to him.

'Sorry, Ben, boys will be boys, you know! Do you have any children of your own?' He swallowed his piece of lasagne down hard, slightly surprised by the question.

'Ah, no!' he replied. 'I'm still single,' he added. It almost sounded like he was making an excuse the way he said it.

'Oh, don't worry about that,' Rita said, in a kind of reassuring way. 'I'll find you a good wife!' Again, she let out that great belly laugh. He couldn't help but smile with her as she looked round at her husband for his reaction.

Eddie shook his head as he chuckled. 'Oh, yes, my darling! If anyone can find him a wife, it's you!'

By the time they had talked a little more about working in the hospital, dinner was soon over and Eddie dutifully made them all a cup of tea. They had just taken the first sip and then Eddie invited his wife to tell him about how she had suffered the injury to her shoulder. 'Well, it happened in my last ever rugby match for my team,' she began. 'And ever since then, I haven't been able to lift my left arm above shoulder height; at least, not without some pain. I've been to a few different physiotherapists and none of them seem to be able to do anything with it.' She held his gaze silently for a moment, waiting for his response.

Noticing the uncomfortable pause, Eddie jumped in. 'But Ben has magic fingers! Don't you, Ben!'

He looked at Eddie's expectant expression. 'Ah well…' he stuttered a bit.

'So come on then, Ben, show Rita the same thing you did with my ankle! Wait till you see this!' he said excitedly as he turned to his wife. They both looked at him and it was then that he knew it was time to deliver on his sending. Gently clearing his throat, as a doctor might before he examines a patient, he got up from his chair and took a few steps round the table until he was standing slightly behind Rita on her left. Rita shuffled a little in her seat and straightened her neck, as if expecting some kind of massage.

'Ah…so where does it hurt?' he asked a little nervously. It was one thing to put his hands on a patient that he didn't know on the ward, but putting his hands on his friend's wife in their dining room was something completely different.

'It's just up around here, really!' Rita replied, circling her finger over the outer corner of her left shoulder. After putting her hand down, he raised both his hands over the area that she had indicated. He could feel Eddie's gaze penetrating right through him. It did make him a little nervous, but now he had to simply focus on what he was doing. He slowly lowered his hands towards Rita's shoulder and then, instantly, he experienced the same feelings that he had on the cardiac ward. His hands felt as if there was a tremendous rush of blood through them so that it felt like they were glowing. Then, when both his hands eventually settled on Rita's shoulder, the pins and needles sensation began buzzing through his fingers. He really wasn't sure what kind of a reaction he was going to see. The reaction from the man in the cardiac ward had been very dramatic and so he really couldn't imagine what was going to happen this time.

At first, Rita gave a quick shiver. Then there was a sharp intake of breath. 'Oh, I can feel something,' she said nervously. Eddie took a step towards her with a bit of a concerned look on his face. The buzzing sensation in his fingers died down as if to indicate that the job was done. He lifted his hands from Rita's shoulder and took a small step back to see what would happen next. He didn't have to wait long. 'Oh, it's getting warmer!' Rita yelped with some alarm. She reached for her shoulder with her right hand and started patting it as if it was on fire. As she did so, she also jumped up from her chair, knocking it backwards into her guest, pushing him back against the wall. The concerned husband started to follow his wife as she skipped into the living room, still patting at her shoulder.

'What's going on, Ben?' Eddie cried in alarm as he set off after his wife. He grabbed her glass of water as he passed the table and proceeded to engage in what could only be described as the funniest dance around a living room that he had ever seen. Out in front was Rita who was jumping and twisting around the living room table as if trying to escape something that had climbed up her back. Not to be outdone, Eddie was keeping up with her, trying to throw some water onto her as she yelped and squealed; doing a second lap of the living room. It was quite a sight to behold and it was all he could do not to burst out laughing.

However, the merry dance around the living room soon came to an abrupt halt. Rita suddenly stopped moving and stuck her left arm straight up in the air. Eddie stopped trying to throw water onto his wife and for a moment there was silence. Everyone stood still, and slowly Rita turned her head to a confused looking Eddie behind her. 'Eddie,' she squeaked nervously.

'What is it, my love, what is it?' asked Eddie frantically.

'I think…I think…' she stuttered; I think my shoulder is better! Eddie took a step back and put his hand to his head. Rita slowly turned around and put her arm down and then she started to rotate it in all kinds of directions, as if to test the joint. Then with a loud scream, she shouted at her husband' 'Eddie, my shoulder is back to normal! I really am healed!'

'Oh darling!' exclaimed a jubilant Eddie and rushed into an embrace with his wife. Tears began to roll down her cheeks and Eddie squeezed her and held her for a few seconds. It was a very touching moment and it made him feel privileged to see a couple so happy. But then, as they released each other from their embrace, they both looked to him where he was still standing with his back against the wall. He hadn't realised it, but he was standing there with a huge grin on his face. All three of them could see the joy in each other's faces and without hesitation, Eddie and Rita both rushed over to him. With a chorus of 'thankyou's,' they both embraced him. Being the size he was and them being the size they were, he was completely enveloped by their embrace. Just as it was becoming difficult to breath, they both released him and took a step back.

Rita was still rolling her newly freed up shoulder. 'Ben, that was amazing!' she said with a true sense of awe. 'How on earth did you do that?' Suddenly, he felt awkward about what to say again.

He opened his mouth to begin, but thankfully, Eddie stepped in to rescue him again. 'I told you darling!' he said, turning his head to his wife. 'This guy has magic fingers! He has the touch! He has the gift!'

Rita turned back to Ben. 'Is that true, Ben? Is this some kind of gift?'

He paused for a second and then decided to go with the flow. 'Ah…yeah, it's a gift!' Rita moved her head back slightly with the sense of being impressed.

'Well, let me tell you, Ben!' she said with a very authoritative Caribbean tone, 'that is some gift! And I just want to thank you from the bottom of my heart.' She pressed down onto her chest with both hands to illustrate where she was talking from and then she embraced him again.

As she did so, he could feel Eddie giving him a few hearty pats on the back. 'Thank you, Ben, thank you! You really don't know how much this means to the both of us!'

With the celebrations over, it seemed that it was time to leave. He thanked them both for their hospitality and remembered to compliment Rita on how good the lasagne was. Perhaps this compliment would result in an invitation back for more. It was certainly something to hope for. After getting his shoes and coat on in the hallway, he bid them farewell and walked back down the road. By this time the stars were out and as he looked up at them and marvelled at their beauty, he couldn't help but wonder at this amazing Sender who had given him this gift. Who was he exactly? Was he someone that could be known? Someone that you could have a relationship with? It really was a big mystery to him. But what he did know was that it was all real! The Sender was real and his sending was real and the proof of that was now there for all to see. All that remained to be seen was where this sending and this gift would lead him.

After catching the bus and getting back into his flat, these thoughts were still rolling around in his mind. The possibilities seemed to be endless, but his energy wasn't. By the time he got his clothes off and got dressed for bed, he was exhausted and as soon as his head hit the pillow he went straight to sleep.

Chapter 9
The Man to See

When he woke the next morning, he felt fresher than he had done in a long time. He walked across the living area in his bare feet and put the kettle on. Once he had a steaming mug of coffee in his hand, he took a moment to stand in front of the big window. There were even fewer leaves on the tree now, but the wind had died down and there was a glint of winter sunshine peeping over the distant rooftops. Everything in front of him was changing. The darkness was giving way to the light and even the deepening winter was full of festive potential. But it wasn't just the environment that was changing, it was him as well. His shattered confidence and shaky faith were now both transformed into a bold conviction. The Sender was real and his sending was real. He was here to heal as many people as he possibly could! He would transform lives and he would change people's minds. The only question was, what would they be thinking when their minds were changed. It was all very well for him to know what he was doing and why he was doing it, but the growing question on his mind was how he was going to communicate this to everyone else. As had happened on a couple of occasions now, people were asking him what happened when he touched people. They were asking how he was able to do these things. Up until now, circumstances and people's willingness to answer their own questions had got him through, but how long would that continue? Eventually, he was going to have to explain what really lay behind his ability. He still hadn't quite figured out how he was going to do that without sounding like a nutter, but he knew that he was going to have to come up with something.

With the last sip of his coffee, he quickly set the cup down on the table in the kitchen area and rushed into the bathroom to get a shower. It wasn't long until he was dressed and out the door. The air was getting gradually colder, but the bright sunshine made up for the drop in temperature. After a quick bus journey, he jumped off the bus with a skip in his step and glided into the foyer of the hospital. He glanced at the clock on the wall above the entrance and suddenly realised that he was actually 20 minutes earlier than usual. His good mood must have got him through his morning routine faster than he thought. Pleased with his early arrival, he slowed his walk down to a more casual pace and sauntered over to the door of the staff room. He opened the door and walked into the room only to find it a little emptier due to the earlier time. Enid was at the kitchen area, setting out some things that she had clearly brought from home and over by the TV at the back of the room, there were three men slouched down in the soft seats. He walked over to his seat and put his bag down at the side. Enid didn't turn around to see who had come in; perhaps she hadn't heard him. But unusually, he saw a couple of the men on the soft seats turn around to look at him. He put his hand up to give them a quick wave and gave an awkward smile. It was highly unusual for the TV zombies to look at anything apart from the TV and very soon it became apparent that they weren't really looking at him for communication, but more out of curiosity. They whispered something to each other and then turned back to the TV again. All of sudden, he felt a bit silly waving to them and got himself seated in his chair in the corner as quickly as he could.

He was just unzipping his coat a little, as he started to feel a bit warmer, when he noticed Enid coming over to the table with a cup of tea or coffee in her hand. She got herself seated at the table facing him, but without looking up. He let a few seconds go by to see if she would lift her head and then when he could wait no longer, he initiated with a greeting. 'Morning Enid,' he said as cheerily as he could. Enid lifted her head a little and with barely a glance in his direction, she whispered a barely audible 'hello.' This was not the Enid that he was used to at all. She was normally the bright sunshine of the staff room, glowing with kindness and fussing over them like a mother hen. But now she was completely different. Ever since that day that Mo had taken her home, she had been withdrawn and even sad. It was then that he remembered something that Mo had said to him the day before. It had something to do with an experience that Enid had gone through back in the Philippines; something which had clearly left her traumatized. After all the kind things that she had done for him, he instantly wanted to help her and so he got up from his seat and walked over to the table. As he sat down at the table next to her, she acknowledged his presence with a small turn of her head.

Leaning over the table on his elbows, he spoke as gently as he could, 'What's the matter, Mama?'

Glancing in his direction again, she replied with a short sigh, 'Oh, it's nothing.' There was a pause as he held his ground, not wanting to back away from her pain. 'It happened a long time ago,' she whispered. 'But it can't be changed now.' This time she turned her head fully to face him. There were tears in eyes. 'Somebody hurt me, Ben.' Her lip trembled. 'Somebody hurt me when I was just a young woman.' She dropped her head down again and a tear dropped from her eyes onto the table. instinctively she began to wipe it up using her hand. 'And I just can't forget it,' she added with a trembling voice. Her right hand was still wiping at the table, drying up the tear drop and without even thinking about it, he put his hand on hers.

Instinctively, she gripped his hand and he responded by gripping hers. 'Enid,' he said with a note of authority which even surprised himself. 'You have done nothing wrong and you have nothing to be ashamed of. You are a good person and nothing that anyone else does to you can ever change that.'

Enid's ears picked up a little when he said this and she turned her head just enough to show that she was listening. 'Are you sure?' she whispered.

'Enid,' he continued, 'we all love you. And the reason we love you is because you are a good and kind person. There is no-one else in this whole hospital who is loved more than you!' Enid now put her other hand on top of his and he returned the gesture so that both their hands were piled up on top of each other. They looked into each other's faces until he started to smile. From behind her tears Enid smiled briefly before she let out a big sigh and pulled her hands back.

Suddenly she slapped her hands on the table and got to her feet. 'OK, I'm going to butter some scones!' she said as she wiped the tears from her eyes. Enid then walked quickly over to the kitchen worktop where she unwrapped a pile of homemade scones and set to work. At that moment, the door opened and in walked Eddie and Mo.

As soon as Eddie saw him, his voice boomed round the room. 'Oh, there he is! Mr Magic Hands himself! Wow, what a job you did on my wife last night!'

'I beg your pardon!' interjected Mo with a wry smile as he collapsed into the chair at the other end of the table.

'Steady, Mo, steady!' replied Eddie quickly as he opened his locker. 'No, we had our friend Ben here round for tea last night and he fixed the wife's dodgy shoulder. Literally, you should have seen it, Mo! One touch from those magic hands and she was right as rain! Even talking about going back to rugby this morning!'

Mo turned to look at him. 'Is that right, Ben? Are you the new quack in town?

He could feel himself blush a little. 'Oh, I don't know about that!' he said rather shyly.

'So, when did this all start? Mo inquired further. Ben could feel himself starting to feel a little awkward now. Eddie wasn't jumping in with his own interpretation; instead, he was being left to answer for himself.

'Well, it just kind of happened, really,' came the vague answer.

'Just happened!' retorted Mo with a note of indignation and a chuckle. 'How on earth does something like that just happen?' Mo was on a bit of a roll now. 'What did you do?' Mo continued with his intermittent chuckling. 'Did you just shake someone's hand one day and accidentally fix their bad wrist or something?' Another pause followed as he was left to answer on his own. He could feel the temperature rising in his face. Was this the time to just blurt out everything that he had experienced over the last few weeks? Was it time to tell them about his encounter with the Sender? He feared that such a confession would make him look like an absolute nutcase. Not really a good look for someone who wanted to get close to people. Instinctively he looked at Eddie, who was waiting for him to answer like everyone else.

'Ahh…' he croaked like a pupil who stuck their hand up in class without knowing the answer. He felt completely flummoxed at this point and even looked at the floor as he continued to croak in his effort to find words.

Eventually, Mo broke the tension when it started to get awkward for everyone. 'Alright, alright, Ben, don't bust a blood vessel or nothin'? I was just asking?' Ben gave a nervous chuckle and gladly turned to Enid as she set two cups of coffee down in front of himself and Mo. 'Oh thank you, Mama!' said Mo, relieved to talk to someone who could answer him; 'And how are you today?'

'Oh I'm fine,' she said in a tone that was suddenly a lot more upbeat than a few minutes earlier. 'And don't you bother Ben with your questions,' she added. 'Can't you see, he's still waking up!' She looked at him with a lovely smile and turned quickly back to the kitchen to fetch the scones that she had been buttering.

'Wait for Ben to wake up,' Mo protested loudly. 'I don't think Ben ever wakes up!' Mo shot a cheeky grin across the table at him.

'Oh yeah, Mo!' came the deep voice of Eddie from the locker. 'That's rich coming from you! The person who arrives late more than most!'

Mo turned to Eddie to continue the jousting. 'Eddie, you know very well that I have a lot of responsibilities at home that keep me up during the night.'

Eddie raised his eyebrows. 'Are you seriously telling me that you are up during the night with the kids?'

'No, no!' protested Mo again. 'Not the kids! I have to keep up to date with the cricket results. Don't you know Pakistan are playing Sri Lanka!' Enjoying the wind-up session, everyone laughed and Mo smiled a big grin as he took another sip of his coffee.

The good-natured banter continued for another few minutes as everyone enjoyed the coffee and scones that Enid was serving up. For a moment, it seemed that things were back to the way they were. Enid was doing much better and everyone was enjoying the banter between Eddie and Mo. But as nice as these moments were in the staff room with his friends, it was never going to be like this again. The more people he healed, the more things were going to change and they were going to change fast. More questions were going to be coming his way and he was going to have to answer them fully. He wished he had more time to think about how to handle everything that was coming, but after a couple more sips of his coffee, Madge arrived at the door and the day was thrown into high gear.

Chapter 10
New Believers

Ben set off from the staff room with a spring in his step. The events of the night before and even his private moment with Enid had given him a big lift emotionally. He was buoyant and optimistic and even though he knew he had to figure out a way to explain his ability, he was sure that there was a way around this problem. It wasn't long before he got to the stairwell and he bounded up the stairs as he usually did. The cluster of student nurses stood where they normally did, halfway between the ground floor and the first floor. But this time, they didn't just have their faces buried in their phones. Instead, they were poking each other and looking at him as he jogged past and then looking back at their phones. He smiled back at them as he passed, but they were busy in conversation once more. He really didn't have a clue who any of them were, but they certainly seemed to recognise him for some reason. He smiled to himself as he reached the first floor. It was probably something as simple as a funny post that Mo had put on social media about him. Mo was not above making a joke on social media, but he didn't really care about social media and therefore he didn't give it anymore thought.

Entering the ward, he was greeted by the familiar sight of people in uniforms of different types scurrying here and there. If Sister Montgomery knew how to do one thing, it was to keep people busy. Even if they weren't doing much, they knew that they had to keep moving, especially when she was watching. Taking care not to get in anyone's way, he carefully made his way towards the nurses' station. On his way there, he could see a different kind of gathering around Dr Pujara who was standing against the desk at the nurses' station. He was wearing a bright blue shirt with a pink tie; both of which looked very expensive. But rather than a cluster of junior doctors hanging on his every word, there was, what looked like a family. A husband and wife and a couple of grown-up children.

The wife in particular was quite animated in her gesturing and by the look on Dr Pujara's face he was enjoying what was being said. Beside the doctor, as always, was Sister Montgomery. She was nodding and smiling and looking as proud as a peacock. Every now and again she would tilt her head towards the tall figure of Dr Pujara as if to bask in his glory. It was a pretty sickening sight, but he had no choice but to get closer. He came to a slow stop a few paces away from the cosy huddle; close enough to hear repeated 'thank you's' coming from the wife and the husband. Eventually Sister Montgomery caught his eye and then she did something quite strange; she actually spoke to him kindly. 'Oh Ben, there you are. Would you follow Dr Black on his ward rounds please? There's a good lad!' she said in a rather posh tone.

'Ah…sure, no problem!' he replied; grateful for not being barked at. No sooner had he spoken than Sister Montgomery went back to basking in the glory of Dr Pujara and his presence was forgotten. He couldn't help but smile at the fact that he had managed to dodge the wrath of the dreaded Sister and with a skip in his step, he went in search of Dr Black.

After poking his head into a couple of bay wards, he eventually found Dr Black standing at the end of the bed of an elderly lady who was sitting in her chair. He had a white shirt with rolled up sleeves and neatly pressed black trousers. Along with his dark hair, he could have been mistaken for a Greek waiter, except for the stethoscope around his neck. Unsurprisingly, he was accompanied by Dr Kanu. She was sitting on the bed talking to the patient. It was always impressive to the see the way that Dr Kanu took time with the patients and you could tell that they appreciated seeing the big smile that she always wore. Not wanting to intrude on the doctor patient conversation, he stood just inside the ward entrance, next to the hand-washing station. The man who was sitting up on the bed nearest to him looked up briefly from the paper he was reading to see who was there. Ben smiled politely at him and said, 'hello' quietly. The man, who was wearing a thick tartan bathrobe, dropped his head back down to his paper; clearly not impressed with the greeting. Just then, Dr Black flipped over the pages of the patient's chart that he was reading.

'Well, Mrs Fogel,' he announced with some authority. It seems that your operation has been a success, but we will need to keep you in for a few more days, just before we let you lose. Now, Dr Kanu here is going to take a few blood tests and then we can sort out your medication.' Having made his announcement to the patient, there was a brief conversation between himself and Dr Kanu about some of the details and then Dr Black went back to the charts to fill in a few details. Dr Kanu picked up a tray of sample bottles and needles in order to begin taking the bloods. Even from standing at the other end of the ward, he could see the look of horror on the elderly woman's face when she saw Dr Kanu bringing the needles in her direction. The patient shifted uneasily in her long floral design nightgown as Dr Kanu sat down on the bed beside her.

Dr Kanu paused for a moment, as if pondering something. She looked around her and suddenly fixed her gaze on Ben.

'Oh, excuse me, Ben. Can you come and help me for a moment please?' she said with that big bright smile that could not be resisted. Slightly taken aback by this request, he gestured to himself just to be sure it was him that she wanted. She laughed with amusement at his indecision and proceeded to wave him over. As he walked over, she pulled the sleeves of her green silk blouse up a little and put on the rubber gloves that were always worn when taking bloods. He came to a standstill just in front of her and the patient.

'Now, Mrs Fogel,' she said as she turned her attention back to the patient. 'This is my friend, Ben, here, and he is going to help us get these samples done; OK?' she said in a reassuring manner. He smiled at the elderly lady, slightly amused at his introduction and purpose in this situation. She smiled back at him with a face that had just gone slightly paler as Dr Kanu rolled up the sleeve on her arm and applied the antiseptic wipe. Dr Kanu prepared the syringe and blood sample tube for collection.

While keeping the needle slightly out of sight, Dr Kanu now turned her attention back to him. 'OK, Ben,' she said cheerfully, 'I just want you to hold Mrs Fogel's hand and while you do that, Mrs Fogel will keep on looking at you and not at me.' They both nodded silently and at that point he took Mrs Fogel's right hand in his left hand and held it firmly.

'Oh!' said the patient with some surprise, 'your hands are roasting! Did you have them on a radiator or something?'

He suddenly felt a little self-conscious and tried to deflect attention away from himself, 'Oh no, it's not me, Mrs Fogel, it's you! Your hands are freezing! But you know what they say, cold hands, warm heart!' he said in a rather rushed manner. Mrs Fogel nodded and winced at the same time as Dr Kanu took the opportunity to get the first sample done.

Dr Kanu continued changing over the sample tubes and in the meantime the conversation quickly dried up as the patient just looked away and closed her eyes while Ben kept holding her hand. Aware of the sudden lull in conversation, Dr Kanu asked out loud, 'So what's all the fuss around Dr Pujara this morning then?'

'Oh, that's the family of the miracle man from yesterday,' came the voice from the end of the bed.

Yeah, his whole family came in to thank Dr Pujara personally,' Dr Black continued. 'Oh, I'm sure he'll enjoy that!' Dr Kanu replied rather wistfully.

Dr Black laughed while continuing to scribble on the charts, 'Yeah, not as much as Sister Montgomery, I don't think!' he added.

Dr Kanu was just about to get the third blood sample when she suddenly turned her attention back to Ben. 'I heard you were in the ward when this patient's health suddenly improved!' she said with her eyes fixed intently on him. 'What did you see happen?' For the second time that morning, he was completely thrown by a question about his activities.

'Oh well...' he began slowly. 'I didn't really see much. He just started moving around in the bed and then you lot rushed in and that was that!'

'Hmmm' came the quizzical tone from Dr Kanu who nodded her head to the side and then continued to get the next sample.

'Don't quiz the poor guy, Mary,' said Dr Black. That's not your line of work is it, Ben!'

'No, no,' he replied shyly. Thankful for Dr Black's intervention, he stood quietly as he watched Dr Kanu finish taking the last blood sample and do all the labelling of the sample tubes. Once again, when questioned about his sending and his actions, he felt completely unprepared, even exposed. It was one thing to heal people, but it was quite another to explain it to people, especially those who were sceptical. But the pressure was building now. He couldn't keep on dodging questions forever. No, he was going to have to take the step of testifying clearly what his sending was all about. He could not be a coward; he was going to have to be honest with others and even honest with himself. This was who he was now, this was the path he was determined to follow and he had to embrace that.

Once Mrs Fogel's samples were taken, he was no longer needed by the two doctors and went back to stand at the entrance to the ward. Having taken all their samples, Dr Kanu handed them over to him with a grateful smile and he set off for the labs. He was already thinking about a form of words that he would use to explain what he was doing; all he needed now was the courage to speak them out loud.

Chapter 11
Fame and Confession

After Ben left the samples in at the lab, it was already time for break, and so he headed round to the staff room. Unfortunately, the labs were at the opposite end of the hospital, and so, by the time he got to the staff room the break time routine was in full flow. Eddie and Mo were already sitting at the table with their mugs of coffee and Enid was at the kitchen getting a few things put on to a plate. He had barely got the door closed behind him when the familiar call rang out from the table. 'Oh, there he is, there he is! Mr Magic Hands himself!' Announced Eddie enthusiastically. 'Come on over mate, come on over!' Eddie pushed one of the chairs out from the table with his foot and motioned for him to join them. Just as he sat down, Enid arrived at the table with a plate that was dangerously overladen with fresh muffins. As soon as the plate hit the table, one of the muffins rolled off the top in his direction and he stretched out his right hand to catch it before it hit the table surface. 'Oh wow, Mama!' he exclaimed. 'Where did all these come from?'

'Well,' she said with a smile that hadn't been seen for a few days. 'You have all been such a great help to me over the last couple of days that I just wanted to treat you all; so I nipped round the corner to the little shop and grabbed a few treats. So, just enjoy them!'

'Oh, thank you, Mama, thank you,' responded Eddie with wide eyes. 'That is a really lovely thing to do! Isn't it, Mo?!' There was no response from Mo, who was clearly in another world, listening to his headphones.

Eddie tried again, 'Mo, aren't these lovely?'

Then without warning, Mo lifted his hands in the air and let out a huge shout! 'Yes! That's another one!' Everyone one jumped at the sudden outburst and then after a couple more shakes of the arms in celebration, Mo seemed to become aware of his surroundings again. With everyone looking at him now, he removed his headphones and explained himself. 'Pakistan have just taken their third wicket of the afternoon!' he exclaimed with some glee. Seeing the shocked look on everyone's faces, he sheepishly put his arms down and then noticed the muffins on the plate in front of him. 'Oh look, muffins!' he said; as if the first person to notice them.

'Yes, muffins that Mama got for us Mo!' said Eddie in a rather unamused manner. 'Wasn't that nice of her?'

'Yeah! Great! Thanks, Mama!' Mo gave a quick glance round to where Enid was standing and then quickly proceeded to lift two muffins off the plate. Eddie glared at Mo disapprovingly for a second and then turned his attention back to Ben.

'So, Ben, did you really like that lasagne the other night?' asked Eddie with a suddenly brighter disposition on his face.

'Oh yes!' he said without hesitation. 'The best I've ever had!'

Eddie leaned back in his chair with a smile of satisfaction. 'Well, I'm glad you liked it! Very glad! And you know…' he added, 'after you helped Rita with her shoulder; which is still doing great by the way; it reminded me of someone else with a joint problem.' As he finished his sentence, Eddie slowly got up from his chair in a way that was clearly leading to something that had already been planned.

Having got to his feet, Eddie turned around to the group of men who were sitting around the TV. 'Hey, Stanley! Come on over!' bellowed Eddie above the noise from the TV. Ben leaned back in his chair to see who Eddie was talking to. They may have shared this staff room with the TV group, but there was very little interaction between them. At that moment, a very thin looking man with a large bald patch got up from his chair. He was dressed in the usual clerical uniform of black trousers and white shirt and he walked quickly from the TV over to where Eddie was standing.

'Alright, Eddie!' said Stanley in a strong cockney accent. 'What's happenin' then?'

Eddie went straight into his introduction. 'Stanley, I want to introduce you to the guy I was telling you about; this is my friend, Ben here,' said Eddie with his arm held out in his direction. Alright, Ben! Nice to meet ya!' said Stanley with both his hands stuck deep into his pockets. Stanley seemed like a plucky sort of fellow, but at the same time seemed a little nervous. Probably aware of the time limitations of tea break, Eddie wasted no time in moving proceedings along. 'Now, Stanley, just put your hand out and show Ben the problem.'

Stanley took a step closer to where Ben was sitting and held out his right arm. 'Right, well…' Stanley began. 'It's some kind of repetitive strain injury or something; and when I bend my wrist or put any pressure on hit, it's absolute agony!' he explained, while pointing to the area of the wrist where the pain was. Ben shuffled his chair a little so that he was facing Stanley's outstretched arm with his whole body. Everyone around the table was transfixed on what was about to happen. Even the cricket match had been forgotten!

With a quick sigh, Ben put his hands over the wrist of the outstretched arm in front of him. 'OK, just hold still,' he said, and with that instruction, he clasped Stanley's wrist with both hands. Suddenly, the heat and the pins and needles sensation rushed through his hands. The response to this contact seemed to come quicker than before, and when it did, Stanley let out a bit of a groan. For a second, his arm trembled a little; then within another couple of seconds it was all over. He let go of Stanley's wrist and Stanley quickly withdrew his arm; rubbing it quickly with his other hand.

'What the heck was that?' said Stanley with some alarm in his face.

Eddie jumped in straight away. 'That was the magic hands, mate! That was the magic hands! Come on try it out!'

Still looking a little unsure of what had just happened, Stanley slowly put his outstretched hand palm down on the table. There was a pause, and then he put more pressure on his hand; and then he moved his arm over his planted hand at different angles. He took a sudden gasp of air. 'That's amazing!' said Stanley with a genuinely surprised look on his face. 'How on earth did you do that?' he said as he withdrew his hand and started moving it around in all directions.

'I told you, didn't I!' declared a joyful Eddie. He has magic hands, doesn't he! I tell ya, he can fix any joint problem you can mention!' Ben could feel himself smile as he watched Stanley try lifting different things that were on the table; even the big plate of muffins with his newly fixed hand. As Stanley put the plate back down on the table, Eddie made a loud announcement from behind him. 'And that's a wrap!' he said with a note of satisfaction. Ben turned on his chair only to find that Eddie had been filming the whole incident on his phone and he was now in the process of doing something with the video that he had just finished.

'Wait a minute, Eddie!' he said. 'Have you been filming this whole thing?'

'Oh yeah! Of course, I have!' replied Eddie with great enthusiasm. 'And now it is on my Facebook page for the world to see!' As he finished the sentence, he emphatically pressed a button on his phone to finish the process. Having finished what he was doing on his phone, Eddie looked at him directly. 'Ben! Everyone has to know about this! They have to know how talented you are! What you can do and how much you can help people! It's amazing!' Eddie's face was full of excitement as he praised him in front of the others, but in his own mind he felt a little stunned. He had been planning to keep a low profile for a while, but now, all of a sudden, his good friend Eddie had basically outed him to the world; or at least, all his friends on Facebook, which was probably legion, given how quickly Eddie made friends.

He was still taking a moment to digest the ramifications of the fame that had just been thrust upon him when Mo interjected. 'OK, OK, hold on a minute!' said Mo with his hands in the air, as if to slow everything down for a moment! Ben!' he snapped in an uncharacteristically serious tone. The sound of Mo calling his name, shook him out of his stunned state and he turned his head in Mo's direction. 'Ben,' he continued. 'All you did was touch that man's hand.' Mo glanced quickly at Stanley who was passively following the conversations around him. 'You didn't feel around his hand, you didn't rub it or press on it, like a physiotherapist or anyone like that!' There was an awkward pause from Mo at that point and a strange soberness descended on the conversation. After a couple of seconds of looking away in deep thought, Mo continued his reasoning. 'So, if you're not working with the muscles or the nerves, then how are you doing this? This is more than just magic hands, Ben!' All of a sudden, there was silence and he could feel the gaze of everyone bearing down on him. The expectation of an honest explanation was getting heavier by the second and there was no chance of anyone bailing him out this time. His mind was blank and he began to look at the floor. The usual fumbling for words began unconsciously.

'Ah…well…um…' he stuttered. It was no use, there was no help coming this time and he could feel the heat rising in his cheeks. His heart began to thump louder in his chest. He looked up briefly at the faces that were looking at him. They were all friends but they all wanted an answer. Then, without warning he just burst into tears. He put his hand to his face to hide the emotion. It was like a dam bursting inside him. He had been holding so much inside him over the last few days, but now it was all coming out.

Straight way, he could feel the big hand of Eddie on his shoulder. 'Oh Ben!' he said with real concern. 'It's alright, mate! It's alright! Don't worry about it!' Ben could sense the presence of Stanley leaving the table at that point. The poor man probably felt a bit awkward about this strange outburst of emotion, but in his absence, Mo and Enid were quick to step in. 'I'm sorry, Ben! I didn't mean to pressurize you! You don't have to explain!' They were kind words from Mo, but there was nothing more comforting than the warm embrace that came from Enid. She stooped over him and put her arms around his head and pulled him into her chest. She held him until his sobbing stopped and he began to breath a bit more normally.

Enid eventually loosened her hug and she spoke softly to him. 'Ben, whatever it is, you can tell us! We are your family and we love you.'

'Yeah, Ben! We love you mate! It's alright!' added Eddie who would not be outdone on the compassion front.

Ben took a deep breath and looked up at each of them. Sensing a freedom that wasn't there before, he spoke to all of them. 'Actually guys, it's not alright. Something has happened to me and I have to be completely honest about it with you.' The faces that were looking at him with such concern now changed back to faces of curiosity. Eddie took the seat next to him, while the other two stayed where they were; all waiting with great anticipation. 'I met someone,' he began. There wasn't a hint of interruption! 'But he isn't a normal person. In fact, I don't even really know who he is at all. All I know is that he gave me this ability to heal people and he has sent me to heal as many people as possible.' He paused and waited for a question, but none came. He smiled a little as he could see the rather stunned reaction in their faces. He continued, 'And that's what I've been doing. I've been healing people on the ward and in here and at Eddie's house. I just put my hands on people and I get a feeling of heat and pins and needles and that's it done.' He shrugged his shoulders, aware of the simplicity of his explanation. 'Whatever is wrong with them is fixed; and that is what I have been sent to do; and that is what I have to keep on doing!'

He could feel a huge weight being lifted off his shoulders now that he had eventually confessed everything that had been secretly going on in his life for the past few weeks. It was also strangely pleasing that the explanation that he had just given came out a lot simpler than he had expected. In fact, the words that he had used actually brought clarity to his own mind; and with that clarity he now felt an even greater conviction about the mission that he was on. As for his captive audience, they all collectively leaned back and took a deep breath. Mo was the first to respond. 'Well,' he said with a sigh, 'it must be Allah! Allah has chosen you, my friend! He is the one who has sent you!' Mo shook his head with a smile; 'and he has given you this power so that you can serve him in this way! Amazing! I never thought I would see such a thing! Wow!'

'Well, you might be right, Mo' Ben replied! But the Sender didn't give me a name! All I know is that he must be pretty powerful!

Mo looked at Ben and the others to reinforce his opinion. 'Well, I say it is Allah! It has to be!' The other two remained silent for a moment and then it was Eddie's turn to speak. He got up from his chair and walked over to where Ben was sitting and put his hand on his shoulder once more.

Standing beside him, he announced to Mo and Enid, 'Well, I don't know who this Sender is, but I believe in Ben! And if he says that he's been sent on some mission, then I'm behind him one hundred percent!' Having made this resolute statement, Eddie gave him a very firm pat on the shoulder, as if to seal his commitment to his friend. The sound of Eddie's hand slapping his shoulder seemed to prompt Enid to speak next.

'Yes, me too,' declared Enid. 'I believe in you, Ben. And whatever your mission is, I will help you in whatever way I can!'

Suddenly aware that he was a little out of step with the rest in his support for Ben, Mo piped up, 'Well, what do we do now?' In unison, they all looked at the leader of this mission.

Shifting a little in his seat, Ben cleared his voice and took a deep breath. 'I think we need to keep this quiet for now. If we draw too much attention to the healings, then we will get more attention than we want.' He turned to Eddie, 'probably best to take that video down that you just posted as well.'

'No problem,' said Eddie and immediately started working on his phone.

Turning back to the other two, he continued, 'If we keep a low profile, then I can get around more patients before things get hectic.'

'Yeah, I totally agree,' came Eddies' voice from behind him.

'But if we don't get back to work now, then we won't have jobs in the hospital at all' Eddie added. They all looked at the clock on the wall and saw that they were five minutes late returning to work. Without hesitation, they all went for the door, with Mo taking one last mouthful of coffee before he ran out last. Their conversation had been brought to a rather abrupt end, but as he hurried back to the cardiac ward, he could feel a new sense of hope. He wasn't carrying this burden on his own anymore; now he had supporters. And with that support he now felt that anything was possible.

Chapter 12
In the Open

Ben sprang up the stairwell feeling a little bit lighter than when he last came down. At last he had told someone what was happening to him! It was such a great relief! But there was more to this confession experience. Up until now, he didn't even know how to explain his experience to himself, let alone others. However, now that he had the experience of telling people face to face, it was as if his experience had now come into sharp focus. He had been sent to do a job; and that was the full story. Of course, if he had been sent, then there had to be a sender, but for now that was a further explanation that he was happy to leave. As he walked onto the ward, he was so focussed on his own story, retelling it to himself over and over, that he was actually looking forward to sharing it with others. This positive attitude was compounded by the fact that even the sun had begun to shine in through the windows of the ward, which improved his mood still further. But no sooner had he stepped onto the ward than a familiar dark cloud made its presence felt.

'Oy! You!' came the shrill voice from further down the corridor. Immediately his feet were rooted to the ground and he got that sinking feeling in his stomach. The lean figure in red began marching purposefully towards him. She was gesturing sharply at the watch on her bony wrist and was wearing a face like thunder. 'What time do you call this?' she barked. With a few more steps until she was right in his face, he braced himself for the onslaught. 'Were you too busy talking to your wee friends, were you?' She now had her finger right under his nose. 'Well, let me tell you something, pal! This is a hospital, not a social club! So if you want to spend time chatting with your wee friends, then you do it in your own time! Are we clear?!' He was about to answer, hoping that the tirade was over, but there was no time to get the words out. Looking him up and down with disdain, she started again. 'I don't know! I could find better workers than you if I threw a stick into a crowd of people and hired the first person I hit! You're workshy, you're shoddy, you're a disgrace!' Her voice seemed to be getter louder as she continued. It was as if she was working herself up to a crescendo. But now the crescendo was over and she took a step back. Composing herself and straightening her tunic she looked at him again with a slightly calmer demeanour. 'Now, if you had been here earlier, then you would have heard that thanks to the professionals in this ward; especially Dr Pujara, we have another miraculous recovery on the ward. Mrs Fogel is now ready to go home and for some reason, which I cannot begin to understand, she actually wants to see you. So as soon as you're done saying goodbye, get on with your duties.' With that, she turned on her heels and started to march back up the corridor. Although she couldn't resist her usual parting shot. 'Now, get on with it!' she yelled with a quick glance back in his direction. A cluster of student nurses scattered as she continued marching in their direction and then there was calm.

Aware of the many faces that were looking at him and the redness in his face, he awkwardly looked around him quickly to find Mrs Fogel. Thankfully he spotted her quickly at the same bed she had been in before and he walked quickly over to her. She was sitting beside the bed in her going home clothes; a pair of beige trousers and a white blouse with a floral pattern. She had her handbag sitting on her lap and a couple of plastic bags sitting on the bed. She was the picture of happiness and sharing in that happiness was Dr Kanu. Dr Kanu was sitting on the end of the bed, filling in some forms, clearly enjoying the company of Mrs Fogel. He was only half way across the floor of the ward when Mrs Fogel looked up and spotted him. 'Oh, there he is!' she cried with delight. Her face lit up like someone who had just found her long lost son.

Ben and Dr Kanu glanced at each other and he blushed; both appreciating the humour of the situation. 'Hello Mrs Fogel! And how are you?' he said as he put on his best smile. She put out her hand for him to hold and he dutifully took it as he came to a standstill before her.

'Oh, son! I am so much better because of you!' A big grin spread across his face. It was all he could do in the face of such happiness. 'Do you realise?' she continued with a little tremble in her voice now. 'Do you realise that since that moment you held my hand, I feel like a different person! All my fear went away and even this old body started to get better as well; and now I feel great!' Aware of Dr Kanu sitting close by, he felt the need to deflect a little.

'Well, Mrs Fogel,' he said, 'let's not forget all that the doctors and nurses have done for you.'

Taking the hint, Mrs Fogel gave a quick look at the smiling face of Dr Kanu and was quick to agree. 'Oh yes,' she said, 'there's no doubt about it, they did their part.' But then her attention came straight back to him. 'But you did something special! I know it! I could feel it when you held my hand! And I just wanted to say, thank you! There is something special about you; and I want you to keep on sharing that special whatever that you have!'

At that very moment, another porter arrived at the bed with a wheelchair to take Mrs Fogel to the front door. She withdrew her hand from his and with surprising energy, she got up and gathered her bags and sat down in the wheelchair. She looked up at both he and Dr Kanu, who had just got up. 'Thanks for everything!' she chirped; and with that the porter spun the wheelchair around and she was away! A little stunned by the sudden departure of Mrs Fogel, he and Dr Kanu just stood there for a moment looking at each other. Gathering her thoughts and sitting down again, Dr Kanu looked directly at him. She may have been small in stature, but Dr Kanu had a subtle authority that commanded your attention when she wanted it. 'So, Ben,' she said with some purpose; crossing her legs under her long green skirt. 'There seems to be a bit of a coincidence here. You were present with Mr James just before his amazing recovery and then you were holding Mrs Fogel's hand just before her sudden turnaround.' She let her words hang for a second, just to let them sink into head. 'Is there something I need to know about you?' she asked. Dr Kanu was now looking at him intently, as if trying to read his mind. Such was the intensity of the moment that his clarity of thought completely vanished. His mind went blank under the gaze of Dr Kanu's dark brown eyes which were burning a hole in his soul. He began to stutter for words, but as soon as he did Dr Kanu cut him short. 'Well, then, I think we need to put this coincidence to the test,' she announced; clearly with a plan in mind. 'For the rest of the morning, you will accompany me on my ward rounds'; and before he even had a chance to respond, Dr Kanu got up and walked across the ward to the patient on the other side. She picked up his chart and started reading it. Then, like a dog-walker whose pet was lagging behind she turned her head and beckoned him closer. 'Come on then, let's get started, shall we?' There was a half-smile on her face when she spoke which put him at ease, and so, he walked over to stand beside her. Before long Dr Kanu was straight into the business of talking to the patient and getting to know him and even making him laugh. She really did have an amazing bed-side manner, but that didn't stop her getting down to the business of treatment. With a quick look in the direction of the nurses, she had them running here and there getting needles and medication and even a cup of tea when she thought the patient needed one. It was a pleasure to watch her command of the situation, but she didn't let him stand idly by either. While she was filling in charts and getting samples taken, she always had him holding the patient's hand or passing things to the nurses. It was some of the most intense work that he had ever been part of!

Unsurprisingly, the time flew by as this high-paced ward round continued, but then suddenly the business came to a halt. Without warning, the tall figure of Dr Black crept up behind them. Ben was holding a patient's hand at the time and turned to see Dr Black peering over the shoulder of Dr Kanu as she was sitting on the bed, wrestling with the pages of the patient's file. He really was an impressive looking man. He was dressed sharper than a carving knife with his shiny black shoes, black trousers and pink shirt. His hair was slicked back and he was clean shaven. It was no wonder that Dr Kanu had a bit of a crush on him. But despite her affections for him, she was not going to be distracted. Without even looking up at him, she acknowledged his presence. 'Hello, Dr Black,' she said with jesting formality and a small grin.

'Hello, Dr Kanu,' came the similarly jesting response. 'How many have you killed today then?' Dr Black said, suddenly ratchetting up the humour.

With a slightly bigger grin on her face, Dr Kanu responded in kind. 'Not as many as you, I suspect, Dr Black!'

'Probably right, Dr Kanu! Probably right!' Dr Black replied with a grin of his own this time. At this point, all present were having a little chuckle, including the patient. Dr Black's attention now turned to him. Without addressing him, he continued his conversation with Dr Kanu. 'Well, I see you still have your new assistant with you today. I don't believe we've been properly introduced, Dr...' After a second of delay in understanding, he leapt into the conversation. 'Oh, it's...ah...Ben, sir! Ben Archer!' Dr Black now stood up straight; no longer looking over Dr Kanu's shoulder who was still writing in the charts. 'So, Dr Archer, how are the patients today?' Dr Black said with the same mocking humour in his voice. Ben hesitated, a little perplexed about how to play this pretend identity that Dr Black had bestowed upon him.

'Now, behave!' came the interjection from Dr Kanu who was just finished filling in the chart. 'Ben here, has been a great help! We have got around all the patients in the ward in no time! Haven't we, Ben?'

'Oh yes' he responded promptly.

'Well, that sounds very impressive!' said Dr Black, putting his hands deep into his pockets and turning to face the one he was clearly there for. 'Which makes me think that you probably need get something to eat now! So, what do you say; down to the canteen?' he suggested.

Dr Kanu smiled; clearly pleased by the suggestion. 'Oh, how could I refuse!' she said and promptly got up from the end of the bed and popped the chart back into its holder. 'OK Ben, thanks for all your help,' she said as she turned to smile at him one last time. 'I'll see you after lunch!'

'Yes, sure!' he replied brightly.

'Goodbye Dr Archer! Nice to meet you!' said Dr Black as he stepped away with Dr Kanu, who gave a him a rebuking nudge on the arm. They both chuckled together as they walked out of the bay ward and in a second, they were gone.

'OK, son, I think your work is done here!' said the patient whose hand he was still holding. 'Why don't you go and get some lunch yourself. I'll still be here when you get back!' It was amazing how quickly the time had passed, working with Dr Kanu and now that lunch had been mentioned, he realised just how hungry he actually was. And so, with a couple of pats on his arm, the patient bid him farewell and in an instant Ben was on his way back down to the staff room.

Chapter 13
Up a Level

As he trotted down the stairwell, the bright sunlight was still shining through the windows in between the grey concrete walls. That little bit of sunshine always improved his mood during the darker months. However, his mood didn't need much improvement at the moment. Despite the dressing down that he had received from Sister Montgomery, his spirits had bounced straight back after his conversation with Mrs Fogel. The time that he had spent working with Dr Kanu had also encouraged him. The young doctor was such a lovely person; although it was pretty clear that she suspected him of having some part in the miraculous improvements of the two patients. The time was coming when he may have to widen his circle of trust to include her as well. But for now, he was happy to keep the truth between himself and his three friends in the staff room.

On arriving at the staff room door, he quickly turned the handle and walked in as he normally did. However, it was not the normal sight that greeted him. Instead of the usual faces shuffling around the kitchen, there was actually a bit of a crowd. There were a few people with white shirts sitting at the table; clearly from the clerical department, and at the kitchen area, Enid was busing handing out cups of coffee and plates of scones to Mo and another friend who were serving. As soon as he closed the door behind him, the conversations ceased and the place went quiet. At that moment, Eddie, who was sitting at the head of the table, looked up at him. 'Oh, there he is, there he is! Come on over Ben!' Eddie got up from his seat and quickly ushered him into the seat that he had just vacated. He sat down rather apprehensively, wondering what was coming next. Was this some sort of intervention? Had they come to the conclusion that he had gone nuts and needed help? These thoughts were running through his mind as Mo set a cup of coffee and a scone on the table in front of him. He looked at Mo who was already on his way back to Enid and then he looked up at Eddie who was standing over him with a big smile across his face. Eddie's face was glowing with anticipation over what was about to begin.

Then suddenly, Eddie decided that the time for waiting was over. With a clap of his hands, he launched into his introductions with his usual enthusiasm. 'Now, Ben, I don't know if you have met some of these guys from clerical. Let me introduce, Tina, Frank and Scott.' All three of them looked at him with rather sheepish grins and said 'Hi.'

'These are all friends of Stanley who thought he would bring them to meet you today,' Eddie continued. Sitting a little further down the table, Stanley gave him a little wave and a big grin. He nodded to Stanley in acknowledgment, suddenly realising the direction that this gathering was going in. 'Now, Ben!' Eddie started again, grabbing his attention from the others. 'Just like Stanley, earlier today, all of these people have various problems with their joints and muscles and they were wondering if you would mind helping them the same way that you helped Stanley.' Eddie paused, waiting for a response.

He looked around briefly at the eyes that were all looking at him with hot anticipation. 'Ahh...well...sure!' he stumbled, not really knowing what else to say. He could hardly refuse and so he might as well go with it. With the response now obtained that he was looking for, Eddie now began to marshal the situation.

'OK Tina, you first,' Eddie said, motioning for her to come forward. Taking a moment to tie her red hair back, the slightly plump figure of a woman, probably in her mid-thirties got up and came to stand beside him. Without even allowing her to speak, Eddie kept the process moving. 'Now, Tina has a case of tennis elbow which is giving her a lot of pain, isn't it Tina.' Tina nodded obediently and presented her right arm. 'OK Ben, it's over to you!' Eddie said and gave him a pat on the shoulder as he stood back to give him room to work.

Looking up at Tina, who was now more than a little nervous, he tried to speak to her as gently as he could. 'OK, Tina,' he said, not really knowing what to do next. 'Ahh...if you just want to put your arm on the table.' Tina leaned over a little and put her arm in front of him. Not looking at her at all now, just at her elbow, he gave one last word of comfort. 'Now, this won't hurt at all.' At which point, he let his hands hover over her elbow for a second, and then he gently gripped her elbow with both hands. Immediately, he could feel the heat flow through his hands and into her arm. Tina flinched a little but then he could feel her relax and in a few seconds, he released his grip. She withdrew her arm straight away and everyone looked at her expectantly. With a slightly stunned look on her face, which was getting a bit red with embarrassment, she tentatively started to flex her arm. With each movement, the stunned look turned to a smile and within a few seconds the joy of being pain free spread across her whole face. 'Oh wow!' she said, completely amazed. 'I can't believe it! My arm hasn't felt like this in ages!' She began to laugh a little and a few tears began to roll down her cheeks.

After a moment of moving her arm around, Enid drew alongside Tina and ushered her back to her seat. 'There you go dear and here's a nice hot cup for you.' Enid said as Mo set the cup of coffee down in front of her.

With one done, Eddie wasn't long in stepping back into the drama to keep the process moving. 'OK, Frank, you're up next! Come on, there's a few more to do after you!' Having seen for himself, the big improvement in his colleague, a slightly older man, with similar slender build to Stanley, dutifully got up and moved round to stand beside him. Eddie, who seemed to know the ailment of each of them, presented the man's condition; and as before he proceeded to heal Frank, just as he had done with Tina. Frank moved his neck around with greater ease than before and went and sat down, only to be followed by Scott who then went through the same routine as the others.

Before long, all three of them; Tina, Frank and Scott were all sitting there in front of him, grinning like school children who had just seen Santa. They were all sipping at the hot beverages that Enid had made for them, looking at each other and even giggling with giddy excitement. Eddie was standing to his right with his arms folded, surveying the situation in front of him with supreme satisfaction; and standing at the kitchen with cup in hand was Enid who had the most beautiful smile on her face. It gave him a wonderful sense of unity to see them all together like this. It may have been him doing the healing, but they were all playing their part, just like a team. Just then, he became aware of Mo speaking to someone in the corner of the room. The person was sitting in his soft seat in the corner and Mo was clearly trying to encourage the person to get up. He was a young man of south Asian origin, who looked painfully thin and weak. Eventually, Mo persuaded him to get up and led him over to the table. 'Ben, let me introduce Sachin to you.' Sachin, whose head was pointed at the ground, looked up from the floor briefly and gave a smile.

'Hi Sachin,' he said, but Sachin's head was now pointed back at the floor. Seeing that Sachin wasn't going to do much talking for himself, Mo stepped up.

'Ben, I've known Sachin for a couple of years now and for all that time he has had really bad diabetes and he really needs your help.' Mo looked at Sachin and put his hand on his back, as if to give him a bit of a push forward.' Feeling the pressure to get closer, Sachin took a short step but then stopped.

Looking up through his long black hair which had flopped over his forehead, Sachin clearly had a concern about what was happening, or about to happen. 'Ahh…how are you able to do this?' he said in a rather nervous tone. Then without really waiting for a response, Sachin continued to explain his concern. 'My parents have been praying and making offerings to all the gods and so have the rest of my family back in India; but nothing has changed. So how are you able to do what you're doing?' It was almost as if Sachin was concerned that he was about to get involved in some strange cult and wanted to be sure about what he was opening himself up to.

Understanding the young man's concern, Ben put his cup down and leaned forward on the table. 'You know what, Sachin,' he said with a calm tone. 'The truth is that I don't really understand it all myself. The only thing I know for sure is that I have been sent by someone or something far more powerful than myself and this is the ability that he has given me. But I understand if you want to take some time to think about it.'

He held the young man's gaze for a second before the young man's eyes began to fill with tears. 'I can't do this anymore,' Sachin said with a voice that cracked with emotion. 'I always feel tired and I get depressed and I just need help.' Sachin's head dropped back down and he looked at the floor as his body shook with his sobbing. After a moment, Sachin looked up and when he did, he could see that there was an arm stretched out in his direction. The situation had now gone beyond words and it was time for action. He held his arm out to Sachin, looking for his response; inviting him to take another short step. Everyone held their breath as they waited to see what Sachin would do. Even the three giddy clerical officers could only hold their cups at their mouths in wild anticipation. It seemed to happen in slow motion. Sachin slowly lifted his right foot and took that final step towards him. At the same time, he held out his bony arm and eventually landed his hand in the one that was stretched out in his direction. In an instant, there was a rush of pins and needles that came down Ben's arm like an electric shock. It was such a surprise that he suddenly gripped Sachin's hand as hard as he could. They both jolted a little with the shock of the experience. Sachin tried to pull away a little, but such was Ben's grip on the young man's hand that he wasn't going anywhere. Within a couple of seconds, the electrical sensation was gone and when Sachin pulled away a second time, he freed his hand with such force that he actually fell over backwards; knocking poor Mo all the way back to the soft seat, which he promptly fell into.

There was a stunned silence as they all watched Sachin lying on his back on the floor. He was breathing heavily and deeply, as though stunned. The first to respond was Eddie who went towards the body lying on the floor and stood over him. 'Hey mate, are you alright?' Eddie inquired gently. After a couple more seconds of panting, Sachin turned his head to the big man standing over him.

'Am I alright?' came the rather strange response. 'Am I alright?' he said again; this time with a chuckle. 'I feel amazing!' he said, getting up from the floor in a flash. 'I feel like I could run a mile!' As if to prove his point, he started to jog on the spot as if warming up for the aforementioned jog. Sachin was as giddy with excitement as the other three, who now gathered around him to congratulate him on his newfound health. But before long, the attention had turned back to the one who had healed them. Sachin moved away from the crowd and walked over to Ben, prompting the others to follow close behind. 'I don't know how I can ever thank you,' he said, with an expression of deep sincerity on his face. A chorus of 'thank-you's' echoed behind him from the others.

'No problem,' Ben said with a smile, as he put his hand up in a gesture of acknowledgement.

But Sachin wasn't finished. 'I don't know who this god is who has sent you, but I believe in him and I believe in you!' Sachin's expression was even more intense now. 'Whatever he has sent you to do, keep on doing it! And you can count on me to help you in whatever way I can!' Sachin then put out his hand for a handshake and from his seated position, Ben obliged.

After another chorus of agreement from those behind him, it was Eddie's turn to take control again. 'OK folks, I think you'll find that lunch break finished some time ago, so let's get moving! Back to work everyone! You can come back later if you want!' Eventually the crowd of visitors turned to the door and filed out of the room. As soon as the door was closed, Eddie slapped his hand down on Ben's shoulder and spoke to the rest who were still in the room. 'Well, everyone, we have done some good work there, I think! Thanks for the drinks, Mama, and thanks for bringing your friend, Sachin, Mo. But now we need to get back to work too! So, let's get moving!' After a quick look at his watch, Mo jumped out of his seat and rushed to the door. Enid, quickly rinsed out a few mugs and started for the door herself. He was about to get up himself but was restrained by Eddie's hand which was still on his shoulder. 'Are you OK, Ben?' he said looking down at his friend.

He looked up at Eddie's smiling face and swung his hand on top of the hand on his shoulder. 'Yes, I'm fine, thanks, Eddie.'

'Alright,' came the immediate response; and with a tap on the shoulder, Eddie led the way back to the wards.

Chapter 14
Cut Short

As Ben got to the top of the stairs near the entrance to the ward, he could hear an unusual level of noise. It was as if there was some kind of emergency going on. Sensing that he may be needed, he picked up his pace a little, but as soon as he got to the ward entrance he was stopped in his tracks. The ward was literally packed with all sorts of people. There were twice the usual number of doctors, all the nurses were rushing from place to place, there were several porters standing with wheelchairs and in the middle of it all there was a scrum of relatives and friends who had clearly come to pick up their loved ones. They were carrying bags that were stuffed with patient's belongings in one hand, and in the other hand they were carrying bags full of medication. In the centre of it all was the tall figure of Dr Pujara. There seemed to be some sort of a queue of people wanting to talk to him, and judging by the huge smile on his face, they were clearly there to thank him for whatever had happened. He couldn't see Sister Montgomery due to her small stature, but there was little doubt in his mind that she was right by Dr Pujara's side, soaking up the glory that was being showered upon him. Having surveyed all that was going on, he figured that it was now time for him to slip quietly into the melee and get to work before anyone noticed how late he was. Such was the business of the crowd that it really shouldn't have been a problem, but he had barely taken two steps inside the ward until his cunning plan went to the wall. 'Oh, there he is! It's the healer!' came the cry from his immediate right. With all the buzz of activity going on in front of him, he hadn't noticed a couple of patients who had been parked just at the edge of the ward exit. Nearest the entrance was a man in his fifties who was dressed quite smartly and to his right there was an older lady who was still in her fluffy pink bathrobe. Her face was full of joy and she had her arms thrust out in front of her, clearly beckoning him to come for a hug. No sooner had the words left her lips than the whole ward fell silent. Literally everyone who was there stopped what they were doing and turned to look at him. He froze and looked around at all the faces with a stunned expression on his face. You could have heard a pin drop, until eventually the silence was broken again by another voice. 'Yes, it is him!' came the cry from one of the patients who was still sitting on a bed in the bay. An elderly gentleman in a brown tank top was pointing the finger precisely in his direction. Having had a few seconds to process this new information, there was suddenly a mass movement of people towards him. All the patients and the relatives starting making a bee line for him and in no time at all he was being embraced from all directions. The ladies were hugging him and kissing him and the men were patting him on the back and the shoulders; some of them a little harder than he would have liked. It was more than a little overwhelming and he really didn't know what to say. There were many voices of gratitude and testimonies of how much better they felt, but it was hard to take it all in. He tried to look at everyone who was talking to him and smile at them all individually, but it was a situation which was hard to keep up with.

Slowly but surely the crowd began to drift out of the ward. Some were helped by relatives while others were wheeled out by porters. He had just finished saying goodbye to the last patient when he looked around to see all the other staff still looking at him. Many of the expressions were ones of bemusement and even laughter, but there were two faces whose expressions were quite different. Standing on the other side of the entrance to Bay 1, was the stern-faced pair of Sister Montgomery and Dr Pujara. They were clearly not amused by the migration of people from them to him. It was OK for people to be praising them, but sharing their glory with anyone else, especially a mere porter, was intolerable. He stood there for a moment, waiting for a sign of some kind and before long it came. Without saying a word, Sister Montgomery, with her eyes flaming with rage, pointed a bony finger to the floor immediately in front of her. After the euphoria of being surrounded by patients thanking him, his heart sank and he walked slowly towards the impending dressing down.

Sister Montgomery was the first to let fly. Withdrawing her pointed finger as he came to a standstill in front of her, she put her hands on her hips, as she normally did on these occasions, and entered into her tirade. 'I simply cannot believe the level of disrespect that you show to this ward!' Her face tightened and her accent thickened; she was only getting started. 'Do you actually, think that you can do whatever you like in here!' He knew better than to attempt an answer to that one. 'You just waltz in and out as if you own the place! Mr Archer, let me remind you that this is the second time that you have been late today! That is completely unprofessional and will not be tolerated as long as I am Sister on this ward!' She paused for a second, holding him with her gaze, like a lion holds onto prey just before devouring it.

Then she leaned back a little and announced, 'Dr Pujara.'

This was clearly going to be a tag team effort. Clearing his throat a little, Dr Pujara looked down his nose at this minor player in his world. 'Mr Archer, these people clearly hold you in high regard for some reason.' The reason for this regard was clearly beyond him. 'But what you must remember is that you are not a doctor! You are a porter! And that is all you are! And you must not mislead the patients into thinking that you can do anything more for them than you are employed to do! We do the medicine around here! You push wheelchairs! Now, just be content with your station in life and don't cause any problems on my ward! Do you understand?' Having finished, he lifted his head a little, signifying his wish for an acknowledgement. No words were required and he just nodded humbly. While this public dressing down was in full flow, the rest of the ward was transfixed by the drama that was unfolding in front of them. Even the pharmacist had stopped giving out tablets to take in the spectacle. He could almost feel the swell of sympathy for him coming from all who were watching, but there would be no mercy today from Sister Montgomery! 'Thank you, Dr Pujara! Very wise words indeed!' She took back the baton with relish! 'Do you understand what we are saying here? You have caused absolute havoc on this ward today! I mean, look at the place!' She swung her arm around in a gesture of exasperation. 'The place is upside down! Nobody knows what they're supposed to be doing! That is not how I run my ward! I run a tight ship, Mr Archer and I will not tolerate any disruptors! Including you!' She finished her last barb by, once again, putting her index finger right up to his face. 'So, what I want you to do now is get out of my ward! You are dismissed for the rest of the day and I am going to make sure that your line manager hears exactly what you've been up to!' She paused to take a breath for one last murderous threat. 'And I hope that you get exactly what you deserve!' After holding him in her gaze for one last moment, she thrust her arm straight out past his head and pointed to the ward entrance. 'Now, get out,' she barked with enough volume to make every single person on the ward jump.

With a cold sweat starting to form on his brow due to the humiliation, he turned slowly to the exit and began his walk of shame. He dared not look up. One glance at any of the faces could have started him crying, such was the high state of his emotions. Instead, he kept his head bowed and walked with increasing pace for the stairwell. He had never been so completely humiliated in front of others like that in all his life. It was an absolutely excruciating experience, to the extent that he almost forgot all the amazing events of the earlier part of the day. As he started down the stairwell, running his hand on the cold surface of the handrail, he tried to take a deep breath and calm himself down. But no sooner was he on his second deep breath than he heard a loud bang from the floor above. It was the sound of the stairwell door banging against the wall after someone had clearly opened it with some haste. He paused his descent and turned around to see who was in such a rush and as soon as he did, he saw Mark, the staff nurse running down the stairs after him. His eyes were wide with excitement and he had a big smile on his face, which was in stark contrast to the faces that he had just been looking at!

No sooner had he caught up with him than he grabbed him by the arms and pushed him up against the wall. 'I know!' he said with a breathless euphoria. 'I know that was you! You were the one who healed those people! That was amazing! Absolutely amazing!' Mark's grip on his arms was getting firmer and his voice was getting louder; something that was bound to attract attention.

'OK Mark, OK! Take it easy!' he said in a soothing tone. 'Yes, you're right! It was me! I healed those people!' Mark's smile got even broader after hearing his admission. 'I have been sent by someone more powerful than me! And he has given me this power to heal the people in this hospital.' Ben wanted to make sure that he had the young nurse's attention and so he looked at him directly in the eyes and lifted his own arms to grip Mark's. 'But, Mark, there are still lots more people for me to help! And if I am going to heal those people, then I need you to play your part.' Mark's breathing began to settle a little at this point. 'Mark, we need to work as a team! We need to keep this as low profile as we possibly can, because if we don't then I won't be able to get near any patients. And if I can't get near them, then I can't help them. Do you understand that?'

Mark nodded his head vigorously. 'Yes, I do! And I want to help, Ben! I'll do whatever!' Mark took a deep breath and let go of his arms and took a small step back.

'Now, Mark,' he said in a deliberately hushed tone. 'I need you to go back to the ward now and say absolutely nothing about what has happened. In fact, pretend that nothing has happened at all. And then when I get back on the ward tomorrow, we can work out what to do next. OK?'

Mark nodded his head again. 'Yes, Ben! You can count on me!' Then Mark suddenly chuckled to himself. 'Oh Ben, you should have seen the look on monster Montgomery's face! She was absolutely fuming!' This observation caused them both to have a bit a chuckle. 'OK, Ben, I'll see you soon!' stated a much calmer Mark, and then, in an instant, the young nurse turned and sprinted up the steps and disappeared back into the ward.

As he was left alone in the stairwell, he felt a sense of calm come over him. There was no doubt about it, the positive encounter with Mark had soothed the pain of the very negative encounter with sister Montgomery. In fact, such was the recovery of spirit that Mark had delivered that he now felt a sense of confidence returning. No matter what sister Montgomery and others threw at him, he would not let himself be deterred from what he was meant to do. He had been given this gift and he would use it to help as many people as he possibly could. With this new surge of determination in his heart, he set off down the stairs with the express purpose of helping one more person before he left the building.

Chapter 15
So Close

There was no doubt about where he had to be now! He had to get back to ICU and help his friends, Jeff and Sharon. It had been far too long since he last saw them; and their little boy, Tommy, desperately needed his help. It didn't take him long to get to ICU, and when he did, Jeff and Sharon were exactly where they had been last time; sitting on the seats at the entrance. They both had cups of coffee in their hands and Jeff was eating a sandwich that he had bought from the shop or canteen. As he got closer, he felt himself slowing down a bit. He realised that he had to approach this situation gently and when he saw them up close, that feeling was confirmed. Both of them looked terrible. Their hair was untidy, their faces were pale and the bags under their eyes told a tale of many sleepless nights. Sharon was the first to look up and when she saw him, she sighed and smiled. 'Oh hi, Ben.' No smile was necessary, but the fact that she made the effort reminded him of just what lovely people they were. However, even that brief greeting seemed to take its toll on her. The greeting was barely off her lips when her head dropped again in exhaustion. He whispered a shy 'hello' back and as he did so, Jeff put his sandwich and coffee down and got to his feet. Jeff hadn't even looked at him, but started towards him and just reached out with his arms. They took each other in their arms and squeezed tightly. They held each other for a few seconds in an embrace that was filled with unspoken emotion. Things were clearly not good which made him even more eager to get in to see little Tommy. As Jeff released him from his embrace, he decided that there was no point in hanging around, he just needed to get to little Tommy as soon as possible. He was about to begin his pitch to see the baby when Jeff put his hand on his shoulder. 'It's not good, Ben! It's not good!' Jeff dropped his head, clearly choked with emotion. 'He's gonna lose his foot, man! They have to take his little foot off!' Jeff lifted his head to look at him briefly. His eyes were filled with tears and in a second, it was too difficult to look at him anymore and his head dropped again; his shoulders convulsing with sudden sobs. He looked at Sharon and she had now put her coffee down and was sobbing into her hands. 'Thanks for coming round, man! Thanks a lot!' said Jeff as his hand slid off his shoulder and he walked slowly back to Sharon. The strong hint was that this encounter was over. It was simply too painful for the two of them to talk to anyone just now. But as he watched Jeff put his arms around his wife, he knew that he couldn't stop there! He had to get in to see baby Tommy!

Without waiting another second, he put his head down and started walking directly for the doors to the ICU. He gave the door a firm pull, but his arm jolted when he realised that it was a security door. He looked for the button that he needed to press and he started to press it repeatedly. He could hear the buzzing from the other side of the door and eventually, there was an audible click and the door lock released. Immediately he pulled the door open and was about to storm into the ward when he almost ran into two men who were coming the other way. His initial instinct was to get past them as quickly as possible, but when he looked up and saw who they were, he froze. One of them was the consultant for ICU, Dr Smith. He was a rather stout man with a terrible liking for striped suits. But it was the other man who really stopped him in his tracks. It was none other than Dr Pujara! They both stared at each other in a sort of stunned surprise for a second. Dr Pujara peered down at him from his lofty height and gave him a look that was filled with increasing disdain. 'Mr Archer! What a surprise!' he said with an acute sense of sarcasm. 'And may I ask what business you have in Dr Smith's ward?'

'Oh-well-ahh-' he stuttered, 'I was just going to visit a friend, Dr Pujara.'

It was so rare for him to talk to someone of such high rank as Dr Pujara that he almost felt he had to bow as he spoke and almost felt himself doing so. Dr Smith reared back on his heels and lifted his head as he silently joined the condescension; his considerable girth now stretching his pinstripes even wider. 'Well, that is all very well, Mr Archer,' said Dr Pujara as he continued his interrogation. 'But as you should well know, visiting time does not begin until 2:30. Now, as you have been sent home for the afternoon, I suggest you go on your way, rather than trying to play doctor in someone else's department!' Dr Pujara's voice became decidedly sterner in tone as he finished the reprimand. Instinctively he stepped back now to let the two doctors pass. As they walked past him, they both looked sideways at him, as if to make sure that he didn't try to sneak through while the door was still closing behind them.

The door closed with a gentle thud and as it did so, Jeff looked round at him. 'That's OK man,' he said in comforting tone. 'You can come back another time.' He quickly turned his head back to his wife and all of a sudden, there was nothing more to do. Feeling a bit disappointed that his effort to get to little Tommy had been cut short, he decided to call it a day and head for home. He had helped a lot of people today and so he just had to be content with that. There would be plenty more opportunities tomorrow; and provided he didn't get the sack, there would be plenty more after that. Having rationalised the day to a positive conclusion, he called into the empty staff room to grab his coat and bag and then headed home. It was rather pleasant to be leaving the hospital while it was still daylight. It was a cold clear day, but he could feel the smallest hint of warmth from the sunshine on his skin. The positive feeling of this winter sunshine stayed with him all the way home and even when he entered his flat, he went straight to the window to continue his enjoyment of the light.

As he stood there, watching the sun, low over the rooftops, he processed the day's events. There was no doubt that it was a day of distinct contrasts. On the one hand, there were the highs of all the healings. Seeing the faces of those people who were feeling so much better was hugely gratifying and even the excitement in the face of Nurse Mark was a big positive in his day. There was no doubt about it, his faith had grown a lot today after seeing the power that the Sender had given him. The Sender was very real to him now and he was quite happy to tell others about him. But it wasn't just the Sender who had become real today, it was also the opposition that he faced on the ward; and this was the source of the other contrast. As high as he felt after healing people, he felt equally low after the humiliating dressing down he had been given by Sister Montgomery. There was genuine hatred in her eyes when she was talking to him; a hatred that he had never encountered before. He would have thought that she and Dr Pujara would be happy to see the patients get better, but instead, it seemed to enrage them! Although, the real source of their rage was probably the fact that they were sharing the credit with a mere porter! However, despite this opposition, he felt the desire to keep going more than ever. The presence of the Sender was more and more obvious to him now. He could feel this power with him at all times; giving him strength and courage and determination; even the ability to tell others about the source of this healing power. It was thrilling to feel this level of conviction. But conviction wouldn't be enough if he was going to continue his work in the hospital. No, he would have to be wise as well, and that meant keeping a low profile. He needed to avoid the sort of attention that he had received on the cardiac ward today. No more healing of large numbers of people in the same place. One here and one there with no apparent pattern; that was the way to avoid unwanted attention. And with the help of his friends and those who believed in him, he could get around every patient in the hospital! It would take a long time, but he believed that it was possible; now more than ever.

Chapter 16
The Crowd

He woke up the next morning to the sound of the alarm clock on his bedside table. He had slept all night but it wasn't a deep sleep. The excitement and anticipation of the next day was too much for him to come to a complete rest. As a result, he still felt a bit tired and had to drag himself out of bed to get the first coffee of the day. With the first dose of caffeine inside him and a shower and a shave to follow, he felt himself slowly waking up. He got himself dressed and headed down the stairs and out of the building and onto the street. It was a much more overcast morning and there was a cold drizzle descending like a mist. Ordinarily, this weather would have felt a bit miserable, but today it was invigorating. The cool damp air enlivened his senses; and with that, his thoughts about the day ahead. This was the day that he was going to put his strategy into effect. He was going to be invisible to all the authorities in the hospital and move around the hospital, quietly helping all that he could. It was a plan that seemed to be without fault; and as he travelled to work on the bus, he felt secure in the knowledge that he had the day under control.

With an air of confidence, he breezed into the hospital lobby and made a bee line for the staff room door. He went to the door handle with the intention of sweeping into the room and greeting all that he saw with a smile. But as he turned the handle, the only thing that greeted him was the hard surface of the door swinging back on him and giving his nose and forehead a solid bump. Before he could think, he instinctively let out a yell of painful surprise. As he took a quick step back and put his hand to his nose to check for damage, he could hear a rumbling of different voices on the other side of the door, urging each other to make way. After a few seconds and a little shuffling, the door eventually opened a little further and he was able to see the familiar bright green of the Pakistan cricket top. It was Mo standing there with a cluster of unfamiliar faces poking

94

out past him to see who it was. 'Ben, come on! Hurry up! Get in here!' he said in a rather flustered tone. He took a step towards the door and as he did so, Mo literally grabbed him by his jacket and pulled him inside the room and shut the door. The door had barely closed when there was an immediate ripple around the room. 'It's him! He's here!' went the wave of whispers from one to the other. He took a second to look around the room and was amazed to see the room absolutely packed full of people. There were people dressed in familiar hospital uniforms from various departments, there were people dressed in regular clothes and there were even a few people there in their pyjamas with their drip stands parked beside them. It was a sight that left him stunned and stupefied! He thought he had a plan for the day, but as a wise philosopher of the boxing ring once said, 'Everyone has a plan until they get a punch in the face.' Still holding his nose and thinking about his plan for a quiet ministry, he was now in full agreement with the philosopher!

He felt another tug on his jacket. It was Mo who was now dragging him through the crowd. He was waving his arm in front of him like an explorer waving his machete as he tries to cut through the undergrowth. 'Out of the way! Make way!' Mo said repeatedly as he led him further into the room. Looking around him for familiar faces, he suddenly found Eddie looking down on him from on high. He was standing on a table in the middle of the room trying to be heard above the noise of all the voices.

'OK, everyone, can I have your attention please. Listen up everyone, I have something to say!' The drone of voices continued as if he wasn't there; they were too busy looking at the person that Mo was dragging through the crowd. Eddie was getting a bit frustrated and decided to drop the polite approach. 'Right, everybody shut up!' Eddie roared like a sergeant major. Suddenly the drone of voices dropped to absolute silence. Still with a loud voice, Eddie continued. 'Now I know why everyone is here! You all want the help of my good friend Ben here; and that's alright! But if we don't get a bit of order around here then no one is getting nuffin', yeah! Alright! So! Without further ado, I want to introduce you to the man with the talent, Ben!'

Having given him this grand introduction, Eddie looked directly down at him and held his arm out straight to welcome him up onto the table with him. Standing beside him like a security guard, Mo put his hands on his waist to help him up onto the chair and then the table. 'This is the servant of Allah,' shouted Mo as he turned to the crowd. 'This is God's power! Now, shut up and listen!'

With the admonishment of Mo still ringing in their ears, Ben looked around the crowd in the room. Over at the kitchen, there was the welcome sight of Enid giving out cups of tea and biscuits and making sure they were passed around; but for the rest of the crowd their eyes were now transfixed upon himself. He felt Eddie's hand on his shoulder.

'Alright, Ben, way you go mate!' He glanced around at Eddie and saw that familiar big smile on his face. Eddie looked as proud as punch to be in the middle of this gathering with his friend. Looking back at the crowd again, Ben could feel his mind go blank. He knew he had to say something and even his mouth was opening with the anticipation of the words but his brain still wasn't quite in gear.

'Hello,' he said. It wasn't much, but it was a start. A few murmured 'hello's' echoed back from the crowd. 'My name's Ben,' he blurted out. There were now a few people in the crowd looking at each other in bewilderment. Had they come to the wrong place? He needed to step things up a bit! 'I have been sent,' he said with some authority beginning to creep into his words. 'I have been sent by the Sender. And I have been sent to heal the sick!'

Another wave a murmuring went around the room. 'What are you talking about? What Sender?' came a rather irate voice from the crowd.

'Yeah, who is this Sender?' came another voice.

'Are you selling some kind of religion or something?' said another. Gradually a few other sceptical voices began to say similar things and before long there was a rising mood of anger in the room. Some clearly felt they were being duped into joining some kind of weird cult.

Sensing the way things were going, Eddie stepped in to save the day. 'Alright folks! Look! I can see that there are some who are finding it difficult to believe all this stuff!' The murmuring settled down a little. Eddie took a long breath. 'And you know what; it took me a little while to get my head around it as well! But this guy is real, yeah! He healed my wife! And I've seen him heal other people as well! And when you see him heal one of you lot then you are going to believe as well!' A hush seemed to fall over the room. Eddie had spoken so powerfully and with such conviction that he felt it was Eddie who should be doing the healing, not him. Eddie saw that he had got the attention of the crowd, but now he needed to drive home the point he was making, and so he singled out one person to be the example. 'Alright, Doris, it's gonna be you!' He pointed to a woman in the crowd with an outstretched arm. Instinctively, everyone in the room looked around to see where Eddie's finger was pointing. One of the patients holding on to a drip looked up at Eddie with a note of alarm in her face. She was a woman in her fifties who was clearly very ill. Her face was drawn and pale and from the way her pyjamas were hanging on her skeletal frame, she had obviously lost a lot of weight as a result of her condition. Now aware of the attention that she was receiving from everyone in the room, she started to shuffle forward, almost involuntarily at first, as if moved by some invisible force behind her. Eddie was holding his hand out to her and beckoning her forward. In response to her shuffling movement, people were trying to get themselves out of her way. Her movement was slow but eventually she managed to drag herself and her drip stand to the table that Ben and Eddie were standing on. Now there was the dilemma of how to get her onto the table. A couple of staff who were standing nearby tried to help her up onto the chair beside the table. The first time she put her foot up she started to fall backwards and had to be caught by her two helpers. There was a sudden intake of breath from the onlookers and quite a few who were holding their breath as she tried again. Eventually, with the help of the two staff members, she managed to stand up on the chair, albeit with a bit of a wobble.

At this point, Eddie made the decision that standing up on the table was going to be too much risk for Doris and that she now needed to stay where she was. With the two staff members holding the chair and Doris in place, Eddie now beckoned him closer. He took a couple of delicate steps forward, very conscious of the edge of the table being quite close. Doris now looked at him intently as he stood beside her. Her eyes were filled with tears; not afraid of him or the crowd, but terrified of being disappointed as she had been on many occasions.

He gently put his hand on her shoulder. 'Doris, don't be afraid. I'm not going to hurt you.' She nodded her head just enough to shake loose a few tears which trickled down her cheeks. 'Now, tell me, Doris, what has happened to you?' Keeping her eyes completely fixed on his, she cleared her throat a little. 'I'm dying,' she said; her voice filled with emotion. Her head dropped for a couple of seconds as she struggled to fight back the tears. She looked back at him once more and continued. 'I got cervical cancer two years ago and I've been on treatment ever since. But it's not working! And I'm scared!' Her eyes widened with the fear that she had just mentioned. Please help me!' This time she took hold of his jacket to emphasise her request.

There was a voice from the back of the room that cut through the tension of the moment. 'What's she saying? I can't hear!'

'Yeah, speak up! We wanna know what's happenin'!'

Standing just behind him, Eddie stepped forward a little and raised his hands. 'Please folks! Be patient! Just wait!' Another ripple of voices of discontent circulated around the room and as it did, Ben could feel himself losing patience with the crowd.

He stood up a little straighter and turned his head to face them. 'This is what the Sender has enabled me to do!' With his hand still on Doris' shoulder, he looked at her and told her, 'Just relax!' He then placed his hand gently on her abdomen. As soon as his hand pressed against her, the pins and needles sensation began to buzz through his whole arm and the heat began to build in his hand. Doris' hands began to pull a little more on his jacket and she closed her eyes as the power of healing began to spread through her body. She sighed heavily and suddenly let go of his jacket completely and opened her eyes wide. He took his hand off her abdomen and stood back a little. Then, without warning her whole body began to convulse. He and the two staff members rushed to stop her from falling. But as the men got close to her, they could hear what seemed to be the sound of laughter. Looking at her face now, they could all see that there was a huge grin of surprise on her face. The convulsion was not pain, it was laughter that was shaking her whole body.

The crowd looked perplexed but the laughter that was coming from Doris now got louder and louder until she was literally laughing at the top of her voice. 'You've done it!' she screamed! 'I'm better! I'm better!' She lunged in his direction to hug him. Ben grabbed her in return, to stop her from falling if nothing else. She was still laughing with joy and now she was jumping up and down. After a couple of seconds, she stood up straight on the chair and started jumping and cheering at the top of her voice as if her team had just scored the winning goal. Her joy was overflowing so much that she was completely oblivious to the fact that her pyjama bottoms had just dropped round her ankles. There was a gasp from the audience and then they instinctively started laughing with her. Ben and Eddie quickly averted their eyes but thankfully the two staff members had the good sense to pull her pyjamas straight back up again. In truth, dear Doris was oblivious to it all; she was just so glad to be free from her cancer for the first time ever! It was now that she decided to get down from the chair. In doing so, she almost jumped on the two staff members who had just pulled her pyjamas up.

They gently got her back on the floor, at which point she began to hug everyone in front of her.

Conversations began to start all around the room. There were the voices of enquiry who wanted to know if she really was healed. These voices were then met by a variety of others; those who just didn't know, those who thought she might be and those who were totally convinced that she was. It was relatively calm at that point, but when some people started pushing to the front and saying, 'I want to be healed now! It's my turn!' there was suddenly a push towards the table that Ben and Eddie were still standing on. Instinctively, Ben and Eddie put their arms on each other's shoulders to steady themselves as the table began to be bumped around by the people trying to get closer to them.

'Alright, folks! Steady on!' came the call from Eddie who was still trying to get his balance. Having steadied himself, Eddie now sought to take control of the situation. 'Now, that's enough everyone! If there's any more pushing, then we'll just bring this to a close right now!' His loud booming voice clearly had the desired effect because the crowd began to take a step back. But as they did so, the people at the front of the room backed into the door as it was swung open. There was a bit of a grunt from the person who got bumped by the door on the inside of the room as well as another grunt from the person on the other side of the door. Eventually the intruder poked her face around the door and it was none other than Madge. At first, she took a bit of a double-take when she saw how many people were in the room. Then she looked even more surprised again to see Ben and Eddie standing on top of the table in the middle of the room.

After a couple of seconds to gather her senses, Madge looked directly at Ben. 'Excuse me everyone! Ah…Mr Archer, can I borrow you for a second?' No sooner had the words left her mouth than she was immediately accosted by a large man with a moustache who was standing beside her at the door.

'Hey, love! We're all here to get fixed! Just wait your turn like everyone else!'

Exasperated now, Madge looked at him again with a bit more determination. 'Ben! Now, please!' she barked!

'OK,' he said, 'just give me a second.' Carefully, with Eddie behind him, he stepped down from the table and then to the ground. As he got to the ground, a voice called out from the crowd, 'wait, where are you going? I want to be healed!'

'Yeah,' came another voice.

'You can't leave us all waiting here!' Very quickly the howls of protest began to build and before long he found it a struggle to get to the door. The crowd was pushing in against him and some were even grabbing at him.

Thankfully Eddie was right there behind him. 'Alright, folks! Settle down, there's no need for pushing! He'll be back later!' said Eddie in a loud voice as he put his arm out in front of him to move people out of the way. Eventually he managed to get to the door with Eddie's help. With a quick push, Eddie shoved him out of the room and slammed the door behind him. He stumbled to a standstill in front of the waiting Madge. They stared at each other for a moment as they both listened to the efforts of Eddie to calm the crowd from the other side of the door.

'Follow me,' she said and marched towards the back of the foyer.

Chapter 17
The Court

He followed Madge as she marched towards the administration section of the building. Her short heels on her shoes clipped the surface of the floor as she sped down a corridor to the left and quickly arrived at a large black door with a brass handle. Seeing that she had arrived at the destination, he added bit more pace to his step to catch up with her. Just in time, he arrived at the door as she spun around to face him. 'OK Ben, come on in.' With that she opened the door and disappeared inside. Tentatively he followed her in and as soon he saw who was in the room, his heart sank. It was Sister Montgomery! She was sitting at one end of a long table with two other people at the other end. He automatically knew this was not going to be a pleasant experience. After closing the door behind him he made his way toward the table where Madge was just taking her seat beside Sister Montgomery. Having taken her seat, Madge looked up at him again and ushered him forward. 'Please, take a seat Mr Archer!' Obediently, he sat down on the chair that had been left on its own facing the panel. After shuffling her papers a little, Madge began. 'Mr Archer, I have called you here today before this panel because, unfortunately, a complaint has been made against you and I would like to get to the bottom of it as soon as possible. Do you understand?'

'Ah, yes, I suppose,' he said a little nervously.

'Very well, then, let me introduce you to the panel and then we can begin. On my right is Sister Montgomery, whom I believe you already know.' He looked at Sister Montgomery briefly as her name was mentioned, only to be met with an icy stare. She was clearly the one who was bringing the complaint. 'And on my left,' Madge continued, 'is Mr Cruickshank, the Head of Personnel, who is here as an observer; and to the left of him is Mr Smith, your union representative. OK, are we ready to begin?' After a quick look around the room and receiving no response from anyone, Madge quickly arrived at the conclusion that they were. 'Alright then,' she said, as she slapped her hands on the table, then let's hear the details of the complaint; Sister Montgomery. Nodding in Sister Montgomery's direction, the Sister duly received her cue and rose to her feet. In her customary manner, she straightened out her red tunic and stood very straight with her hands behind her back. He could feel himself wince with anticipation, and then it began.

'I don't know about you, Madge, but I pride myself on running a tight ship in this hospital!' There was a quick look from the other panellists in her direction; not sure if there was an intended insult there or not. However, this was not a concern for Sister Montgomery who was getting herself into full flow. 'And when I say, running a tight ship, I mean, running the most efficient and effective ward in this hospital. And I have awards to prove that!' Her gaze did not move away from him at all. 'But I can only maintain the highest standards on my ward if every member of my team is up to the task! And this individual is not one of those people!' Suddenly she shot out her arm to point at him with one of her bony fingers aimed directly at his head. If she had a gun, she would have shot him right between the eyes. She paused for effect and then quickly put her gun back in its holster. 'He arrives late on a regular basis; which is one of the worst things an employee can do in my opinion! And even when he does arrive, rather than attending to his duties, he harasses the patients, prevents other team members from going about their work, and causes serious disruption throughout the ward. Madge, this individual is a disruptor! He lowers the standards of this hospital and puts its very reputation at risk. Therefore, it is my professional opinion that his employment here should be terminated!' With a slight rise in the volume of her voice to finish, Sister Montgomery gave him one last glare and took her seat.

There was silence! Mr Cruickshank and Mr Smith both gave a collective sigh with eyes wide in response to the horror show that had just been unleashed in front of them. In order to break the tension a little and get things moving again, Madge cleared her throat authoritatively. 'OK, well, ah…thank you for that Sister Montgomery,' she said with a hint of irony in her voice. 'So, Mr Archer, you've heard the accusation that has been made against you; and now you have a chance to respond. The time is yours!' All of a sudden, he could feel the eyes of all four of them closing in on him; especially those of Sister Montgomery. He shifted awkwardly in his seat and looked at the floor for a moment to escape the attention that was now on him. He could have taken this opportunity to fight back and tell them all how terrible Sister Montgomery was to work with and how rude she was to the other staff; however, he had a sense that they already knew this.

The problem with fighting back, though, was that it might jeopardize his chances of getting back onto the wards. Management might even decide to suspend him if they thought that his presence was going to make the working environment even more difficult. This would bring his ministry to an abrupt halt and he didn't want that. No, instead, the best thing to do now was keep things as calm as possible and show management that he wasn't a trouble maker. This would keep him in the hospital and give him the best chance to use his gift. Having reasoned his response briefly through his mind, he now raised his head to face them. 'Madge,' he addressed his line manager directly and kept his eyes on her alone. 'I realise that my time keeping has not been what it should be lately and I apologize for that. From now on, I will improve my time keeping and stick to the duties that I am given. I am glad to have this job in the hospital and I will do my best to work with everyone else in the team.'

There was another moment of silence as the panel absorbed his contribution. Madge scribbled for a moment on the page in front of her and then looked up at him again. 'OK, thank you, Mr Archer! Um…' for a moment Madge seemed a bit lost, but she quickly regained the situation. 'Does anyone else have anything to say? Mr Smith?' She looked at the union representative with an air of expectancy. Slowly Mr Smith got up from his chair. He was taller than he had seemed when he was sitting down and rather surprisingly, he became a dominant presence in the room. He had a head of thick brown and grey hair which hung loosely over his forehead and was dressed in a mix and match jacket and trousers with a beige jumper that covered his shirt and tie.

'Well, thank you, Madge! Yes, there is something I would like to say!' He spoke softly, but with an air of intent that made the rest of the room brace itself. Out of the corner of his eye, he could even see Sister Montgomery tensing up. This was clearly not the first time that these two had locked horns and she seemed to know what was coming. 'This man,' Mr Smith continued with a gesture in his direction and one eye on Madge, 'has an exemplary record! He has worked here for a number of years and does not have one complaint against him!' Mr Smith's volume was increasing, as was the emphasis that was injected into the end of his sentences. 'And yet, all of sudden he is being described as the potential cause of the downfall of this institution! And for what reason? He's been late a few times and he takes a bit of an interest in the patients! I don't know about you Madge, but the last time I checked, the whole point of working in the health service is about taking an interest in the patients!' Mr Smith was visibly getting revved up now for his main point. 'But you know, Madge, let's face it! This is not the first time we've had these sorts of accusations levelled against our staff! Time and time again, there is one ward in this hospital that seems to take delight in dragging good workers over the coals for the slightest of infractions! And to be honest with you, Madge, for me it is actually borderline harassment! And if it doesn't stop soon, then the union will have no other choice than to examine the behaviour of certain senior individuals in the hospital and make them sit in that chair rather than one of our workers! This harassment of staff has to stop!' With those closing words, Mr Smith banged his knuckles on the table and sat down.

At the other end of the table, Sister Montgomery stuck her chin in the air as if to dismiss everything that Mr Smith had just said. There was another moment of awkward silence as Madge scribbled a bit more on her notepad. For the first time in the meeting, Sister Montgomery wasn't looking anywhere near him. She was looking as far away as she could out of the window, as if the farther she looked, the farther she could get away from the stinging rebuke of Mr Smith. Madge stopped scribbling and leaned back on her chair. As she did so, the quiet Mr Cruickshank leaned towards her and he spoke softly into her ear.

There was a brief exchange between the two and then Madge leaned forward again. 'OK, Mr Archer, we've heard what everyone has to say and…well…' she hesitated, 'we are pleased with your apology.' There was an immediate spitting sound from Sister Montgomery as she reacted with disgust. Madge stiffened a little following that expected reaction, but then carried on. 'However, given that there has been a problem with your time keeping, I am going to recommend that you are put on probation for the next three months and if you are late again in that time, then further action may be required. Do you understand?' He couldn't help but smile in response and nodded in assent. 'Well, in that case you may go; and thank you to the rest of the panel.' The words were barely out of her mouth when Sister Montgomery stood bolt upright and marched furiously across the room in front of him. As she passed him, she made sure that she caught his eye with a withering stare and then swung the door open violently and disappeared out of the room.

Next out was Mr Smith. He swaggered past him and patted him on the shoulder. 'Don't worry,' he said as he looked down at him, 'you're not the first.' And with that he sauntered out of the room. That left him in the room with the other two who were now in conversation. At last, he felt he could breathe again. He took a deep sigh of relief and walked towards the door. He had won this battle, but if he was going to keep on healing people, he was going to have to act fast. He may have wanted to take things slow and quiet, but that was no longer an option!

Chapter 18
Open Hostility

Without delay, he walked straight to the stairwell that would take him up to the Cardiac Ward. The events of the disciplinary hearing were still going around in his head as he bounded up the stairs, so much so, that he almost walked straight into the familiar group of student nurses who inhabited that part of the stairwell. At the last second, he pulled back from the collision. Sensing the sudden movement in their proximity, all three of them looked up at him from their mobile phones. With all three of them now looking at him, he excused himself from their gaze and went to move on past them. But just as he turned his back on them, there came a quick outburst from one of them. 'Oh! It's you!' He stopped in his tracks and turned to face them. 'Yes, it is you!' cried the girl in the middle. She was Chinese in her appearance and had her hair dyed orange. Excitedly, she was showing what was on her phone to her friends either side of her. They both looked at the phone and then looked at him.

'Oh yeah!' they exclaimed in agreement and then burst into a fit of giggles. Suddenly, he felt like he was back in high school, being laughed at by the cool kids; an experience that he was sadly very familiar with. He smiled awkwardly because what else can you do when a group of girls is giggling at you? He was about to turn and walk away again, when the nurse in the middle spoke again.

'Can we take a selfie with you?' she asked in her strong London accent. For a second, he was stunned with the request. His lower jaw hung open as he audibly pondered the request. Without thinking he then accepted their offer.

He wasn't looking for fame, but if someone asks to take a picture with you and they seem friendly, then why not! 'Uh, where do you want me?' he asked. Without hesitation, the leader of the three asked him to stand in the corner. As soon as he did so, the three of them clustered in around him and after a short moment of jostling and positioning of heads, he soon found himself staring at a smart phone on the end of a selfie stick. Somehow it seemed that he was not the first person they had done this with.

'OK, ready!' the nurse announced and with a smile and a click it was all over. 'Oh, thank you so much! Really appreciate it!' said the orange-haired nurse, and with that, he moved out of the corner and proceeded up the stairs. Glancing back down at them as he ascended, they were already clustered round their phones again; probably busy sharing the recently taken photo. It was a rather surreal experience, but it was also oddly encouraging because it had taken his mind off the disciplinary hearing completely. However, that good work was about to be undone! Standing at the entrance to the ward, waiting for him, was the imposing figure of Sister Montgomery. She had both fists firmly fixed on her narrow hips and was wearing the most unwelcoming of expressions. There was no telling how long she had been standing there like that, but if it was any length of time, then who knew how many people had already turned away in terror. As she caught his eye coming through the door from the stairwell, he could feel his pace of walking slow down instinctively. He almost came to a standstill when the arm suddenly shot from the hip into a deadly point in his direction!

'You, get in here, now!' she shrieked with even more malice than usual. She turned on her heels and marched out of sight into the ward. Shaking himself out of his state of fear, he quickly sped off in pursuit. This was one appointment that he could not afford to be late for; not by a second!

He quickly caught up with her just before she got to the nurses' station in the middle of the ward and was standing just an arm's length away from her when she suddenly stopped and swung around to face him. With a violent movement that was intended to make him flinch, she pointed her finger very close to his face.

'Now, you listen to me, Ben!' she said with her teeth clenched. 'You do not move from this spot! Do you understand me!' This question was clearly rhetorical; he stayed silent and nodded. 'You do not speak! You do not do anything unless I tell you to! Do I make myself clear?' He was so terrified by this hardened Scotswoman that he decided to just keep on nodding, for fear of saying something stupid. 'Well,' she demanded. 'Do I make myself clear?' A verbal response was now a must!

'Yes, Miss Montgomery,' he blurted out, immediately realising his mistake. In that second, her face went a shade of scarlet that he had never seen on a human face before.

'It's Sister Montgomery! You idiot! Sister! Sister! Sister!' she screamed in his face, not caring who was watching now. But people were watching. Slowly her pointed finger retracted and became a tightly clenched fist which seemed, for a brief moment, to be getting closer to his nose. Then, as quick as a flash, she spun away, marched to the Sister's office and slammed the door behind her.

There was a stunned silence around the ward. All eyes were on him; patients and staff. To the sudden relief of everyone on the ward, Dr Black spoke up from where he was standing just outside one of the bays. 'OK, everyone let's get back to work, please!' His words cut through the tension like a knife and gradually everyone came back to their senses and resumed their business. He breathed a big sigh of relief. It felt like he hadn't been breathing for the last five minutes. He looked at the door to the sister's office and thankfully it remained closed. Every minute that the dragon remained in its cave was another minute to recover. Eventually his heart stopped beating quite as hard as it had been and he even sensed a note of normality returning to the ward. With his breathing back to normal, he began to relax a little and as he did so he began to look around the ward. All the beds that had been emptied the day before had been filled again with new patients, all in as much need of healing as the previous occupants. It was a sobering reminder that the job of a healer would be never be complete. No matter how many people he healed, there would always be more! This was the reality of the world that he lived in and it would only change if someone was able to heal the world itself; someone with much greater healing powers than himself.

As he mused on these profound matters, his eyes roved around the beds and the patients who were now sitting on the chairs beside their beds. Most of the faces were unfamiliar to him, but then his eyes settled on a face that was not unfamiliar. It was dear old Mrs Moore. She was a kind-faced older lady, probably in her eighties. She had been in the ward for about a week now and was probably due to leave very soon. He studied her as she turned the pages of one of her women's magazines. Then, without warning, she looked up from her magazine directly at him. He automatically switched his gaze away to another patient, as if to mask the fact that he had been looking at her. After a suitable delay in looking everywhere else but at Mrs Moore, it was now time to look back at her to determine if she was still looking in his direction. She was! Immediately he kept his head turning in a vain attempt to look natural, but it was clear that she had caught him. Then out of the corner of his eye, he could tell that the woman's magazine had now been put down and she was going for her zimmer-frame. A feeling of dread began to soak through him. He couldn't move and he couldn't say anything! It was like being in one of those horror movies where the victim is utterly helpless in the face of advancing doom. In this case the doom took the shape of a woman in her eighties on a zimmer-frame which wasn't quite the same as the few horror movies he had seen. However, it was her slow advance that remained just as terrifying. With every shunt of the zimmer-frame in his direction, the danger of a much greater threat was increasing. He watched the door of the Sister's office with increasing alarm as the noise of the zimmer-frame grew louder. He allowed himself a quick glance in Mrs Moore's direction. She greeted him with a kind smile to which he responded with a rather nervous one of his own. The poor dear had no idea of the peril that she was putting them both in. Perhaps she was simply at that stage of life where all caution is thrown to the wind, but what she may have missed in her calculations was that he wasn't!

No sooner had he smiled at her, than the inevitable sound of a door opening hit his ears like a thunderbolt. Both of them froze like a pair of deer in the headlights. They stared at the door way of the Sister's Office with their eyes peeled wide with horror! There she was in all her tremendous fury; the dragon was awake! Fists on hips and eyes like fire, she took a short step out into the ward. 'Mrs Moore!' she thundered. 'Get back to your bed, at once!' Poor Mrs Moore quickly started the fastest about turn that could possibly be imagined using a zimmer-frame. It bounced around the floor like a skimming stone and off she shot back to her chair. As the sound of a bouncing zimmer-frame faded into the distance, the whole ward froze with anticipation of what was coming next. He fully expected the dreaded Sister to be over to him in a shot, ramming her finger up into his face, as was her habit. But in an unexpected act of mercy, she disappeared back into her room almost as quickly as she had appeared. After another moment of breath holding, the sense of danger was gone and everyone, especially himself, let out a huge sigh of relief. He looked over towards Mrs Moore very briefly. Her head was buried deep in her woman's magazine once more. She had clearly learned her lesson! Even at her stage of life, there were still things to be cautious about.

With another little drama coming to a close, the business of the ward resumed automatically. This time there was no need for Dr Black to intervene, he mused to himself. However, now that the name of Dr Black crossed his mind, he started looking around the ward to see where he was. It took him a while, but before long he could see him standing at the other end of the ward, near the entrance. He was standing with his hands in his pockets and his stethoscope around his neck looking down at the much smaller figure of Dr Kanu. There was no doubt that she had the power to attract all of his attention; which was not surprising because she oozed feminine charm. Her hair was always carefully styled and she always wore floral, colourful dresses like the yellow, patterned one she had on today. But it wasn't just the way she looked; it was also how she carried herself. She was always softly spoken and kind; never arrogant but clearly a dedicated clinician. However, from what he could see of her now, the body language was showing that something was definitely bothering Dr Kanu. Her easy-going manner was now replaced with a rather more forceful stance. She was clearly trying to make a point to her boyfriend and was even doing a bit of hand waving to get her message across. Then suddenly, they both looked in his direction. Once again, he had been rumbled. It was becoming a bad habit. As before, he looked away quickly, although he sensed that they had not. He looked at the floor for a good thirty seconds and then let his eyes roll around the ward until he casually looked in their direction again. This time it seemed like the conversation was over. There was no more exchange between them and for a moment they were still facing each other but were looking elsewhere. Whatever they were talking about, whether it was about him or not, he really did hope that they were not falling out. The last thing he wanted was to see Dr Kanu being upset.

Chapter 19
Battle Lines

The rest of the morning had passed rather slowly on the ward. Break time had come and gone and while he would have liked to get down to the staff room to see Eddie and Enid and Mo, he thought it best to go the extra mile on the ward, simply to stay out of trouble with Sister Montgomery. She had sent him on a couple of errands here and there; taking patients to scans of various kinds, but for the most part he had been left to languish at the nurses' station; simply watching the world rush past him as if he was quarantined. Eventually the time for early lunch break came along and it was at this point that Dr Pujara appeared on the ward. He walked up to the door of the Sister's office and lightly tapped the door. Within a couple of seconds Sister Montgomery appeared at the door wearing a light navy cardigan and a small black handbag over her right shoulder. She smiled sweetly at Dr Pujara who nodded back at her with a smile. It was probably the only time that he ever saw the dear Sister with a smile on her face. Before long they were on their way past him. Thankfully, neither of them even glanced in his direction. Once they were through the doors and out of sight, it was as if there was a quick flurry of excitement. Nearly everyone started talking to each other as if they had been starved of conversation the whole morning. It was pretty obvious who they were talking about and for a moment he felt a little alone, but that didn't last long because within a minute of them leaving, Mark, the Staff Nurse came bounding up to him. With his usual enthusiasm, he gripped him by the arms. 'Ben! Are you OK, man? That was insane this morning!' It was funny that they were both still looking left and right to see who was watching, but the danger was gone.

'Yeah, I'm fine, thanks,' he said casually; not really knowing if he was or not!

'Man, you have taken some punishment from that old woman, haven't you! But listen, Ben!' Mark pulled him a little closer; such was his usual intensity. 'Ben, I believe in you,' he said nodding in assent to his own statement. 'I do! I believe in you! I believe you are here to help people! And more than that! I believe I am here to help you do that! And so, whatever you need, you can count on me!' At this point he stood back a little and gave a him a good old slap on the side of the arm. 'So, what do you want me to do?'

Ben stood dumbstruck for a second, a little stunned by the offer. 'Um…' came the inspiring response. Once again, he was a little thrown by Mark's very direct brand of enthusiasm. 'Well…look, Mark, it really does mean a lot to have your support, but to tell you the truth, I'm still trying to work out my next move. A lot has happened this morning and at the minute I'm still trying to process it all.' It was interesting to find himself being so honest with Mark.

Perhaps it was Mark's positivity that made him feel that he could be truthful. In any case, every word was going in because Mark was nodding his head with every syllable. 'Yeah, yeah! I get it man, I get it! We're gonna play it cool! No problem! But remember! You can count on me, yeah!' Mark spluttered, while adopting a somewhat casual stance that he was clearly not comfortable with. His hands were on his hips, but then he put his finger up to make one last point. 'But remember, Ben! I believe in you! I believe! OK?' He put his hands up to acknowledge his young friend's sincerity.

'Yes, Mark! I know! And thank you!'

'OK,' said Mark with a big grin on his face. 'Well, in that case, I will see you after lunch!' And with that, Mark turned on his heels and went marching down the corridor to the exit.

As he watched Mark disappear around the corner, he couldn't help but smile to himself. No matter how bad the opposition that he faced was, there was always a friendly face around the corner to keep him going, whether it was the student nurses in the stairwell or Mark on the ward. It was almost as if the Sender had put them there to make sure that he didn't give up. While he was pondering these things, it wasn't long before he had another person to talk to. This time it was Dr Black. He was smartly dressed, as usual, in his blue shirt and tie and his long dark hair was neatly swept back into perfect position. At first, he thought that the doctor was going to send him on another errand and so he dutifully stood up straight and got ready to go. But as Dr Black got closer, he could see him adopt that stance with his hands in his pockets, which generally meant that he wanted to talk. 'Hi Ben,' he began. 'Bit of a rough morning then?'

'Ah, well, you could say that.,' he said with a bit of an embarrassed chuckle. 'Yeah, now about that,' Dr Black said as he clearly set himself for getting to the heart of the matter. 'You see, Ben, we all have our beliefs, don't we! And coming from your background, you have your own beliefs too.' He wasn't entirely sure what background Dr Black was referring to, but he was willing to give him a pass on that one. Dr Black continued, 'Now, there's nothing wrong with beliefs, although I just believe in science myself; but when it comes to work, it is best just to keep your beliefs to yourself! Do you know what I mean?' He could sense the level of condescension building in Dr Black's voice and although it made him uncomfortable, he just kept quiet and nodded. 'Good!' said Dr Black sharply. 'Because the one thing that we don't want to do on the ward is confuse the patients! You see, the patients look to us, the doctors, for guidance. And if that guidance is getting confused with what other people do and say, well…you can see what that results in, can't you!' Ben nodded in agreement. 'And we don't want you getting into any more trouble either, do we?' He nodded again; feeling yet more condescension being heaped upon him. Dr Black straightened himself up for one last word. 'Well, then, chin up old boy! Just keep your nose clean and you'll be fine!' The doctor smiled at him, as a teacher to a child, pleased with the little pep talk that he had just delivered. And with a quick tap on his left shoulder, off he walked back to the computers at the nurses' station.

It was hard not to be angry with Dr Black for the way he had just spoken to him. He was not Dr Pujara or Sister Montgomery and yet he spoke as if he was very much on their side. What made this even more confusing was the fact that he was so close to Dr Kanu. Perhaps it was his relationship with such a wonderful person that made him expect more from Dr Black. If a person spent any time at all with Dr Kanu; especially if they were in a relationship with her; then her kind nature should definitely have had an effect on them. As he pondered these things, his mind drifted back to the conversation that he witnessed between them earlier in the morning. Their apparent disagreement was maybe a sign that Dr Kanu was not having the effect on Dr Black that she had hoped.

Suddenly, a hand came from nowhere and grabbed his left arm. He was jolted out of his daydream and looked round to see his assailant. He was shocked to see that it was the very person that he had just been thinking about, Dr Kanu. But this time she did not have her usual cheerful facial expression. This time she had a look of serious determination on her face. 'Come with me,' she said in a flat hushed tone, and while still holding his arm, she led him straight across the corridor and into the nearest side ward and closed the door behind them. Without saying a word, she walked to the end of the bed and lifted the chart of the patient in the bed. While she was reading and turning the pages in a hurry, he stepped slowly further into the room so that he could see the patient. Thankfully the patient was sleeping and therefore he didn't need to make up an excuse for being there. After a few more seconds of reading Dr Kanu put the chart down. She straightened herself up and with one hand on the end of the bed, looked directly at him. 'Ben…' there was a pause as she looked for the next word. As she looked at the floor for a second, he could tell that she was nervous.

'It's OK Dr Kanu, ask me anything,' he said, knowing full well what this was about.

'OK,' she said, looking up at him again. 'I believe that you are healing people in this hospital. Is this true?' it was refreshing to be asked such a direct question and so he repaid her in kind.

'Yes, I am,' he said with a smile. Dr Kanu took a deep breath, as if to help process the previous question and answer.

'OK, then,' she said. 'And how are you doing that?' This time it was he who needed to take a deep breath.

'Well,' he began; 'I have been sent. I don't know who the Sender is; maybe it's God, I don't know, but he has sent me and he is the one who has given me this ability. All I know now is that I am here to use it as much as I can.' Before he had finished speaking, he could see the tears welling up in Dr Kanu's eyes. Without warning she rushed over to him and threw her arms around him.

'Oh, thank you, Ben! Thank you,' she said with the sound and pressure of her rushed emotional breathing pervading their embrace. She hugged him tighter. 'I believe again!' she said in a voice that was cracked with emotion. 'My family believes in the Sender and now I believe too!' After whispering this revelation in his ear, she released her embrace and stood in front of him while holding his hands. For a moment, he wondered how Dr Kanu and her family knew the Sender, but it didn't seem like the time to ask.

After a brief moment of looking at each other with smiles on their faces, as if coming to some mutual understanding, Dr Kanu took another deep breath and pulled down hard on his hands. 'Right, Ben!' she said, with a look of renewed determination on her face. 'You've been sent to heal, so let's get you healing!'

She released her grip on his hands and she walked round to the other side of the bed. Encouraged by Dr Kanu's newfound faith and enthusiasm, he dutifully followed her to the bed and stood facing her on the opposite side. She looked at him with a look of pure excitement on her face. 'OK, Ben, I've seen you do it before, so use those magic hands of yours!'

'OK!' he said with a smile of his own. The patient was still sleeping; a man who seemed to be in his sixties with a full head of grey hair and moustache. Since the patient was sleeping, he decided that he would try to do this without waking him and causing a fuss. Slowly he stretched out his hands and lowered them gently onto the man's chest. In no time at all, the tingling sensation pulsed through his arms and through his fingers and then it was gone. As he lifted his hands from the man's chest, the man took a deep breath and shifted a little in his bed. Both he and Dr Kanu looked at each other. There was a look of sheer delight on her face, as if she had just seen Santa put presents under the tree. He would have laughed out loud if he wasn't afraid of waking the patient. Quietly, Dr Kanu clasped her hands together to express her great joy at what she was witnessing. She looked at the patient and then looked back at him and nodded in the direction of the door for them both to leave. Their work here was done. Carefully they left the room and Dr Kanu closed the door behind them. They stepped away from the door and further into the corridor; almost back to where he had been standing beforehand. Still looking at each other, their broad smiles burst into muffled laughing. 'Wow! That was amazing!' she said with a chuckle.

'Yeah, I know!' he replied with a chuckle of his own. At this point, they actually found themselves a bit breathless due to their efforts to keep quiet while filled with excitement. But now they were also filled with adrenaline because this was only the beginning. They now had the rest of the ward and even the hospital to get around. However, their ambitions were about to be cut short.

Suddenly an alarm went off above the side ward that they had just exited. The red light flashed above the door way and the siren boomed through the whole ward. Both of them instinctively looked down the corridor of the ward to see who was there. There was one nurse and Dr Black at the nurses' station and both were already on their feet. But it was the sight at the end of the corridor that chilled them to the bone. It was Dr Pujara and Sister Montgomery, just back from their lunch. Even from long distance, he could see the rage building up in Sister Montgomery's eyes. He looked back at Dr Kanu, but she was already on her way into the sideward, quickly followed by Dr Black and the staff nurse. He took a quick step back in order to resume the exact position that he was standing in previously, as if to mask the fact that he had ever moved at all. Once in position he looked down the corridor again and by this stage, Sister Montgomery was almost upon him. The modest heels on her black shoes were nearly producing smoke, they were pounding the floor that furiously as she shot towards him. Dr Pujara followed on at a magisterial pace, bringing all his formidable authority with him. The Sister slammed her handbag down on the bench at the nurses' station and with her clenched fists running down her legs, she let rip at him.

'What have you done now?' she screamed with all the venom she could muster. Without stopping, she swept past him and into the side ward. Eventually, Dr Pujara arrived on the scene with an air of calm that was unperturbed by the drama unfolding in front of him. Without looking at Ben and keeping his chin up high, he drifted towards the doorway of the sideward, from which there was emerging quite a noise of different voices. He peered in for a little while. The clamour of voices was getting louder. It actually sounded like there was a bit of riot going on in there. Dr Pujara eventually put his foot out to step inside the room, but as soon as he did so he was nearly run over by the nurse who shot out of the room in front of him.

'Sorry! Excuse me!' she shouted as she ran past what was now a startled Dr Pujara! He rolled back on his heels and stared after her for a short while. After regaining his composure, the good doctor turned to make his way into the side ward for a second time. Unfortunately, the efforts were thwarted again, this time by another nurse coming steaming out of the room. Unfortunately, this particular nurse happened to be Sister Montgomery. Her face was red with rage and she walked right up to him with her right arm fully extended and finger pointed.

'Well, what have you done? What have you done?' she screamed at him with unbridled anger. He stood with his back to the wall, getting as far away from that finger as possible. 'Were you involved in this?' Her eyes were literally dancing with fury. 'Answer me,' she barked! For a second, he considered answering but then thought better of it. Seeing that he had been struck dumb with fear, Sister Montgomery continued to vent. 'I told you to stay where you were! That was all you had to do! And you couldn't even do that! No, instead you have to turn my ward into a circus!' Sister Montgomery's face was getting redder by the second, so much so, that her fury began to trigger her asthma. She started to wheeze a little, but even as she struggled for breath and raised her inhaler to her mouth, she still kept her rage-filled eyes fixed on him.

As Sister Montgomery took two heavy puffs from her inhaler, he could see the family of the patient being led into the room in front of him. All sorts of questions suddenly rushed through his mind. Had something gone terribly wrong? Had the healing not worked? Was this man now at death's door? The whole ward was in complete confusion. Meanwhile, Sister Montgomery was getting herself even more worked up! 'You are completely and utterly unprofessional,' she raved! 'You give this ward a bad name! You give this hospital a bad name! Hell, you even give porters a bad name! So, tell me now, what have you done?' There was no way he was answering that question, but he didn't have to.

'He was in the room. I saw him go in!' came a voice from behind them. It was Dr Black who had just come out of the side ward and was standing in the doorway. He calmly walked over to where the confrontation was going on. At this point, Dr pujari decided to give up his efforts to enter the side ward and moved over to join them. It was now three against one. There he was with his back against the wall and in front of him were the three most senior staff on the ward. Sister Montgomery glanced left and right quickly and then looked back at him with an evil smirk.

'I told him not to go in, but he went in anyway and within a few seconds of him coming out, the alarm went off.' Dr Black was back to his condescending tone and looked towards his senior colleagues as he testified against him. He was, of course, not being entirely truthful. It was actually Dr Kanu who led him into the ward, but on this occasion, he was glad of Dr Black's dishonesty because the last thing he wanted was to get Dr Kanu into any trouble.

'Well, well, Mr Archer,' it was time for Sister Montgomery to get her oar in again. 'You really are a piece of work, aren't you,' she chuckled malevolently. 'You come into my ward and you think that you can just mess up everything that Dr Pujara and I have worked so hard to create! Well, let me tell you something, kid!' She leaned in towards him with the finger nearly touching his chin and the Scottish accent at its thickest and most threatening. 'I am going to make sure that you are never allowed on this ward again! Isn't that right Dr Pujara!' She said it without even looking at Dr Pujara, but he couldn't help but glimpse over at him. In his usual manner, the consultant lifted his chin as he was about to speak, but before he could get the words out, he suddenly found himself catching a falling nurse. Sister Montgomery literally threw herself into Dr Pujara's arms, who dutifully caught her. Ordinarily this would have been a situation that Sister

Montgomery would possibly have enjoyed, but on this occasion, neither the throw nor the catch was voluntary. No, instead, what had happened was that no less than four members of the patient's family literally rammed into their little meeting at full steam. With the result being that all three of the senior staff members were scattered like pins in a bowling alley.

With the pins out of the way, there was now nothing between the four relatives and himself. A brief moment of alarm crossed his face as he wondered if this was a lynch mob who had come after him for killing their loved one. His fears were quickly allayed as the woman at the front of the mob threw her arms around him. The raincoat and scarf that she was wearing suddenly engulfed him. 'Oh, thank you for saving my, Bobby,' she cried! 'Oh, thank you so much!' And she began kissing him repeatedly on the cheek. Following quickly behind her were three more. They looked a little younger and therefore he assumed they must be the grown-up children. There were two sons and a daughter and were all of similar size. As they piled into the collective embrace, he could feel the pressure building between him and the wall. It was even getting a little hard to breath!

Amidst the chorus of thankyou's, he was just about able to get out words, such was, 'you're welcome' and 'no problem,' but as he was doing so, he couldn't help but notice the other gathering that was going on just beside them. The bowling pins that had been scattered so unceremoniously had now reassembled and were deep in conversation. Except this time, it was Dr Pujara who was looking more animated than anyone. He was not used to having this type of situation on his ward and much more than that, he didn't like his people whizzing past him and almost over him. It just wasn't the way that he wanted his ward to be run!

Eventually, the grateful relatives took a step back and left him able to breathe again which was a huge relief. Before long they had turned and gone back into the side ward to see their loved one who was now walking freely around the room, looking very cheerful indeed. Presumably the alarm went off because he removed the sensor pads from his own chest. The lack of signal therefore caused the heart monitor to alarm, which in turn, set off other alarms. But now that all alarms and celebrations were over, there was a bit of calm descending on the ward once more. In the midst of this calm, he looked over at the other group that had been meeting a few feet away. It seemed that their meeting was now over. Dr Pujara lifted his head and looked towards him. It seemed that he was going to be doing the talking. Slowly and carefully Dr Pujara walked over to him with Sister Montgomery and Dr Black following after. As he stopped in front of him, he straightened himself up and cleared his throat. 'Mr Archer,' he began. 'This sort of activity cannot continue! This is a ward, not a circus! And we cannot have people running in and out of here as if it is! We are here to help people get better and we cannot do that if the ward is in chaos! Do you understand?'

'Yes, Dr Pujara,' he answered. Dr Pujara wasn't quite as scary as Sister Montgomery and so he felt able to get a few words out. But Dr Pujara wasn't done. 'Now, Mr Archer, it appears to be that lately you seem to bring chaos wherever you go and what is worse you seem to be giving people the idea that you are some sort of healer.' He squeezed the word, 'healer' through his teeth with utter contempt and after he did so he furrowed his brow a little more and leaned towards him. 'Now, this is behaviour that we just can't tolerate on this ward. It just isn't professional and if you can't behave in a professional manner then you simply don't belong on this ward!' Dr Pujara slowly raised his voice to give added emphasis to his words. He held his gaze for a moment and may have been ready to say something else but then he was interrupted again.

'But he does belong on this ward!' said Dr Kanu. She suddenly emerged from behind Dr Pujara and came to stand beside him. With his brow still furrowed, he turned his gaze towards the junior doctor.

'I beg your pardon, Dr Kanu,' he growled. The Consultant was not in the habit of being contradicted by one of his subordinates.

'Dr Pujara, just hear me out!' Dr Kanu swallowed nervously. She realised that she really was going out on a limb here. 'Sir, I have seen this man do things that I have never seen anyone else doing. Please, just give him a chance and let him show you what he can do!' Dr Pujara raised himself up straight once more and this time with a look of disgust on his face.

'Dr Kanu,' he bellowed. 'Are you telling me that you had something to do with this incident?' Dr Kanu bowed her head for a second, but then lifted it up suddenly in defiance.

'Yes,' she announced with brave clarity. 'I did! And just look at the results,' she said, gesturing with her right arm to the side ward. 'This man had severe cardiac failure! He may have needed bypass surgery! And now he is perfectly healthy!' This really was an impassioned plea from Dr Kanu. He had no idea that she was so brave! But what made it all the more impressive was that she was doing it for him; someone she barely knew! However, as brave as it was, it was to no avail.

'Dr Kanu! That is enough!' Dr Pujara raised his hand and shut his junior staff member down in an instant. 'You are a doctor! And as a doctor you must behave professionally, not get involved in hocus pocus nonsense with some trickster like this man! I'm sorry, but I am going to have to send you home for the rest of the day while I decide what to do with you! This is a black mark on your career, Dr Kanu! Now, go home!' For a second, Dr Kanu's eyes filled up and then she turned on her heels and walked straight out of the ward with Dr Black following her. At that moment, all he wanted to do was rush to Dr Kanu's defence, but there was nothing he could do. He was one of the most junior staff on the ward and had no authority to challenge anyone. After they had all watched Dr Kanu and Dr Black leave, he turned back to Dr Pujara who lifted his chin up even higher; satisfied that he had put this little insurrection to rest.

'Now, Mr Archer, you run along for your lunch break and we will decide what to do with you when you get back!' And with that, he and Sister Montgomery walked into the Sister's office and closed the door behind them.

Chapter 20
Healing Unleashed

As he took the long slow walk out of the ward, it felt like the eyes of the whole ward were on him. He kept his eyes firmly on the ground as he moved towards the exit with increasing pace. There was a mixture of emotions racing through him; the intensity of which brought burning tears to his eyes. On the one hand, there was the positive love and hope that had been raised up with the healing of the patient and the warm embrace of the grateful relatives. But on the other hand, there was the bitter and nasty opposition that he faced from Dr Pujara and Sister Montgomery. They should have been happy that another one of their patients had been healed, but instead they were filled with hatred and anger. And what made it worse was that those who supported him; Dr Kanu in particular; were also being attacked and hurt because they supported him. It was becoming clear to him now that there could be no middle ground in what he was doing. People either wanted to heal or to hurt. It was a mystery to him, but that's the way it was! Therefore, he wasn't going to tip toe around those with the opposite agenda anymore. He was going to heal as many people as he could and if others didn't like it, then that was their problem and they could do whatever they wanted to stop him.

As he stomped down the stairwell, the crystallization of his resolve to fulfil his sending overcame the emotions that had welled up inside him. This settling of his emotions was timed perfectly with his arrival at the ground floor and his encounter with a frantic looking Mo. He was barely off the last step when Mo swung open the door to the stairwell. Mo stood there wide-eyed and almost breathless with intent. 'Where have you been, Ben? We have been waiting for you all morning and the queue is running out the door! Come on, man! Let's go!' Ben smiled slowly with a hint of curiosity on his face. As he stepped closer to where Mo was standing in his purple scrubs, Mo instinctively reached out and grabbed him by the shoulder and lightly ushered him out into the hallway. Letting the door close behind him, Mo skipped out in front of him to lead the way to the staff room. It was refreshing to meet someone who was almost aggressively in favour of him healing people, instead of the response he got on the ward moments earlier. 'So, there's a lot of people then?' he said casually and a little hopefully.

'A lot?' said Mo quizzically as he looked around with a gleeful grin.

'You must be joking, mate! The whole place is going mad because of you!' Mo seemed to be picking up the pace with every word he spoke and then he looked around again.

'Oh, Ben! You are going to love this! This is going to be amazing!'

'Oh, cool!' he responded with a bemused smile. Compared to what he had just come from on the ward, this overwhelming enthusiasm from Mo was a lot to take in. However, it wasn't just this change in attitude that he had to consider now, it was also the increasing pace that he had to maintain to keep up with Mo. His friend was nearly at jogging pace now and he had to speed march just to keep up with him.

In no time at all, they rounded the corner and the entrance to the staff room came into view. He hadn't really thought that much about Mo's description of the scene before they got there, but when he saw it for himself, he was so shocked that he almost came to a complete standstill. Just like Mo had said, there was literally a queue of people running right out of the door of the staff room; and not just out of the door, but quite a distance beyond it! There must have been a line of people, about twenty in number, stretching all the way to the main entrance in the lobby. There were people in their pyjamas from the wards, there were people in staff clothing, including a couple of nurses, and there were also people in plain clothes, as if they had just stepped in off the street. They were all talking to each other, busy comparing their different aches and pains as Mo arrived. Mo clapped his hands to get their attention.

'OK folks! We are ready to begin! The servant of Allah has arrived!' Suddenly everyone looked in his direction! There was silence! Then a couple of people burst into a few muffled sniggers. A rather loud whisper of, 'he's just a porter' went up and down the queue quickly and three or four people began to walk away while looking back and laughing and shaking their heads. He was quickly reminded of his realization of the division in attitudes to his acts of healing, but he wasn't going to let that get him down anymore. He knew what the Sender had sent him to do; he knew that he had the power to do it; and that was exactly what he was going to do!

After slowing down in pace, he accelerated his walk to the door of the staff room and got right behind Mo as he pressed his way in past the queue. Just like earlier that morning, the room was filled with the same mix of people. There were people from the wards and staff and elsewhere, but this time everything seemed a little more ordered than before. There was no sign of Eddie on the table in the middle of the room, but rather there were lots of cups laid out with a couple of tea pots and half a plate of biscuits with a lot of crumbs around it. Mo continued his progress into the room and announced his arrival at the same time.

'Make way, make way, the servant of Allah is here!' There was a ripple of murmuring and excitement around the room and many people checking their phones to look at the various postings on social media that had been put up since the healing of the lady with cancer that morning. They were moving deeper into the room now and just as they were squeezing their way round the table, Enid appeared carrying a jug of milk. As soon as she looked up and saw him, she gasped and thrust the jug of milk into Mo's hands. Immediately, she threw her arms around him.

'Oh, Ben, it's you! Thank the Lord! We've missed you!' After a tight embrace, she stood back but still kept her hands on his arms and looked him up and down. 'Now,' she said with a mother's look. 'How are you feeling? It has been a tough day for you!' He wasn't sure just how much Enid knew about his day, but it was just lovely to find someone who was genuinely interested in how he was!

'Oh, I'm fine, Enid,' he answered with a shrug. 'Just want to get on with helping people.'

'Yes!' Enid acknowledged firmly. 'But I am here to help you! So, here is a cup of tea and a biscuit to keep your strength up and make sure that you finish them both before you heal anyone!' It seemed like a rather odd demand, given the circumstances, but the words were so full of affection and genuine warmth that he gladly accepted the cup and piece of shortbread that were thrust into his hands. She leaned forward and gave him a kiss of the cheek and then she quickly turned around and went back to the kitchen area to keep everyone refreshed.

'OK, lover boy!' said Mo with a laugh, 'let's go!' While carefully balancing his tea and munching his biscuit, he followed Mo carefully through the crowd, smiling and acknowledging everyone as he brushed past them. As he got closer to the back of the room, he could hear Eddie talking to everyone around him. He and a friend were standing in the corner of the room with clipboards and pens in hand, questioning everyone around them. Eventually Mo broke through the crowds and emerged in the little space that Eddie had partly cordoned off with a few neatly arranged chairs. 'Look who I've found,' he announced as he stepped over the chairs in front of him. Eddie and his other porter colleague both looked up and Eddie gave a great cheer.

'Yeah, Ben, the man of the moment! Come on in my friend! Come on in!' He smiled in response and then looked for somewhere to put his half empty cup.

Noticing his awkwardness, Mo was the first to respond. 'Here, Ben, gimme that, will ya? Mo said with his hand out. He took the cup and put it on the television stand which had been pushed off to the side of the room. Having got rid of his cup, Ben joined Eddie and Mo inside the little circle of chairs. After handing his clipboard to his assistant, Eddie put his hands firmly on Ben's shoulders.

'OK, Ben!' Eddie said with a big grin on his face. 'Are you ready to do this?'

'Yes, I am,' he said with a grin of his own.

'Well, in that case, step this way,' said Eddie as he turned with his arm outstretched, gesturing towards a seat in the corner. Ben looked at his seat and he couldn't help but smile. They had moved his old seat from the other end of the room to the opposite corner.

'You like that, do ya?' chirped Eddie with a big laugh as Ben walked over to the chair and sat down. No sooner was he seated than Eddie clapped his hands loudly and got everyone's attention.

'OK folks, now the healer is ready to begin and so are we. So, my friend Mo here is going to keep the queue moving and once you have been seen then please make your way out of the room so that others can come in.' Having made his announcement, Eddie came over to stand beside him. Eddie's assistant who was a lean little man with heavy stubble, stood beside Eddie. The assistant handed Eddie his clipboard and Eddie was ready to begin.

He checked the first name on his clipboard and looked up at the first person in the queue. 'Angela, please come forward,' Eddie said in a much softer tone. Eddie turned to him as Angela came and stood in front of him. She was a young woman in her twenties and was wearing the uniform of a clerical worker. 'Now, Ben, Angela here has a bad case of psoriasis and she's had it for a long time and would really like to be free of it. So, can you help her?'

'Yes, I certainly can,' Ben said to Angela with a smile.

'Please, Angela, come forward,' he said as he sat up a little straighter in his seat. The young lady stepped forward rather timidly. At the same time, she undid the cuff button on the arm of her blouse and rolled up her sleeve. She held out her arm and Ben could immediately see how bad her psoriasis was. All the way down to her wrist there was red, blotchy skin that looked very uncomfortable. After a moment of looking at the outstretched arm in front of him, he looked at Angela who already had tears in her eyes.

'OK, Angela, just relax, this won't hurt.' He then took her gently by the hand and immediately he could feel a great surge of heat rushing through his fingers. His hands were soon pulsing and tingling as he could feel the power transferring from his body to Angela's. Angela gasped a little, indicating that she could feel something happening. Eddie and his assistant looked over to see if there was any change and then they gasped too, this time with shock. Right before their very eyes, the red blotchy marks began to disappear. The psoriasis could actually be seen retreating back up her arm! Then Angela began to chuckle in amazement with tears now running down her cheeks. She put her other hand on her upper arm and down her leg. It seemed that the healing effect was covering her whole body. Eddie and his assistant could only stand there with their mouths open in amazement. A ripple of murmuring went around the room as what had happened was relayed down the queue. It was one of the most amazing healings that he had ever done. It was the first time that he had actually seen the healing occur visibly. But in a couple more seconds it was over. He released Angela's hand and as soon as he did so she fainted and collapsed in front of him. Thankfully she didn't hit her head on any of the furniture around them. Eddie and his assistant immediately rushed over to her and within a few seconds they had her on a seat and she began to come around. Not long after, Mo arrived with a cup of water that he had got from Enid at the kitchen. Within a few minutes she came around and was on her way, with Mo helping her.

With the drama of that first healing over, Eddie returned to his position and ushered over the next patient. He was an elderly man in a wheel chair and Eddie introduced him as Trevor. An elderly woman, probably his wife, was pushing his chair and she wheeled Trevor around until he was stopped in front of him.

'Now, Ben, Trevor has a problem with his legs. He has suffered some nerve damage which means he has lost power in them. Can you help?'

'Yes, no problem,' Ben said; and without delay, he put his hands on Trevor's knees. Trevor closed his eyes, partly in apprehension and partly in hope. His wife did the same. A couple of seconds passed and the energy in his hands died down.

'OK, you're done,' he said to Trevor. Trevor opened his eyes and thought for a moment. Then he looked at his wife who looked straight back at him with wild curiosity. Then suddenly, without warning, Trevor slapped his hands down on the arms of his wheel chair and thrust himself forward. The poor wife gasped with terror, thinking that he was going to fall over and even Eddie readied himself to catch the man. But rather than falling forward, Trevor stood bolt upright. There was a moments' silence as the crowd in the room watched on. Then a little smile began to spread across Trevor's face and he started to march on the spot like a soldier on parade. The whole room erupted in a great cheer of celebration and began clapping the marching Trevor as he began a very elaborate march around the little corner of the room. Now his wife was clapping and Trevor was punching his arms in the air. The crowd loved it and cheered even more.

With a sudden about turn, Trevor marched over to where he was sitting. He grabbed the hands of his healer and began thanking him. 'Oh, thank you sir! Thank you so much! I will never forget you and my wife will never forget you! You have given me and my wife our lives back.' Tears began to fill the old man's eyes. Trevor stared at him for a second and then got down on his knees. 'Would you please do one more thing for me, sir?'

'Of course!' Ben responded. It was all he could say in the face of such sincere gratitude.

'Would you please heal my wife's headaches? She really does get terrible headaches! Please, sir, heal my wife too?' He smiled at Trevor. He couldn't help but love this guy and his concern for his wife was touching. Trevor looked around at his wife who was crying profusely at this point. He gestured for her to come over and stand beside him. Walking around the unused wheelchair she came and stood beside her husband and put her hand on his arm. From his seated position, Ben put his hand up towards her head and she leaned over to let his hand rest on her forehead. He could feel her breathe deeply as the healing took place and then after a few seconds she stood up straight. She had a bit of a shocked look on her face at first. It was like a weight had been lifted off her. Then she smiled the broadest smile and looked down at her husband who looked back at her with a smile of his own. Trevor got to his feet and he and his wife embraced each other. It was one of the most beautiful moments he had ever witnessed and all the people in the room agreed with a few cheers and flutters of clapping. They both looked at him with smiles and tears and then both walked out together with Mo leading the way and pushing the wheel chair that was no longer needed.

Chapter 21
Can't Be Stopped

Trevor and his wife had only just left the room when Madge appeared at the door. She stepped inside the room with a look of disgust and confusion on her face. 'What is going on here?' she exclaimed loudly.

'We're getting the healing, love!' came the cheerful response from one of the patients in the queue.

'Healing!' she exclaimed again, loudly. 'What is this nonsense about healing? This has to stop!' she said, shaking her head. The people at the other end of the room began to look around at who was making this protest. It wasn't immediately clear to Ben what was happening from where he was sitting, but when he and Eddie saw that it was Madge, Eddie stepped in front of him so that Madge couldn't see him. Madge began to make her way through the room but was soon blocked by the chairs and the people in front of them. From where she was, she called over to Eddie. 'Eddie, what is going on here? Where is Ben?' she demanded angrily.

'He's busy, Madge!' replied Eddie firmly. 'He's busy helping people.' Ben wasn't sure if Madge could see him or not but he decided to remain seated and let Eddie do the talking.

'Well, that's all very well,' said Madge rather dismissively, 'but I need to see him now! We have to put an end to this nonsense!' Just then, one of the crowds turned around to face Madge.

'Excuse me, Madam, but you will not be putting an end to anything.' She was a middle-aged woman who was slightly overweight and was wearing blue jeans and a tracksuit top. She did not move from her place in the queue but had her hand raised towards Madge to make her point.

'Look, I don't know who this Ben guy is; and frankly, I don't care! All I know is that I have seen people walking out of here healed from their conditions and I will not let you or anyone else stop me from getting that same healing! My mum died from cancer and now I've got it too, so don't you dare get in my way!'

After a brief moment of the whole room being reduced to silence, including Madge, there was a shout from the other side of the room. 'Well said!' came a man's voice.

Then a couple of people shouted their agreement; and before long, the whole room was chanting, 'out, out, out,' at poor old Madge. Her face fell. Any resolve or anger that she had before was gone. She had lost all authority in this room and was probably beginning to fear that the crowd might get violent. After a few seconds of considering how to handle this, she decided that retreat was the best option and she hurried for the door, with the chanting of the crowd still ringing in her ears. As soon as she left the room, there was another great cheer of victory. It seemed that he wouldn't be getting summoned to another disciplinary panel today. And with the repelling of this threat to his ministry he could also feel a great swell of confidence filling his chest. There was a sense that people were really coming together around his ministry; not just Eddie and the others, but people he had never met before. The number of people who believed in him was growing; and it was a belief that they were now prepared to stand up for. It seemed that the Sender really was opening up the way for him to fulfil his ministry. Perhaps this was the Sender's way of getting people's attention so that he could then tell more people about the Sender. Who knows? Maybe the Sender would give them abilities too. But whatever the Sender's plan was, the possibilities now seemed endless.

Not long after Madge had disappeared out through the door, Mo appeared in the opposite direction. 'Hey! Hurry it up, will you? The queue is getting longer out here!' It was clearly getting more difficult to manage the queue and so, without delay, Eddie started looking at his clipboard again while clearing his throat to indicate the resumption of business. The next person dutifully stepped forward with the prompting of Eddie's assistant. Without looking up from his clipboard Eddie announced the details of the person's condition.

'Now this young man has a broken arm and a broken leg after falling off a roof and he wants to get back to playing rugby as soon as possible!' Eddie clearly enjoyed the rugby playing part of the description, but as soon as he looked up, there was confused silence from all around him. They all looked at the patient who had stepped forward and then they looked at the patient who was next in line and then after another second or two, they all burst out laughing. The patient who had stepped forward was not young at all and she was certainly no rugby player. She was an elderly woman with a walking stick and severe curvature of the spine. It was actually the next patient who was the young rugby player with his arm and leg in casts. Amidst the laughter, Eddie quickly looked back at his clipboard and stepped forward to put his hand on the elderly woman's shoulder.

'Oh dear, Mrs Anderson, I am so sorry! I do hope you will forgive the confusion! But don't worry, you can play rugby too when you're healed!' After a bit more laughing, Ben decided to get up from his chair and stand with Mrs Anderson.

'OK, Mrs Anderson,' he said reassuringly, 'just relax.' Then he put his hand on her back and almost instantly there was a series of loud cracking noises that came from her body. So loud were the cracking noises that it almost sounded like something violent was happening. People who were watching began to wince with every loud cracking sound, suspecting that this dear old lady was about to break in two. But in a matter of moments, the eyes that were wincing were soon wide with amazement. Right in front of them, the elderly woman seemed to grow about six inches in height as her back gradually straightened into a healthy posture. It was a stunning sight and once again the crowd in the room reacted with a lot of cheering and clapping. With a smile on her face, Mrs Anderson threw her walking stick at the wall and walked out of the room to yet more cheering and clapping, with Eddie's assistant walking beside her.

With no more interruptions and a system in place for getting people in and out of the room, the healings now continued at pace. Those with cancer came in with their faces full of gloom and sadness, but left with faces bright and cheerful. It was the same for those with severe diabetes and intestinal problems. Then there were those with all kinds of muscle and joint problems. They came in hobbling and wincing with the pain, but as soon as he put his hands on them, their whole posture changed. Those with hip and knee problems could walk with ease and perhaps most satisfying of all were those with multiple sclerosis and motor neurone disease who erupted into floods of tears when they realised that they could walk and move with strength. It really was the most uplifting experience that all of them had ever had! And in the midst of it, Enid had kept them all fed and watered with cups of tea and biscuits and even the odd sandwich every couple of hours. They were all working as a team with great cheer in their hearts and big smiles on their faces.

Chapter 22
Friends Reunited

It was about 5 or 6 that evening that the queue began to die down and by that stage they were all exhausted. There was a late flurry of people with eye problems and after he had touched their heads, they all threw their redundant glasses onto a chair that was already overflowing with them. After checking that there was no-one else waiting, Mo closed the door with a bang. 'Wow, praise Allah! I can't believe we got through so many people! That was incredible!'

'Yes, it was my friend! Yes, it was!' said Eddie while hammering his pen on his clipboard. 'Now, folks, let's all take a break!'

'Yes!' agreed Enid from the kitchen. 'We are going to take a break and everyone is going to sit around the table! So, come on everyone!' As Enid carried a freshly made pot of tea across to the table and set it down, everyone else followed her lead. They all slumped into their chairs and took a moment to stare at the selection of pancakes and sandwiches that Enid had generously prepared for them all. Then Eddie said something that came as a complete shock.

'OK, Ben, you say grace!' It took him a bit by surprise, but it showed him that ever since the healings had begun, there had definitely been a spiritual awakening amongst his friends. Rather awkwardly he put his hands together in front of him and closed his eyes as the rest of them bowed their heads. After a second or two of wondering what to say, he spoke,

'Oh Sender or God, I don't know. Thank you for helping us today and healing all those people. Thank you for my friends and we thank you for this food. Amen.' They all chimed with his 'Amen' and all began to reach out for the food. They were clearly as hungry as he was.

'That was a lovely grace, Ben, thank you,' said Enid as she was buttering her pancake.

'Yes, Ben, very nice! Very nice indeed,' echoed Eddie with a smile as he took a big bite of his sandwich. The amount of encouragement that he got from his small team was amazing. They never ceased to be positive with him, which was a very welcome contrast to what he had received on the ward.

As they all continued to eat rather quickly, such was their hunger, he couldn't help but think about the people on the ward, especially Dr Kanu and Nurse Mark. They had tried to encourage him, but unfortunately, they were brutally put down for doing so by Dr Pujara and Sister Montgomery. He was just beginning to wonder where they were and how they were doing, when suddenly, he didn't have to wonder anymore. The door opened wide and Dr Kanu and Nurse Mark burst into the room. They both had their coats on over their work clothes and both were wide-eyed with excitement. 'What is going on out there?' they both said, almost in unison. They both walked over to the table while taking their coats off.

'The lobby is packed with people laughing and crying and celebrating and there's a big pile of wheel chairs and crutches lying just outside the room!' said Mark in his typical excitable manner.

'Ben!' exclaimed Dr Kanu, leaning over the table with great focus. 'Is it you? Have all these people been healed?' Ben looked briefly at his colleagues who were at the table and smiled at them and they smiled back at him. Then he put down the biscuit he was eating and leaned back in his chair, still smiling at Dr Kanu. It warmed his heart to see her.

'Yes, they have all been healed, Dr Kanu. And my friends here have been helping me all afternoon,' he said. He could see Dr Kanu's eyes filling up a little. Then Mark jumped back into the conversation like a man who had been restraining himself from speaking for the last few seconds.

'Helping them!' he exclaimed with unrestrained glee. 'I'll say you've been helping them! It's like Glastonbury out there! People are hugging each other and taking selfies and everything! It's a flamin' carnival!' Ben couldn't help but giggle at the colourful description that Mark gave and there were a few giggles from the rest of them at the table. Then suddenly Ben realised that the people at the table probably didn't know the two newcomers. He stood up quickly.

'Oh, I am so sorry,' he said to Dr Kanu and Mark. 'I haven't introduced you to my friends.' He then proceeded to go around the table, telling everyone their names and where they worked in the hospital. After all the, 'hello's' and 'how do you do's' were out of the way in a very English manner, Eddie interjected.

'Well, now that we all know each other, take a seat!' Eddie then jumped up and darted across the room to drag over a couple of chairs and put them in place at the table. He never failed to think of the practical things and then Enid interjected in the area that she never failed at. 'Now, both of you must be starving! I'll get you some tea and sandwiches!' she said with some authority. There was no question about it, they had to receive refreshment. As Ben watched her skip over to the kitchen, he realised that the whole team had become energized by what was happening. They had all risen to the challenge and were using their individual strengths with an air of confidence that he had never seen before. It was humbling to see and made him realise what great friends the Sender had given him to accomplish his mission.

It wasn't long before Enid had returned with steaming cups of tea and a full plate of sandwiches. At this stage in the day, it was perhaps no surprise that the only sandwiches left were tuna and onion. In Ben's experience, these were always the last to be eaten. However, it did not seem to bother Dr Kanu and Mark who were quick to take a few bites. It seemed their excitement had added to their appetite and they seemed very glad of the refreshment. After they had eaten half a sandwich and had a few sips of tea, it seemed like the time to enquire about what had been happening on the ward since lunch. 'So, tell me about the ward.' Ben said, leaning forward with some curiosity. Dr Kanu and Mark both suddenly stopped eating and looked at each other, as if remembering the actual reason they were both there.

For once Mark remained silent. It was clearly Dr Kanu's place to relay this message. 'Oh, Ben!' she said with her face and her voice dropping to a very serious tone. 'I am so sorry; I should have said as soon as we arrived.' She looked again at Mark briefly, who was also wearing a much more sober expression. She looked back at him. 'Dr Pujara and Sister Montgomery have done something terrible! They have been telling lies about your healings! They are saying that you have been stealing medicines from the pharmacy and have been using them to make it look like you are helping people and they are going to have you arrested!' Dr Kanu finished what she was saying with a note of breathlessness, as if it had been a trauma for her to say it. That was further evidenced by the fact that she immediately put her head in her hands when she stopped. Mark instinctively put his hand on her shoulder to offer some comfort while the rest of the table sat in a stunned silence.

'Dr Kanu! Is this really true?' inquired Mo, in the most serious tone that Ben had ever heard him speak with. Dr Kanu wasn't quite ready to respond just yet.

'Well, if it is, then we need to get you out of here, mate!' said Eddie, bringing his fist down firmly on the table while turning to face him. They were all looking at him now, waiting for his response. Ben dropped his head to look at the table and gave himself a few seconds for contemplation. It was, of course, the logical thing to run. If he was arrested now, then there would definitely be no more healings; not for a while, at least. But if he did run, then it wouldn't be long before the police would arrive at his door. He was pretty sure that Dr Pujara and Sister Montgomery would be only too happy to assist the police with their inquiries. Besides, if he did leave then he would be abandoning all the patients in the hospital who were still in need. How could he live with his conscience if he left them to suffer another day? No, he was determined that he had to stay and heal as many people as possible!

Having come to his conclusion, he looked up at them again with an air of determination in his face. 'No, I can't leave now!' he said firmly. 'I have a responsibility to the patients of this hospital. This is where the Sender has placed me and this is where I must persevere until the job is done!' He looked around the table at a mixture of expressions. Eddie and his assistant and Mo and Enid all looked a bit bemused; still trying to figure out if this was the right thing to do. However, the expressions on the faces of Dr Kanu and Mark could not have been more different. Dr Kanu pressed her hands firmly against her chest with delight and Mark gave his usual loud response by clapping his hands together with zeal and a big grin!

'Alright then!' announced Mark with great enthusiasm. 'Let's get started! Which ward should we go to first?' Then suddenly, as Mark was rubbing his hands together, Dr Kanu quickly put her hand on one of his arms to stop him in his tracks.

'Oh wait!' she said with a note of alarm. Mark stopped rubbing his hands with a look of confusion on his face. 'We can't get into the wards!' she said solemnly. There was a moment of stunned silence.

Then Eddie sought an explanation to the statement. 'What do you mean we can't get into the wards?' Eddie enquired.

She looked at Eddie and then looked at Ben with a note of hesitation. 'There was one other thing that I forgot to tell you about Dr Pujara's plans,' she said. 'As well as making up accusations against you, they have also put security guards at the entrances of many of the wards so that you can't get in. Ben, what are we going to do?' she pleaded!

It seemed that they were in an impossible situation, but despite that he responded to her almost automatically. 'Don't worry about it! The Sender will make a way for us to get through! All we need to do is stay here and we will figure out a way to get into the wards tomorrow.' The words were out of his mouth before he even had time to process them himself. His own faith had clearly grown and from the looks on the faces around him, it was clearly making an impression.

'Yes! That's it, Ben!' said an excited Eddie as he thumped his fist triumphantly down on the table. 'We will not be moved! We will not let them force us out! We are going to dig in and finish the job!' The enthusiasm was catching and now it was Mo's turn. He stood up suddenly and without warning gave Eddie's assistant a firm slap on the shoulder; to his surprise.

'Yes! We will not be stopped! The enemies of Allah will not stand in our way!'

'And I'll make sure there are plenty of sandwiches for everyone!' announced Enid with her hands together and a look of glee on her face. There was no way she was going to be left out of this mission!

'And what about me?' said Dr Kanu, leaning over the table with a look of renewed excitement on her face.

'And me,' said Mark, chiming in.

'Well…' he pondered for a moment. 'The best thing for you two to do, is go home.' Both of their faces dropped with disappointment. 'Look!' he said, quickly following up on their disappointment. 'With both of you still in your posts on the ward, you will be able to help us get access to different parts of the hospital; and you'll be able to keep us up to date with what is going on, just as you have done now. But the only way you will be able to do that is by carrying on working as normal!'

Both of them gave a reluctant nod of understanding. 'Yes, I suppose you're right,' said Mark with a note of resignation. Dr Kanu looked down at the table for a second and then looked back at him.

'Yes, OK, that will do. But we will be back here at the crack of dawn!' she said resolutely.

'And I think you should do the same, Sid!' Eddie said to his assistant. 'No point in you I' into bother as well!' Sid nodded obediently, and with that, he, Dr

Kanu and Mark got up and put their coats back on. After they all got to their feet, Ben and Eddie walked over to the door with them. Mark walked on out through the door with Sid, but Dr Kanu suddenly turned around and flung her arms around Ben.

'Oh Ben!' she said, holding him tight. 'Thank you for helping us believe!' She was clearly filled with emotion once again, but she didn't want to make a fuss and so she released him and followed Mark quickly out the door. As the door closed behind her, Ben and Eddie looked at each other briefly. A knowing grin crept across Eddie's face as if he knew something more about the relationship between Ben and Dr Kanu than he should have. Ben blushed a little and then shook his head dismissively. Eddie was probably going to say something more, but then Enid interrupted. She brushed between them with her purse in hand.

'OK, I'm going over to the shop before it closes.' She opened the door and just before she left, she instructed them, 'now make sure you all get a nice comfortable seat that you can sleep in and I'll be back soon.'

'OK, Mama!' they both said in unison and then did as they were told.

Chapter 23
Big News

Each of the three men in the room set to work on their own version of a makeshift bed, using various arrangements of chairs and tables. They were all examining them and testing them when Enid arrived back with an armful of sandwiches and various other snacks. 'OK,' she said, 'I've got a few different things for you for supper, but unfortunately all the sandwiches are gluten-free. The girl at the shop said that as soon as all the coeliac people got healed, they came straight in and bought up everything with gluten in it.' She dropped everything she was carrying onto the counter and then turned to them with a bit of a chuckle. 'In fact,' Enid continued; 'they told me that in some cases, they had the stuff half eaten before they even got to pay for it!' The idea of these gluten-obsessed people gorging themselves on food that had been off limits for a long time gave them all a bit of a laugh.

Enid finished putting some of the food away in the fridge and then she turned to face them all. 'Now, that's me all done here, and I will leave you all to settle down, and I will be back with the others early in the morning.' It really was wonderful to have someone like Enid to look after their needs with such kindness and it filled his heart again with great thankfulness to have friends like these. As he felt this swelling of thankfulness within him, he moved instinctively across the room and when he got to Enid, he gave her the best hug that he possibly could.

'Oh, thank you, Mama!' he exclaimed.

'Oh, thank you, Mr Healer!' she replied with an emotional voice. They were still locked in their embrace when they heard a familiar clap of the hands and a loud laugh from Eddie.

'Yes! That's what I'm talking about!' he cried with excitement.

'OK, let me get in on this action!' Eddie declared; and within a couple of seconds both he and Enid felt Eddie's big arms surrounding them both. With all three of them locked in this embrace, Mo was left standing on his own, looking a little awkward. Ben could see him out of the corner of his eye and quietly gestured to him with his free hand to come over and join them. With a bit of a shy grin, Mo ambled over towards them and joined the embrace.

'This is it, folks! This is it!' declared Eddie triumphantly; and with one last squeeze around all of them, he released his grip on the huddle and they all did likewise. It was amazing to feel how their love for each other had grown over the past week. Their collective sense of mission had definitely deepened their relationships and a visible sign of that was the tear that Enid wiped away from her cheek.

'OK, boys, now be good and I'll see you in the morning.' She made her way to the door and was just about to put her hand on the door when there was a loud knock from the other side. It made Enid jump with surprise and for a second, she hesitated to open the door. Sensing her apprehension, Eddie dived in front of her and opened the door just enough to see who was knocking.

'Hi, I'm from the 'Good Morning London' newspaper and I just want to ask a few questions about reports of people being healed, if I may.' The voice was that of a woman and sounded charming but business-like.

'Oh, OK then, come on in.' Eddie replied with a note of curiosity. He subsequently opened the door wide and as the reporter stepped in, Enid stepped out.

The reporter closed the door behind her and Eddie took a step back to welcome her into the room. She was a rather tall woman, almost as tall as Eddie, in fact. She had long straight dark hair that hung down over her shoulders and was wearing a light grey trouser suit with low-heeled black shoes that had clearly walked a few miles. Ordinarily it might have been a bit awkward for a woman to be standing in a room with three men but this particular woman did not appear to be the least bit nervous.

'OK, then,' she announced with some authority, 'which one of you is doing these healings then?' They all looked at each other for a second, not sure how to respond to such a direct question.

'Oh well, that would be, Ben,' said Mo rather shyly, gesturing in his direction. Without hesitation, the reporter immediately walked right up to him and introduced herself. She put out her hand to shake his. Her grip was a lot firmer than he expected and she gave his arm a thorough shake.

'Hello, Ben! Lovely to meet you! My name is Janice Perkins, I'm a journalist with the Good Morning London newspaper and I'd like to ask you a few questions, if I may? Is that alright?' Keeping her grip on his hand, she awaited his response. He smiled awkwardly, somewhat taken aback by the rather forthright request.

'Ah well, sure,' he said timidly.

'Great!' Came the immediate response which seemed to snatch his assent right off his lips. 'Now would it be possible to sit over here, just you and I, and then maybe I can talk to your friends here later on?' she said, as she gestured to the corner where the healings were done.

'Yeah, no problem!' Ben replied, submissively. We'll be over here if you need us.' Eddie said with a wave, and he and Mo settled down at the table where both of them started tapping on their phones.

Janice turned to him with a smile and held her hand out towards the corner of the room. 'Lead the way!' she said politely but firmly. Following her prompt, Ben went over to the chair in the corner and sat down. No sooner had he got himself comfortable than Janice pulled a chair up close to face him. As she sat down, she pulled her red handbag off her shoulder and lifted out a voice recorder and a note pad and pen. Pulling another chair up slightly in front of her, she set the voice recorder on the chair that was now partly between them and pressed a button to start it recording. Now that she seemed ready to begin, she thrust herself back in her chair, crossed her legs and set her notepad on her thigh. She looked up at him with a deep breath to ready herself.

'Now, Ben, you are claiming that you are healing people, is that correct?' Getting used to her direct questioning by now, he gave a straight answer, but still a little timidly.

'Ah…yes,' he answered.

'OK,' she nodded, 'and what do you mean by heal?' He hesitated, a little baffled by the simplicity of the question.

'Oh, well…I just make people better, I suppose. I take away their pain.'

'And how do you do that, precisely?' she fired back.

'Well, I touch them. I mean, I put my hands on them.'

'You put your hands on them,' she added with a note of curiosity.

'Is that all?'

'Ah, yeah,' he said. 'You see, when I put my hands on them,' he continued, feeling the need to explain a bit more; 'I get this feeling like pins and needles in my hands. It's as if there is some sort of power or heat travelling down my arms and into the patient that I am healing.'

'Right,' said Janice with a little raise of her eyebrows. 'And is this something that you have always been able to do or is it something that has started recently?'

'Oh no, this is only a recent thing! Just the last couple of weeks, in fact!' Ben felt himself becoming a bit more candid now.

'I see,' said Janice, ponderously, now making the first inscription on her notepad. 'And how did this all start, Ben?'

'Oh, well, it started with the Sender.'

'The Sender?' Janice straightened up a little, and made her second inscription on her notepad.

'Yes, the Sender!' he responded promptly. 'I'm not sure who He is, but he has appeared to me on a couple of occasions and he has made it clear that he is the one who has given me the power to heal.'

'He has appeared to you!' said Janice rather quizzically, raising her eyebrows even further this time. 'And when he appears to you, this Sender, what does he look like?'

'Oh well, he doesn't actually appear as a person. You see, what happens is that the room that I happen to be in at the time will be filled with some kind of mist or smoke and then out of the mist, there is a voice.' He could sense how strange this testimony was, but after the practice that he had telling others about the Sender, he now felt more confident to tell his story.

'Right,' said Janice, who was now looking openly sceptical. 'So, when you say it was a 'he' that was speaking to you, you can't really be sure if this Sender was a man or a woman.'

'Oh well, I never really thought about that,' he said, rather bemused at the interest in the gender issue.

Janice took another deep breath and leaned back again in her chair. 'Well, Ben, I have to say that a lot of people will find this hard to believe! I mean, all this stuff about a Sender and smoke and healings! Do you know what I mean?' Her scepticism was becoming a bit more blatant now, but he wasn't perturbed.

'Oh yeah, sure! I understand completely! I mean, it took me a while to get my head around it too!' He was about to continue with the story of his own conversion, but Janice quickly cut back into the conversation.

140

'You see, Ben, there are a lot of accusations going around about these, so called, healings! And I'll give you a few of them,' she said as she turned a few pages over on her notepad. Finding her place, she continued,

'A patient on your ward claims that you pretended to be a doctor and you gave her an injection of some unknown substance. A nurse claims that she saw you do this, and a pharmacist claims that she has seen you hanging around the pharmacy department a lot over the past week. Now what do you say to those accusations?' As she finished speaking, she leaned forward as if to press for the answer. It took him a moment to process the accusations that she had just listed and he couldn't help but look rather bewildered.

'Ah, well, they're not true.' The words eventually tumbled out of his mouth. Janice gave a derisory snort and a smirk at his response.

'Well, Ben, with all due respect, these are well-respected health professionals we are talking about here! Why would they lie?' The question was left to hang in the air for a second or two while he tried to come up with an answer.

But Janice continued, 'Ben, you're talking about some spirit appearing to you, you're talking about healing people, even though there are witnesses who have testified against that, I mean let's face it, it's all a bit far-fetched, don't you think!' She really was trying to get underneath his skin now and was almost glaring at him. 'Ben, why should anyone believe you?' Still leaning forward, she waited for his response. He would have loved to have thought of some clever response at that moment, especially after listening to the condescending tone that Janice was using, but all he could think about was the fact that he was telling the truth.

'Well, the reason that people should believe me is because people have been healed.' It took him a second, but his memory began to catch up. 'There are many people who were on the cardiac ward this week with serious heart failure, but they are better now. There were people with late-stage cancer here earlier today and now they don't have cancer. There were people with diabetes and digestion problems and now they can eat what they want. There were people with eye problems and ear problems and now they can see and hear as good as anyone else.' Giving this list of healings was starting to fill him with confidence again. Telling the truth was putting fire in his belly and was far better than coming up with some clever response to the reporter's insults. He could tell that this was the case because the list of his healings had caused Janice to sit back a little from her position of confrontation. She sighed a little. Not the same snorting derision as before.

'Well, Ben, that's all very well and it sounds very impressive, but you and I both know that there are a lot of hoax healers out there; so again, why should anyone believe you? What makes you different from all the rest?' He responded more decisively this time.

'Well, Janice, I've told you about all the healings that I have done. That is my evidence and that is what people will have to look at and then make up their minds.' Janice dropped her head this time. She wasn't making a dent in his story and so she resorted to one last jibe.

'Ben,' she looked at him again. 'Are you dangerous? Are you giving false hope to people who are desperate?' This time it was his turn to lean forward. His eyes met hers head on.

'Janice, I am here to help people, that's all! Because that is what I have been sent to do!' Her eyes quickly looked at the floor.

'OK, that'll do!' she announced rather abruptly, gathering her things. As soon as her notepad and pen were in her handbag, she stood up. He promptly stood up with her.

'Well, Ben, thank you for your time. I'll show myself out.' After a quick shake of the hand, she turned on her heels and was on her way to the door.

'Oh ah, thanks, bye,' he called after her. She was past Eddie and Mo before they even realised she was leaving. They looked up from their phones with a bit of surprise on their faces and they both just managed to lift their hands to wave and say goodbye when she had the door opened and closed behind her.

'Oh! All done already?' said Eddie looking back at him after the door had closed.

'Ah, yeah,' he replied.

'And how did it go? What did she ask you?' continued Mo. He was getting tired and didn't really fancy explaining the whole conversation.

'Oh, it was fine. She just asked a few questions about the healings, that's all.' Eddie and Mo both nodded their heads in response to his answer. It seemed that they were too tired to discuss it further as well.

'Well then,' said Eddie, standing up, 'in that case, I suggest we all get some sleep now.' He turned and headed for the makeshift bed that he had put together for himself with a few chairs and cushions. He and Mo followed Eddie's lead and before long they were all settled for the night.

Chapter 24
Night Life

It was hard to tell how much time had passed while they were all sound asleep but when there was a knock at the door all three of them woke up straight away. Ben was still rubbing his eyes when he saw Eddie jump out of his makeshift bed and grab the door handle. As Mo walked unsteadily over to join him, clearly still waking up, Eddie pulled the handle down and opened the door just enough to see who it was. 'Hello, who are you?' came the rather abrupt greeting from Eddie to the person on the other side. By this stage, Ben was making his way to the door from his own makeshift bed on the other side of the room. He was just close enough to the door to hear the hushed voice from the other side.

'Ah, hello,' the voice began nervously, 'I'm sorry for calling so late but my name is Dr Nelson, Adam Nelson, and I would like to speak to the guy called Ben, if that's OK.' Mo was standing by Eddie and he pulled the door open a little wider so that he could see Dr Nelson too.

'Yeah, what do you want with, Ben? I hope you're not another reporter!' said Mo in a surprisingly aggressive tone. He knew Mo wasn't a morning person and now he could see he wasn't a middle of the night person either. Eventually arriving at the door, he tried to calm the situation down.

'It's OK guys, let him in. I've heard of Dr Nelson.' Rather reluctantly Eddie and Mo opened the door and stood back. Dr Nelson stepped into the room rather sheepishly under the suspicious glare of the two door men. As soon as Dr Nelson saw him, he rushed over to shake his hand.

'Ben!' he exclaimed rather urgently. 'I need to talk to you about everything!' he said as he shook his hand a little too long. It seemed a rather extreme request, but he was pretty sure what Dr Nelson was really referring to. Eddie closed the door gently as both he and Mo observed the conversation with interest.

'It's OK guys,' he said to his two friends, 'I'll just take Dr Nelson down the other end for a chat.' Eddie and Mo gave each other a quick glance and, with a nod, they both went back to their makeshift beds. They were both clearly happy with the arrangement and were also quite happy to get back to sleep.

After the initial greetings, he invited Dr Nelson to follow him to the back of the room where they both grabbed a chair and sat opposite each other. 'Alright, Dr Nelson, what can I do for you?' he said with a sense of authority. It was a little strange that he had grown so comfortable with this sort of situation so quickly.

'Well, Ben,' he began a little breathlessly, I don't know what to make of what I've seen.' Dr Nelson paused and shook his head a little, still wrestling with what was on his mind. 'I had a few patients on the oncology ward, the cancer ward; and they were at a pretty late stage in their condition; I mean they were pretty much terminal! There was very little we could do for them!' The doctor was looking at the ground while he was talking, trying his best to keep his thoughts in line. 'But then they went down to see you…and when they came back…they were completely better! And I don't just mean there was an improvement! I mean all their cancer, all their secondary's, all their symptoms were completely gone! They were completely healthy! Healthier than me!' He paused for a second, seemingly fighting back his emotions. 'And they were happy! They were happy, Ben! And I have to know where that came from!' For a second, he wasn't sure whether Dr Nelson was asking about the happiness or the healing. No longer was he looking at the ground but he was looking at him with a face full of emotion and sincerity. It was hard not to be moved by the sincerity of Dr Nelson's inquiry and he leaned back in his chair to give a moment's consideration to his response. It would have been easy for him to launch into the direct explanation of his encounter with the Sender and then add to that the rest of his testimony, but in this case, it seemed like a different approach was called for. This young doctor wanted to understand – that was for sure – but first, Ben wanted to know what answers the doctor was prepared to hear. 'Well, where do you think it came from?' he said with his elbows planted firmly on the arms of the chair and his hands crossed in front of him. At first, Dr Nelson looked a little stunned at the question. His mouth dropped open a little,

'Aaahhh…' he stalled, as if stumped by a consultant on the ward rounds. His eyes darted around the room for a little while, looking for the answers on the walls and the ceiling, and then eventually they returned to the questioner.

'Well, look!' he said, regaining a little composure; his experience as a senior doctor kicking in to stop him falling over completely. 'My dad was a doctor and my mother was a science teacher. So, ever since I was old enough to learn anything, I have learned that science explains everything! It explains the world around us through evolution and it explains the bodies that we live in through medicine! That is what I know and that is how I understand...' he paused and for a moment he got lost; 'that is how I understand life!' Each statement that the young doctor made was punched out from his mouth with utter conviction and almost a demand that these things must be accepted as true and unassailable facts. However, beneath his powerful assertions, there was, at the same time, a subtle, but detectable fragility. His whole worldview hung on what he had learned through his education, but now his experience on the ward had set the whole bookshelf of his learning at a precarious angle. 'Now, there must be a scientific and rational explanation for these people getting better, I am sure of that! And I know the accusations that have been made against you, and that might satisfy some people, but they don't satisfy me! Even the best fake doctor could not possibly do what I have seen!' He paused again, this time to take a deep breath. It was clearly an exhausting struggle that was going on in this man's heart and mind. He was taking his reasoning of the situation as far as it could go and therefore it was time to lead him a step further.

Sitting up a little straighter in his seat, but keeping his arms firmly fixed in their crossed position, he got ready to give the young doctor his next prompt. 'Dr Nelson, do you really think that human science and knowledge can explain everything in this world?' Dr Nelson looked up at him again with another long sigh.

'Well, that's what I've been taught!' he stated with some deflation. The doctor's reasoning had hit the buffers and now he was open to something new.

'Well then, maybe you need to be taught a little more!' Ben said with a big smile on his face.

'And can you teach me?' said Dr Nelson with the most serious expression.

'Teach you?' Ben said with a chuckle. 'No, Dr Nelson, I will show you!' At the same time as making this statement of intent, he got up to his feet and stood in front of the doctor with his hand gesturing towards the door.

'Lead the way!' he exhorted Dr Nelson, who duly responded by getting to his feet and making his way towards the door. Eddie and Mo were both still fast asleep and didn't move a muscle as they both left the room. No sooner had they left the room than Dr Nelson, all of a sudden, injected some pace into his walking, so much so that Ben found himself almost breaking into a jog to keep up. They got a strange look from the security guard at the main entrance as they disappeared down the corridor towards the back of the building. Ben already knew where the oncology ward was and so he had no problem following Dr Nelson, even at the fast pace that he was setting. It wasn't long to the cancer ward; up just one flight of stairs and then left towards the back of the hospital. He caught up with Dr Nelson on the stairs, but when they got to the top and were about to enter the corridor, Dr Nelson suddenly stopped and put his arm out to stop him. The doctor took a peek down the corridor and then looked back at him with caution in his face.

'Wait here and I'll get rid of the guard,' he whispered. Ben nodded in agreement and at the same time smiled inside himself. The doctor's words made it seem like they were on some covert military operation.

Dr Nelson disappeared around the corner and Ben quickly took his place, peering around the corner to see what was happening. All he could see was Dr Nelson's back at the entrance to the cancer ward and then he heard his voice. 'Hi Malcolm! Hey, listen, you wouldn't nip round to the canteen for me, would you, and get me a coffee from the vending machine. The coffee round there is much better than the machine we have here! And while you're there, get one for yourself too!'

'Oh yeah, sure, no problem doc!' came Malcolm's voice during the handover of some change that rattled between their hands. Ben ducked back behind the corner he was hiding behind so that he wouldn't be seen and it wasn't long before he could hear Malcom's footsteps marching past him on his way to the canteen. Once the security guard was well past him, he came out from hiding and walked on down to the ward to join Dr Nelson who was waiting for him at the entrance. Once Ben caught up with him, Dr Nelson nodded in the direction of the ward and without words, he opened the door and led them both through. As the door closed behind them, they both found themselves standing at the end of a long corridor with many individual patient rooms down both sides. All of them had a wall of glass which made it easy to see all the patients who were there. There were many older patients, all with varying degrees of hair loss and some women with the characteristic head scarfs. But then, saddest of all, were the younger people who were there. Some were very pale and some were much thinner than they should have been. It was a tragic sight to see, but thankfully all of them were asleep. They may have been sick, but at least they could rest.

After a moment to take in the surroundings, Dr Nelson looked at him.

'OK, show me!' he said. At last, this was the moment he had been waiting for. No Sister Montgomery or Dr Pujara to stop him; he could simply get around the whole ward and do what the Sender had sent him to do. He smiled at Dr Nelson with supreme confidence and walked straight through the door to the first patient. Dr Nelson followed him in and closed the door behind him. Ben walked over to the side of the patient's bed and Dr Nelson stayed at the door, clearly wanting to be able to see everything that happened next.

'He has lung cancer,' came the advice from Dr Nelson in a hushed tone. He looked down at the man in the bed. He had clearly been through some chemotherapy already, given the rather unnatural appearance of his lack of hair. He wasn't as old as some others on the ward; probably in his late fifties, early sixties; and there was ample evidence of the cause of his cancer in the stained tips of his fingers. Ben felt a little judgment rising within him because of the self-inflicted nature of the patient's suffering, but he quickly pushed that feeling down. The Sender had only sent him to heal, not to judge. He looked briefly in Dr Nelson's direction and he could see the young doctor's face full of anticipation; examining his every move. It was time to satisfy the young doctor's curiosity, and so without waiting any longer he reached out his right hand and put it gently on the man's chest. As expected, the pins and needles and the heat came to his hand quickly and then as quickly as it came, it went. He pulled back his hand and watched. Suddenly, the man's shallow breathing became a sharp and deep intake of breath. Then he began gasping. Dr Nelson took a few quick steps towards the other side of the bed. But then, before he could get to the man's side, the breathing settled down into a slow and deep rhythm. Dr Nelson stood for a moment and peered down at the patient; examining him as much as he could with his eyes. After half a minute of examination, he looked up at Ben with a face full of curiosity.

'It's done, Dr Nelson!' he said in rather casual way. Still looking back at him, Dr Nelson chuckled softly with bewilderment. The doctor then leaned back and walked out of the room. It was time to move on to the next patient. The night was already getting old and it wouldn't last much longer. There was much to be done!

Quickly he followed Dr Nelson out of the room and into the next one. Again, Dr Nelson stood at the door as he went over to the bed and laid his hands on the relevant part of the person's body. This process repeated itself for the rest of the night with varying responses from the patients. There were those who made little or no reaction at all and there were others who moved around and made various noises. Thankfully none of them woke up, or if they did, they didn't really care who was in the room with them. They had suffered so much by this stage that personal privacy wasn't a big concern. Dr Nelson watched on eagerly to learn whatever he could from the experience and as Ben entered every room, he could feel Dr Nelson's inquisitive gaze bearing down on him. There was no conversation other than the routine informing of where the cancer was in each patient and so they got around the ward without much interruption.

Eventually they came to the last room in the ward. It was a room that wasn't automatically visible from the ward's entrance and unlike the other rooms in the ward the glass walls were part-frosted to prevent anyone seeing in. However, floating above the frosted part of the glass were a couple of children's balloons which were covered in familiar cartoon characters. Dr Nelson reached for the door and this time he stopped before entering and turned to face him.

'This one's special!' he said, with an air of excitement. They entered the room as normal and there in front of him was a little girl with the most peaceful face he had ever seen. She had a pretty red scarf on top of her head and a small brown teddy bear pulled close to her chest. The sight of this little girl, who was clearly very ill, stopped him in his tracks. He took a few seconds to marvel and to mourn at one so young being in this ward. Dr Nelson leaned over to him,

'I told you she was special!' he said with a knowing grin. At that moment, Ben became overwhelmed with emotion. He could feel his eyes filling up and a lump building in his throat. It suddenly hit him; the realization of what this gift meant to people. It meant hope! It meant the end of sorrow and tears! It meant saving people from the worst pain in the world!

Without realizing it, he could feel himself walking over to the bed where the girl was still fast asleep.

'She has leukaemia,' came the voice from behind him. He found himself standing over her and held his hand above her head. He looked at the teddy bear that she was holding tight and he could feel himself filled with emotion once more.

'This should never happen,' he said to himself. And with that thought, he brought his hand down gently on the little girl's head. She pulled her teddy bear closer for a few seconds and then it was over. The pale skin became a little rosier, the tight curl that her body was in became a little looser, the breathing a little stronger; the leukaemia was gone. He lifted his hand from her head although he didn't want to. He and Dr Nelson stood on opposite sides of the bed and just looked at her for what seemed like a solid five minutes. This was why they were here! It was to help take away the pain! There really was no other feeling like it in the world and they both wanted to savour it for as long as they could. The fact that this little girl had leukaemia and now she didn't was all the motivation he needed to carry on, no matter how tough the opposition might be. Even if he had to go to prison for ten years in order to have the chance to heal another child like this one, then every one of those days in prison would be worth it. Then suddenly, he remembered who that child was. It was little Tommy.

As soon as he remembered this baby boy and his parents, a sense of emergency jolted him out of his daze. He looked briefly at Dr Nelson and then walked over to the door to leave the room. As soon as Dr Nelson realised that his partner was moving, he followed him out of the room and back down the corridor to the entrance to the ward. They both stopped at the door and he turned to Dr Nelson. He was about to speak but Dr Nelson got there first.

'Ben! I don't know what to say!' he laughed in disbelief. 'I've never seen anything like it!' Suddenly his mind turned back to the conversation that had brought them to this point.

'Dr Nelson, science doesn't explain everything! But what science can do is prove that what you just saw is real. So, do me a favour; run all the tests that you need to run to prove that all these people have been healed. Make sure that no-one can deny what has happened. Then, when you've done that, the science that you believe in, will point you to the truth that science can't describe.' Dr Nelson was nodding his head vigorously as if he was getting instructions from his consultant. He then put his hands on Dr Nelson's shoulders.

'Now, Dr Nelson, there is one more thing that I need you to do for me; I need you to get me into ICU. Can you do that? There is someone I need to see, there!' Dr Nelson stopped nodding his head. He thought for a moment and gritted his teeth at the challenge that had been laid down. Eventually he sighed,

'Well, Ben, I'll try, but as you know, security has been bumped up here and while I have a bit of authority in this ward, I'm not sure that will work the same for another ward.' He took his hands down from Dr Nelson's shoulders to mull over what the doctor had said. After a couple of seconds of looking at the floor, he came to his conclusion.

'OK, let's give it a try,' he said and then opened the door.

No sooner had he opened the door than he realised his mistake. There in front of him was Malcolm, finishing the cup of coffee that he had brought back from the canteen. He lowered the cup from his mouth and glared at the intruder. 'And what do you think you're doing here?' he said aggressively. Malcolm was not much taller than he was, but was considerably more muscular. He clearly took full advantage of the hospital gym! As he stood in front of this imposing figure, he was at a complete loss for words. Thankfully, Dr Nelson jumped into the situation as soon as he saw what had happened. He stepped into the space between him and Malcolm and in the process bumped him backwards. He stumbled a little but regained his footing and quickly stepped off to the side, out of Malcolm's eye line.

'Oh Malcolm, there you are!' said Dr Nelson with some bullish good cheer. 'So, what about that coffee?'

'Oh…ah…' said Malcolm, suddenly having to shift his thoughts to a different subject.

'Oh yeah, the coffee! Yeah, I left it at the nurses' station in the ward because I couldn't see you when I got back. Probably a bit cold now, I'm afraid!' While Malcolm was explaining the coffee situation, he took his chance to move past Malcolm and down the corridor towards ICU. As he disappeared down the corridor and turned left, he could hear Dr Nelson keeping up the charade.

'Oh, don't worry Malcolm, I'll just warm it up in the microwave later. Well…ah…I'm just nipping out for a moment. Be back in a minute.' There was a barely audibly, 'alright doc,' from a rather bemused Malcolm and then the sound of Dr Nelson's feet catching up with him.

As Dr Nelson rounded the corner with some haste, he jumped a little with surprise when he saw him waiting. 'Oh! Ha!' He laughed. The young doctor was clearly a little on edge with all the excitement of the night. Not stopping he continued on down the corridor towards ICU which was at the very back corner of the building. As he followed Dr Nelson at a distance, he could see that there were at least a couple of security guards at the door to the ICU ward. Not wanting to get involved in another confrontation, he hid behind the entrance to the catering department as he watched Dr Nelson approach the two security men at the door. As he began talking to the guards, they listened to him intently for a little while but then both of their heads began to shake and one of them put his hands up with his palms facing Dr Nelson. The body language said it all. After another couple of go's at talking his way into the ward, it quickly became clear that that these guards were not letting anyone in. Eventually, Dr Nelson put his hands up in defeat and turned and walked away. As the doctor got closer to him, he stepped out from the catering entrance into the corridor. Dr Nelson shook his head as he saw him and stopped in front of him. With a sigh, the doctor sunk his hands into his pockets and looked at him and shook his head, 'There's no way we can get in there,' he said despondently. 'The guards are under strict orders not to let anyone other than ICU staff in or out of the ward. I'm sorry, Ben, but there's no way I can get you in there!' He looked at the floor with disgust at the doctor's words. After feeling such a high from healing all the people in the cancer ward, he felt as if his heart was in his boots. Dr Nelson didn't know what to say and neither did he. After the brief moment of freedom to get around a whole ward of patients, it was very hard to accept this latest setback. He mulled the situation over for a moment in his mind and eventually he looked up at the doctor again.

'OK, Dr Nelson; there's not much more we can do tonight. You had better get back to your own ward and run those tests now. Best that you are not seen with me too much by the guards.' They both sighed and looked at each other for another couple of seconds. They both desperately wanted to keep going, but there was nothing they could do.

'Alright,' Ben said, breaking the silence, 'let's go!' Silently they walked back down the corridor. Dr Nelson took the right turn to the cancer ward, while he kept on walking to the stairwell at the back of the hospital in order to avoid another encounter with Malcolm. The air in the stairwell was cooler than in the rest of the hospital and by the time he got to the bottom, the cool air seemed to have calmed him down. The day and night that had just passed had been such an emotional rollercoaster that his body had been constantly filled with adrenaline. But now, he could feel that adrenaline draining away and it left him so exhausted that by the time he got back to the staff room, he felt that he was crossing the finishing line of a marathon. He crept past Eddie and Mo who were both snoring and before long, so was he.

Chapter 25
March of the Angels

He wasn't sure how long he'd been sleeping when he was awoken by the sound of the door opening and people walking into the room. 'Good morning, everyone,' came the sound of Enid's cheery voice as she turned on the lights. There was an immediate reaction to the lights being turned on from all those who had been sleeping. They all turned on their makeshift beds and began rubbing their eyes.

'Oh, hello guys,' came the voice of a croaky Eddie, who was already getting onto his feet. As he roused himself to sit upright, he could see that Enid was not alone. Close behind her were Dr Kanu and Nurse Mark who were both carrying plastic bags.

'Oh Enid! Tell me you haven't!' said Eddie in a very hopeful voice after seeing the bags being put on the table. He walked over and began to have a poke at them to see what was in them.

'Ah, Eddie! Not until the tea is ready!' warned Enid who was already in the process of getting the kettle on. Eddie put his hands up in surrender to Enid's demand and went back to his makeshift bed to restore the chairs to their normal arrangement. Ben could hear the kettle beginning to boil and felt that he had to get up now. He got to his feet and began to make his way over to the table with his eyes fixed on the floor.

'Ah, there you are, sleepy head! Have a good night?' said Mark in a voice that was way too cheerful for this time in the morning. He reckoned that Mark was probably the type of person who jumped out of bed as soon as the alarm went. 'Oh, hello, Mark,' he said rather sleepily as he got to the table and put his hands on one of the chairs and leaned over it. He was still coming to his senses and hadn't really become fully aware of where everyone was. It was in this relaxed state that Ben looked up to see Mark standing on the other side of the table with a big smile on his face; but then he could see that Dr Kanu was standing right beside him. She was dressed immaculately, as always, this time in a white floral wrap-around dress with a black overcoat. Ben's eyes immediately jolted open.

'Oh…ah…good morning, Dr Kanu!'

'Morning Ben!' she replied with a warm smile. Suddenly he felt a little embarrassed about his dishevelled state and immediately tried to correct his posture.

Mark laughed, 'Oh, don't worry, Ben, you look gorgeous!' The nurse laughed again, even louder; clearly taking great amusement at his belated efforts to impress the doctor.

Eventually they all got to the table and pulled out a chair and sat down. The only exception was Mo who was still getting up from his bed very slowly. Enid carefully carried over a full pot of tea. This was followed by cups and plates; after which she proceeded to lift various kinds of pastries and fruit out of the grocery bags. 'Mama, this is lovely! Thank you so much!' Ben said and everyone else at the table echoed their own 'thankyou's.' Eddie kindly offered to pour the tea for everyone and before long they were all tucking in to their choices of fruit and pastry.

Mark and Eddie were already starting into their second plate of food when Mo eventually managed to make it to the table. He had picked up the local paper that had come with the groceries and slumped into one of the chairs that was at the table. 'Oh dear me, Mo, you look terrible!' said Enid in an unusually blunt way. It was so uncharacteristic of her that Eddie burst out laughing.

'Yes! Mama, you tell him!' Realising just how blunt she had been, Enid put her hand to her mouth in surprise at the words that had just come out of her own mouth.

'Oh, Mo, I'm so sorry! You actually look lovely!' Eddie now laughed even harder and banged the table as Enid tried to back-peddle. Everyone else at the table couldn't help but snigger, however, Mo retained his sombre expression.

'It's OK, Enid! I know that you care, even if…' Mo suddenly stopped mid-sentence as he ruffled the paper in front of him. 'What on earth is this?' he exclaimed after a couple of seconds of reading the front page. Mo then proceeded to read the main headline.

'Hoax healer in local hospital!'

'You what?' exclaimed Eddie, suddenly losing any trace of his laughter, and leaned towards Mo to see the story for himself. Mo continued to read, 'In an exclusive interview, our reporter, Janice, gets to the bottom of some outrageous claims from a porter that he has been healing dozens of seriously ill patients without the knowledge of doctors or nurses.' Mo slammed the paper down on the table in disgust.

'I do not believe it, Ben! That reporter has stitched you up!' said Eddie in a rage.

'Reporter? What reporter?' asked Mark, who looked completely confused.

'Ben, what happened last night after we left?' said Dr Kanu with a follow-up inquiry.

Now all eyes were directed towards Ben. He took one more quick sip of his tea and put his cup down with a sigh. 'Alright,' he said, 'I'll bring you all up to date. Last night, just after you guys left, a reporter arrived, wanting to find out about the healings. So, I told her the whole thing. We had a good chat; she mentioned the false accusations and I told her the truth.'

'Well, this isn't the truth on the front of this paper!' Mo protested as he bounced his index finger up and down on the paper in front of him.

'Oh, that is typical newspapers, isn't it!' said Eddie, in total agreement.

'It is fake new, Ben! Fake news!' added Enid with a resolute tone. There was now a unifying sense of righteous indignation going around the room and Dr Kanu didn't want to be left out.

'Yes, you are absolutely right, Enid.' she said with some gusto and Enid responded immediately to her support.

'Thank you, dear!' Enid said brightly and tapped Dr Kanu on the hand. Ben couldn't help but smile and nod as the newspaper was roundly condemned by everyone. It wasn't nice to have the reporter tell lies about him, but it was lovely to see how the circle of friends pulled together so forcefully in his defence.

But then he remembered that there was a bit more to the story of last night that he hadn't told any of them about. 'Oh wait!' he announced suddenly.

'There's more!' Everyone looked at him again.

'After the reporter left, there was someone else who came to see me. It was Dr Nelson from the cancer ward.'

'Oh yes, I know Dr Nelson!' Dr Kanu interjected.

'He's a nice guy!'

'Well,' he continued, 'He came into the staff room and he was full of questions about the healings. Some of his patients had been healed and so he wanted to know how it had happened.'

'So, what did you say?' asked Mark, breathlessly.

'Well, rather than explain it to him, I simply went up to the cancer ward with him and he watched me heal all the patients in the ward.' As soon as he told them about healing all the cancer patients, all of their mouths fell open.

'Wait a minute, wait a minute!' exclaimed Eddie with shock. 'Did you just say that you healed all the cancer patients in this hospital?'

'Ah…well…yeah,' he replied with a smile, suddenly realizing the enormity of what he had just said.

'Oh Ben! That will make so many people so happy!' said Enid, getting a little emotional.

'Well, surely they can't stop you now, Ben! Not now that they have seen what you can do!' added Dr Kanu with a hint of hope in her voice. He was about to respond when the door opened and a couple of young porters came in.

'Morning,' they said, and threw their bags down at the lockers. As they opened the door Ben could see that a number of people were assembling in the foyer outside. Conscious of the extra noise outside, Eddie turned to the two men who had just entered.

'Hey, guys, what's happening out there?' The taller one turned to him, 'oh I think it's gonna be some kind of press conference or something. Looks like they're nearly ready to start actually!'

Eddie looked round at them all and for a second, they sat in silence, trying to work out what this meant. 'Oh, Ben, what if they're coming to arrest you now?' Dr Kanu suddenly cried out in alarm.

'No, no! That's not going to happen! Not on my watch!' said Eddie, resolutely. Then Eddie turned and looked at him, 'but what are we going to do now, Ben?' Ben sighed and leaned back in his chair, not really sure how to answer his friend. They all looked in different directions for a while, not sure what to say, but eventually Enid spoke. She looked at him and put her hand on his.

'Ben, I think we have to try to pray.' He looked back at her with a little shock in his face. He had never prayed before and didn't really know how. That was when Mo piped up. He had been quiet for a while as he read through the article in the newspaper, but now he felt that he could contribute!

'Oh, praying! That's easy!' he exclaimed with some enthusiasm.

'Right! Everybody put their hands out in front of them, palms facing up!' After a little hesitation, everyone followed Mo's example.

Then Mo turned to him, 'OK, Ben, lead away!'

'Oh, right!' he said, with a sense of nerves rising up inside him. This was not something that he had done before and just like the first healings, he did not feel sure about himself at all.

'OK, let's pray!' he said and he bowed his head and closed his eyes and all the rest did the same. After a couple of seconds of awkward silence, he began with the name that he knew.

'Sender,' he said softly. 'We need your help. There are people outside who want to stop people getting healed. Help us, please, amen.' It was short and to the point and he was quite happy to keep it that way. They all opened their eyes and then Mo jumped to his feet.

'OK, let's see what's happening out there!' It was as if he was so convinced that the prayer would work that he wanted to see the results of it straight away. He spun away from the table and opened the door wide. All the rest of the people at the table crowded round the doorway with him to see what was going on. Meanwhile, the other two staff who came in earlier took up their seats around the TV at the other end of the room, clearly not interested in what was going on at all.

As they all pressed against the doorway, they could see a small podium being set up in the middle of the foyer. There were a couple of general maintenance workers hurrying here and there in their navy uniforms, setting up the microphone and then testing it. It was still a bit dark outside but in the gloom at the entrance to the building, it was possible to see a few journalists and men with cameras. By now, Mo was actually standing slightly outside of the room, in the actual foyer itself. 'Hey, Ben, there's your friend, Janice!' said Mo turning to him with a cheeky grin. They all looked at the entrance and sure enough, there she was with the other journalists, checking her notes.

'Yeah, here to write more lies, no doubt!' piped up Eddie with some indignation. They were all peering down towards Janice at the entrance, when suddenly their attention was drawn back to the podium because there were now some people walking towards it from the other end of the foyer. When they saw who it was, there was collective intake of breath from all of them. It was Dr Pujara and Sister Montgomery and a few other people in suits. He wasn't sure who the people in suits were, but one of them looked like he was quite senior. He was wearing a dark grey suit and had a full head of thick white hair which was tidily swept back. It wasn't long before all five of them were gathered around the podium, conferring with each other. As they did so, the journalists also noticed their presence at the podium and they began to make their way towards them. It was clearly time for the press conference to begin.

'Oh look, it's about to start!' exclaimed Mark in his usual giddy tone.

'I wonder what they're going to say?' mused Dr Kanu who looked round at him briefly. He raised his eyebrows in response and then realised how peculiar it was to have Dr Kanu with them. Here was a beautiful, intelligent doctor who had a great career, but she chose to be with them instead of with her professional colleagues. Her choice was a clear testimony to the strength of her character. But it wasn't just Dr Kanu, it was all of them. They had all chosen to stand with him in his time of need. As he was admiring the faithfulness of all his friends who were huddled around the doorway, he was soon distracted by a few more people joining the crowd of journalists in front of the podium. There was actually quite a crowd of them by now; about twenty or so. This was also noticed by the group of five and it was clearly agreed among them that it was time to begin. Dr Pujara and Sister Montgomery stood close to the man with the white hair who stood at the podium. The other two men in suits stood on the other side but a little further back. The man with the white hair then took the folder he was carrying and set it on the podium. He set his hands on either side of the podium, cleared his throat a little and tipped his head back slightly in advance of uttering his first words. But just as he was drawing breath to speak, a hand went up from one of the people at the back of the crowd of journalists. 'Ah, excuse me!' came the timid, yet clear, interruption. All the journalists turned around with a look of disgust to see where the interruption had come from. It had come from a woman who was dressed in jeans with a long cardigan that hung down to her knees.

'Can you tell me where the healer is, please?' she continued. The man at the podium was a little thrown by the question, but soon gathered his wits.

'Ah, well, Madam, if you don't mind, we will wait until the end of the press conference until we take questions,' he said in a very authoritative tone. Once again, he cleared his throat and set himself to begin and while he did so, another ten people joined the group of journalists that was beginning to turn into quite a crowd.

'Now, I'd like to begin by introducing myself. My name is Michael Turner and I am the communications director for the local hospital trust and I am here today to address some recent reports that have been coming from this hospital.'

Mr Turner was about to continue when another raised hand appeared at the back of the crowd. 'Ah, excuse me!' came the same words, except this time from a different person. Again, the rest of the crown turned around to see who was interrupting this time.

'Is the healer still here?' Asked a short round man in jeans and a brown jacket. Mr Turner dropped his head in exasperation and then turned to his two colleagues who were standing behind him. He gave one of them the nod and that person immediately set off towards a couple of security guards who were standing near the shop entrance. It was at this time that the little group standing at the door of the staff room began to realise what was happening. Enid, who was peeping out from the left side of the doorway turned to him in wonder,

'Ben, I don't think those people are here for the press conference, I think they're here for you.' There was no need to respond because it was all happening before their eyes. At regular intervals now, there were groups of six or seven coming in through the main entrance to join the crowd at the press conference; except these people clearly weren't reporters. They were people who had heard the news about the healings, either by social media or by word of mouth; and now they wanted some healing themselves and they were determined to get it! But the gathering crowd which was now over fifty in number, wasn't the only thing going on in the foyer. There was also a gathering number of security guards as well who were assembling at the hospital shop. They had clearly been sent for and after about ten had gathered, they started moving to the other side of the foyer, towards the staff room. About five of them took up positions between the staff room and the crowd and one of them, a tall man with a shaved head and tattoos on his neck walked over to them.

He stood in front of Mo, towering over him, 'Right! Can you get back inside the room, please!' he said in a way that told everyone this was not a request.

'Alright, alright!' said Mo rather indignantly, not pleased about being bullied by the big security guard. They all moved back slightly to let Mo back into the room, but they kept the door open so that they could still see what was going on.

The big security guard took his place in the line with his colleagues, which was clearly designed to keep the crowd from getting near the healer. However, they could still see the podium and now that the security guards were getting into place, Mr Turner deemed that it was now possible to resume the press conference.

'OK, sorry for the delay there,' he said, putting his hands down firmly on either side of the lectern.

He took a deep breath, 'Look, folks, there is something we need to be very clear about! There is no healer in this hospital! If there is any healing going on here, it is solely down to the hard work of people like Dr Pujara and Sister Montgomery and their colleagues!'

Dr Pujara lifted his chin a little higher in the air and Sister Montgomery straightened herself like a little peacock.

'However,' continued, Mr Turner, 'I can understand why some of you are here today to see this, so called, healer. There have been a lot of stories circulated on social media that this individual has been able to help a lot of people, including those who are severely ill. But what I am here to tell you today is that all those stories are fraudulent!' Mr Turner was raising his voice a little more now in order to emphasize his message. It may also have been because he could see the crowd in front of him getting bigger at an even faster rate. More security guards were arriving all the time and were taking up positions near the podium and at all points of access to the foyer. Small groups of people were also congregating at the back of the foyer as well; patients and staff and some others who were coming from the wards and the adjoining hospital carpark. The situation was actually becoming a little tense.

'It has been reported to me by many witnesses,' Mr Turner continued, 'that the individual concerned has been presenting himself as some kind of miracle worker, when, in fact, he has been secretly administering medicines that he is not qualified to handle; thus endangering the lives of those he is claiming to help!' Mr Turner was still increasing the volume of his voice in order to get above the murmurings of the crowd that now filled the front part of the foyer. 'This is dangerous behaviour and we will not tolerate such behaviour in this hospital!' Mr Turner paused for a moment. He was becoming visibly concerned at the growing crowd in front of him. He signalled again to one of his two colleagues and made a gesture towards the front entrance. In response, four security guards, who were standing nearby, started to make their way to the front door of the hospital.

From the relative safety of the staff room, the little group of friends watched on with amazement. But there was also anger at what Mr Turner had just said. 'I can't believe the lies that this guy is coming out with!' said Eddie with real frustration in his voice.

'Yeah, talk about fake news! Who does this guy think he is?' added Mark with his energetic indignation. From where he was at the back of the huddle, he could see all of them following the unfolding events avidly. It was great to have them stand with him, but at the same time, he didn't want them to get in trouble on his behalf.

'Look, guys,' he said to get their attention. They all turned their heads to look at him. 'I have a feeling that something might kick off here and I don't want any of you to get hurt, so…look…I think it might be better if you took this chance to get somewhere safe.' There was a couple of seconds silence as they collectively tuned out of the events they had been watching and tuned in to this new conversation.

'No!' said Mo suddenly and rather loudly. Even one of the security guards in front of the entrance turned his head briefly to see what the noise was. 'We will not abandon you!' Mo added with his face full of sincerity. Dr Kanu then put her hand on his shoulder.

'Ben, we believe in you!' she said. Eddie looked at him and shook his head,

'Sorry mate, you're stuck with us! You're family and that's the end of it!' Ben could feel his eyes filling up with tears. There was no way that he deserved this kind of loyalty from anyone and it reduced him to silence.

'Oh look,' said Mark, suddenly breaking the silence. 'They're trying to stop people getting in.' Everyone looked towards the entrance and, sure enough, there was now a line of security guards blocking the front door. They could see that the people outside were not happy and even at this early stage there was a small crowd of them waiting to get in. Then their attention returned to Mr Turner. He stepped closer to the platform once more and continued where he had left off.

'As I was saying, we will not tolerate fraudulent behaviour in this hospital! The safety and treatment of our patients is our highest…' Mr Turner was about to finish his sentence when the frustration in the crowd eventually gave way. 'Are we going to get to see this healer or not?' shouted an older man from the back. There was an angry tone to his voice and very quickly his frustration was echoed around the crowd with a few shouting their agreement.

'We're not here to see you, fancy pants! We're here to see the healer who was on Facebook!' shouted another person from the middle of the crowd. She was a younger woman who was shaking her arm in the air as she was talking.

There was a brief ripple of laughter around the crowd at the woman's description of Mr Turner. But then a voice spoke out in Mr Turner's favour.

'Oh, for goodness' sake! Can't you see he's a fraud!' This time the intervention came from the small group of reporters at the front of the crowd. The little group in the staff room all looked to see who it was, and to their surprise they actually recognised her; it was Janice, the very same reporter who had written the negative article about him in the paper that very day. The problem for Janice on this occasion, however, was that she was now in a position where people could fire back at her and that was exactly what they did.

'Oy, fake news! Shut it!' Came the very abrupt response from the same woman who still had her arm in the air.

Seeing that things were getting out of hand, Mr Turner tried to take control again. 'Look!' he said, quite loudly, 'This is a hospital, not a Church! We practice science here, not religion! And therefore...' Mr Turner stopped again. It was no use; there were more of the crowd who were calling out to see the healer and they had no interest in anything he had to say. Mr Turner was now getting visibly frustrated with the crowd. He gave a quick instruction to one of his assistants, who quickly got on his phone and then he went back to the podium. It was then that he made a huge mistake!

'This hospital will not tolerate imposters! And if you think that this man is a real doctor then I am here to tell you that he is not!' It was with those words that he looked directly into the staff room and pointed directly at Ben. All of the group of friends around him instinctively turned to look at his face; but they weren't alone in doing so! Mr Turner probably hadn't planned on it, but he had now identified the healer to every single person in the foyer and every single one of them was now looking directly at him. For a moment, there was a hush that descended over the crowd as the attention shifted from Mr Turner to the staff room. Then the silence was broken.

'That's him! That's the healer!' came a shout from the crowd, and before Mr Turner or anyone else could react, the whole crowd started moving in the direction of the staff room. Almost immediately, the crowd started pressing up against the line of security guards who were stopping people from getting to the staff room. The situation really was getting out of hand now and Mr Turner was desperately trying to regain control from the podium.

'Right! That's it! I am now asking everyone to leave the hospital! You are endangering the staff of this hospital!' It was no use! The crowd had stopped listening to him as soon as he had pointed out where the healer was. Now, the only thing on the crowd's mind was getting to the healer. The pressure on the line of security guards was getting heavier and heavier. Other guards had to come from different places, including the front doors, in order to help them hold the line; but the crowd was determined and they even began to chant.

'We want healed,' they said in unison. It began with a few voices, but before long, the whole crowd had taken up the anthem; and that crowd was growing by the minute. The foyer was filled with people and there was a large crowd outside wanting to join them. It was becoming more and more difficult to see what was happening outside, but in the midst of the chaos outside the hospital, they could now see blue flashing lights and even a couple of TV cameras.

The crowd in the foyer was now so large that there was a very real danger of some people getting crushed. Aware of this fact, Mr Turner was growing increasingly desperate and irate at the microphone. 'You must leave the hospital!' he shouted.

'The police have been called! You must leave the hospital!' He repeated himself again and again in the midst of the chanting crowd. The noise in the foyer was now deafening. The tall security guard who was showing signs of physical strain against the crowd turned to them with raw anger in his face.

'Get back inside, and close the door!' Obediently, they all took a step back and allowed Mo to close the door a little, but not much. It was a sight that they just couldn't stop watching! Between the shouting of Mr Turner into the microphone and the chanting of the crowd and the shouts from some of the security guards, it was a whirlwind of activity. However, even in the midst of the whirlwind, there was an unmistakable sound that suddenly rung out around the foyer. It was the sound of a bell giving a single ring. At first, no-one paid much attention to it, but then it happened again. It was Mr Turner who stopped shouting first. He stopped what he was doing and turned around and stared up at the balcony that overlooked the foyer. The bell rang again. This time some of the crowed who were closer to the balcony also stopped to look; and with another ring of the bell, the whole crowd quickly became silent. All of them stopped pushing and they were all now transfixed on the sound of the bell and what was happening on the balcony.

The little group who had retreated into the staff room now ventured forward to see what was happening. The sound of the bell was still going off every few seconds like a slow fire alarm. The sound was almost hypnotic and certainly seemed to have hypnotised everyone in the crowd. But what was it that they were looking at? He pushed forward from the back of the group so that he could see what was holding everyone's attention and then he saw them. The first few were walking down the steps in single file into the foyer; each of them carries plastic bags of varying colours. They were the patients from the cancer wards and everyone knew it! The bell that was ringing was their end of treatment bell and the way that they all looked was the same for all cancer patients. They were thin, they were bald and they wore the head scarfs that had become synonymous with the condition. Each one of them beamed with the joy of life and they were beautiful! The bell continued to ring as each patient came to the top of the stairs and began to make their way down to the foyer. The sound of the bell seemed to make people's mouths hang open in shock and wonder every time it rang out. But the best was yet to come because as soon as they reached the crowded foyer, the sea of people in front of them parted to let them past. Slowly and purposefully, they walked through the crowd, still with faces full of inexplicable joy. They did not look to the left or the right, but kept their heads forward, as if drawn by a light in front of them. Then suddenly that light came into view! It was their families! As if from nowhere, the parents and spouses and children and friends of those restored to life appeared in front of them. The plastic bags were dropped like stones and the healed and their families rushed to embrace each other. As well as mouths hanging open, eyes began to fill up as emotions erupted in front of them. Whole families were locked into the tightest embraces; husbands wept and wives cried out in joy and relief, and the bell kept on ringing. Then, as if anything more were needed to add to the occasion, the crowd began to clap. Within a few seconds, the clapping had spread to the whole foyer and even to the crowd outside. People began to cheer and shout. From being a situation that was fraught with tension and frustration only a moment ago, the situation had now changed to one of rampant euphoria. People were literally celebrating as if they were in a football stadium, except here, they were celebrating the sick and the dying being restored to their families.

This rejoicing seemed to go on forever, but no-one was complaining. Even Dr Pujara and Sister Montgomery had to give a reluctant clap as they stood right in front of the family reunions. However, Sister Montgomery still had a face like thunder. Her heart was so hard that the celebrations only seemed to make her more angry. But it didn't matter, because her resistance was no match for the overwhelming goodwill that had swept through the hospital. For as long as the bell kept ringing, the celebrations and cheering continued as the former cancer patients made their way from the top of the stairs, all the way to the street outside. It was like a victory parade that seemed to have no end. But eventually that end did come, although it came with a twist, because the last person to ring the bell was the little girl. She rang it three times as you would expect a child to do, and therefore the attention of the crowd shifted back to the top of the balcony. The cheering of the crowd died down again and even the other cancer patients who had not yet left, stopped to look back. She was carrying her teddy bear in her right arm and after ringing the bell, who else but Dr Nelson took her by the hand and led her carefully down the stairs. She was wearing a smile that, literally lit up the room. The smile was so bright that you could easily have forgotten it was winter. The whole of the foyer stood motionless so that they could bathe in the radiance of her health and happiness. He could see the tears rolling down the cheeks of Enid and Dr Black and even Eddie. He expected that the clapping would break out any second now, but instead something else happened. 'Anna! Anna!' Came a loud scream from the front of the foyer. A woman in a long green coat with soaking wet hair was scrambling through the crowd. Eventually, she broke free and began running as fast as she could through the gap in the crowd and towards the little girl.

Still screaming her name, the woman raced up to the girl who now let go of Dr Nelson's hand and cried out with glee, 'Mummy!' The woman stopped running and stood briefly in front of her daughter to look at her. She put her hand to her mouth as she gazed at her healthy daughter in disbelief. Anna put her hands reassuringly on her mother's arms.

'It's OK, Mummy, I'm all better!' she said with a huge smile; at which point her mother got down on her knees and gathered her daughter into her arms. Now the cheering began! It began with a single audible clap, which then became an avalanche of applause; and was quickly followed by shouting and cheering from all parts of the crowd.

The clapping and cheering seemed to go on and on without fading in volume. In the midst of the incredible noise Anna was picked up by her mum, who then began carrying her towards the exit; but they had barely got two steps before a man ran up to them. His eyes were as wide as saucers and his hair and clothing made him look like he had just run a one hundred metre sprint. He slowed down for a second and then launched himself at Anna and her mum. He opened up his arms and wrapped them tightly around them both. Anna, in turn opened up her arms and put them around the man's head; 'Daddy!' she shouted with delight. 'I'm better, Daddy! I'm better!' The man's whole body convulsed with emotion as he held his family tight. In response to this new embrace, the crowd descended into full blown hysteria! The clapping died away and now people were just bouncing up and down and cheering with all their might. It was the most jubilant celebrating that he had ever seen; and the most remarkable thing about it was that it was over nothing more than a husband and father hugging his family. The love of this family was being celebrated as if a national team had just won the most coveted of all world competitions! It was one of the most remarkable things he had ever seen and heard and the noise of it just kept on going as the husband led his wife and child through the crowd and out of the hospital.

As the family left the building and disappeared into the crowded street outside, the cheering and celebrating eventually died down; at which point a familiar voice rang out in the foyer. It was Mr Turner trying to assert himself in his role as communications director, except this time he came to the podium with a rather humbler tone. 'Ah, listen, folks…' he began with some hesitation, not sure how to follow what he had just witnessed. At this stage, the four police officers who had entered the building were now standing beside Mr Turner and he looked at them nervously.

He then looked back at the crowd again, 'I know a lot of people are very emotional at this point in time, but I'm afraid that this situation is now beyond my control. It has become a public order matter and therefore I am handing over control to the police who are now going to take the healer, I mean, Mr Archer out of the building so that order can be restored.'

There was an immediate reaction from the crowd to this announcement from Mr Turner. A few people shouted; 'You can't do that,' 'That's not fair!' and then the chanting began all over again. It was hard to make out where it started from in the crowd, but as soon as one person started shouting it, the whole crowd, inside and outside the building, joined in almost immediately. Within a matter of seconds, the hundreds of people who had been cheering the reunion of a little girl with her family were now shouting aggressively their one demand, 'We want healed!'

Once more, Mr Turner tried to appeal to the crowd. 'Please remain calm, we must let the police do their job!' he shouted desperately, but it was too late for the voice of moderation. The crowd had one thing on its mind and that was to get into the staff room. The crowd surged towards the open door from where the little group of friends were watching events unfold. The line of security guards, which was now bolstered a little by some porters, was being buffeted and stretched by those desperate for healing. But it wasn't just at the front of the foyer where this line had to be strong. There were also growing numbers of people at every entrance to the foyer, both from the front of the hospital and from the back, including the balcony and stairs. It was a situation of growing tension and the lines of security guards and porters at every entrance were struggling to cope with the surge of people. It seemed like the space in the middle of the foyer was getting smaller and smaller by the second as more and more people kept on pushing in from every angle. If the security cordon broke now, there would, almost certainly be a crush of people trying to get into the staff room. But the crowd didn't care about that; all they wanted was that touch of healing that they had seen others get on social media. He couldn't blame them for wanting to get healed, but such was the size of the crowd that this situation was getting dangerous. He looked at the faces of his friends around him. He could see that they were getting alarmed. He wished that he could do something to get them to safety but all he could do was stand there and watch as the four police officers made their way swiftly to where they were standing. Collectively, they all stood back from the doorway in anticipation. The police had arrived.

Chapter 26
Louder and Louder

At first, the little group of friends expected to have some sort of conversation with the police men who were on their way towards them, but as they got closer to the staff room, it became apparent that the pace of their arrival was not slowing. Suddenly, the Sergeant who was leading the way, pulled his baton from his belt, and with a flick of his wrist, extended the telescopic baton to its full length. 'Get back inside the room!' he roared as he got to the door way. He was a man of average height and build, but his aggressive manner was very intimidating. Instinctively, Mark and Eddie pulled Dr Kanu and Enid out of the way of the officer who charged through the door way, with the other three officers following close behind. Mo stumbled backwards away from the advancing officers, and in doing so, bumped into Ben. As Ben landed on the table behind him, he could see Mo putting his hands up to try to calm things down.

'OK, OK! Take it easy! We don't want…' Mo's efforts to calm things down were not heeded by the Sergeant. With a huge swing of his arm, the officer landed a huge blow right in the middle of Mo's rib cage. Such was the force of this blow that it sent Mo hurtling to the side of the room where he crashed into the cupboard doors of the kitchen. As soon as he hit the cupboard doors, he crumpled into a heap on the ground and began clutching his side and writhing in agony as he gasped for breath. Immediately, Dr Kanu and Enid ran over to him.

'What do you think you are doing?' cried Dr Kanu as she knelt down to help her new friend. Two of the officers went over to see what the women were doing and how the man was, while the fourth officer stood guard at the door next to Eddie. He watched for a moment in stunned silence as Enid helped Dr Kanu examine Mo's injury. Then suddenly, it dawned on him; what was he doing watching when he had the power to help? Lifting himself up off the table that he had been leaning back on, he started to move towards his friend who lay injured on the ground. Then the sergeant, who was momentarily distracted by the activity on the floor, grabbed him with both hands and shoved him back against the table.

'And where do you think you're going, mate?' growled the Sergeant in an aggressive cockney accent.

'The only place you're going is where I tell you! Do you understand, sir!' The Sergeant shouted the warning into his face and gave him a shake to help get the message through.

Ben's adrenaline was spiking and he could feel his heart thumping in his chest, 'But, officer, I can help my friend!' he spluttered.

'No! No!' shouted the officer with the same aggression and pushed him further back over the table and further off balance at the same time.

'You've done enough helping today, mate, you're coming with me!' There was nothing he could do now. All he could do was watch Enid and Dr Kanu try to get Mo into a more comfortable position.

Once more, Dr Kanu turned to the officer who was holding him over the table. 'I'm a doctor and this man needs to get to the Emergency Department!' she said with all the authority that she could muster.

'Yeah, well, you'd better call an ambulance then, hadn't ya!' the Sergeant fired back with snarling sarcasm as he pulled Ben off the table and started to walk him out of the room with a firm right hand on the back of his neck. Ben took one last look at Mo and the two women who were tending to him. He felt so guilty for the danger that he had put them in and now he even wondered when he would see them again. He looked at the floor again and was about to walk through the door way when, suddenly, he was grabbed by a pair of huge arms. It was Eddie. He had been standing quietly on the other side of the door way while everything had been happening inside the staff room, but now he had decided to make his move. As soon as Eddie had him in his arms, he pulled him away from the Sergeant who had detained him and stood in the door way against the door post.

'I'm not leaving my friend!' Eddie shouted in defiance. But this only enraged the Sergeant who had lost his man. Immediately, the Sergeant rushed at Eddie and grabbed him by the shoulder and pushed him up against the doorpost. The Sergeant's face was red with rage. At the same time as he was pushing Eddie up against the doorpost, he swung his baton down hard against the back of Eddie's knee. Eddie flinched with the pain, but the Sergeant didn't stop; he wanted to make a point. He kept on swinging the baton against Eddie's leg at various points. Each hit drew a groan and then a shout from Eddie, but Eddie still didn't let go. His friend must have been in agony. The Sergeant took a step back and was actually panting with the exertion of the violence.

'I'm not letting him go!' Eddie shouted again, while choking back the pain and emotion. The other officers were watching their colleague, not sure what to do. The officer at the other side of the door was clearly very conscious of the watching public, including the media, while the other two officers were dealing with the reactions of Enid and Dr Kanu.

'Leave that man alone!' shouted Enid with surprising volume. She got up from where Dr Kanu was still dealing with Mo and went to intervene but the two officers who were on that side of the room simply stood in front of her. It was hard to tell what she was saying but Enid was looking directly at the two officers and waving her finger under their noses while Dr Kanu was also contributing at regular intervals. Those officers were finding out that although these two women were the smallest people in the room, they were more than ready to fight.

While the other officers were somewhat distracted, the Sergeant was not going to be denied. He straightened himself up, and with his face contorted with anger, he stepped forward with his baton raised high over his head. With a roar, he brought the baton down hard on one of the arms that Eddie hard wrapped around him. He could feel the impact vibrate through Eddie's arm and Eddie cried out with pain. Again, the Sergeant raised his baton and brought it down hard on the same area of Eddie's arm. Each time, Eddie screamed in pain, but then the officer changed the angle of his swing. He tried to hit Eddie's arm from the side rather than from above and this time the blow slid off Eddie's arm and crashed into Ben's forehead, just above his left eye. Immediately there was a trickle of blood that started to flow down his face. He couldn't help but cry out in pain and swung his head away from the blow.

'Ben! Are you alright?' shouted Eddie in a panic. His could feel his head spinning a little, but he quickly regained his senses. Thankfully, so did the police.

'Sarge! Sarge!' shouted the officer who was standing at the door, trying to get his colleague's attention. The Sergeant stood back from his latest assault and caught his breath.

'Sarge! There're people watching!' the officer at the door shouted again. At that moment, the Sergeant took a brief look out through the door and suddenly realised that he was not completely hidden from the glare of the public and the media. He took a second to reassess the situation and then he looked around at the officers who were holding Enid back.

'Right, you two! We're on the move!' he shouted at them with his baton pointed in their direction.

'Me and him lead and you follow!' All the other officers responded immediately to their instructions. The Sergeant walked around Ben and Eddie to stand in front of them in the door way. The two officers who had been standing in front of Enid now moved across the room to stand behind them. They were now surrounded by the four officers; two in front and two behind them. This was going to be their escort out of the building.

As the officers assembled around them, he could hear Eddie moaning a little. 'Are you alright, mate?' Eddie whispered close to his ear. Eddie was clearly in great pain, but was still concerned about him.

'Yeah, I'm fine; don't worry about me. What about you?' he said in response.

'Ah, don't worry about it! Let's just get you out of here safely!' Eddie whispered again. He was about to say something about healing Eddie's wounds when they both felt themselves suddenly jolted towards the door way. The Sergeant had grabbed Eddie by the collar and pulled him close.

'Right, you pair! Whenever I say move, we move! Understand? Now get ready!' No sooner had he shouted this warning into their faces than he turned his head away to speak into the radio on his stab vest.

'This is Bravo Delta, Sergeant Stokes, to control! My team and I are at St Mary's Hospital and we are escorting two males out of the building. All pedestrian access appears to be blocked! Where is my assistance?' There was a quick buzz from his radio as he ended his message. Then, after a couple of seconds of waiting, there was a voice from the other end.

'Sergeant, be advised, there has been a delay to your assistance due to heavy congestion on the streets around St Mary's. The only possible way for you to be extracted safely from the building is by vehicle. Can you get to the adjoining car park?' Once again, the radio crackled and went silent. Sergeant Stokes looked briefly at the other officer who stood on the other side of the door way. The other officer clearly had nothing to offer and so Sergeant Stokes leaned out of the door way and into the foyer to assess the situation. As he did so, he and Eddie were pulled with him. They both looked out into the foyer and they could hardly believe their eyes. The foyer was almost completely full of people. The space in the middle of the foyer had reduced down to a small path that led from one side of the foyer to the other. In that space, there were only a few people. They were all employees of the hospital, including Dr Pujara and Sister Montgomery. Both of the cardiac ward staff looked confused and alarmed by the situation that they now found themselves in. Then, suddenly, as he was looking over the shoulder of Sergeant Stokes, Sister Montgomery looked directly at him. As soon as she caught sight of him, her eyes immediately narrowed with spite. Even at a distance, she was able to pour out her intense hatred towards him. It was a chilling sight and actually made him feel glad that he was surrounded by the police.

Thankfully, the visual connection between him and Sister Montgomery didn't last long. After half a minute or so, Sergeant Stokes leaned back from the foyer and pressed down on his radio once more.

'Bravo Delta to control, be advised, I have identified a route to level one of the car park at St Mary's. We will hold the suspects there until you arrive! I repeat, level one of the car park!' Sergeant Stokes now took his hand off his radio and turned to his fellow officers.

'Right guys, we're going up the stairs to the balcony! Ready to move! Ready to move! Move, move, move!' As soon as he started shouting this latest command, all the other three officers pushed in close to Eddie and himself. Then they were on the move. Sergeant Stokes had his hand grasped firmly around Eddie's collar, while the other officer had a firm grip on Ben's. With short steps, they moved slowly out into the foyer. As soon as they did, they were hit with a barrage of noise. The crowd became even more frenzied as they realised that they were seeing the healer taken from them. They pushed against the line of security guards even harder, so much so, that the small squad of six men was buffeted from the left and the right. People on either side of the security cordon were reaching out to him with their hands, hoping to be able to make some kind of contact with him. However, Eddie still had his arms firmly wrapped around him which meant that his arms were pinned to his side.

The progress towards the staircase that led to the balcony was slow. Then, suddenly, someone from the crowd broke through the cordon of security guards. He squeezed himself under their arms and stumbled out in front of the police escort. He was a relatively short man and was dressed in a very normal-looking pair of trousers and a shirt. However, as normal as he may have looked, he was clearly desperate. As soon as the man regained his balance, he put his hands up to the police, as if to make some sort of appeal to them, but Sergeant Stokes was having none of it. He, immediately, reached for his CS spray and pointed it in the man's direction.

'Get back! I have CS spray and I will use it!' he shouted forcefully. The man in front of him, whose face was covered in desperation was about to speak, but Sergeant Stokes had no interest in what this man had to say. Before he could even get a word out, Sergeant Stokes blasted the CS spray into the man's eyes. Immediately, the man reeled backwards, putting his hands to his face and screaming in agony. As soon as Sergeant Stokes had put his CS spray back in this belt, he leaned forward and quickly grabbed the man who was blindly stumbling around in front of him and flung him to one side. With the obstacle out of the way, Sergeant Stokes then led them forward once more.

However, as a result of this latest drama in the foyer, there was now even more jostling from the crowd. It was a very bumpy ride, but the four police officers remained steady and kept moving forward with short steps. People from the crowd were calling out to him continually.

'I want to be healed!' cried one. Help me, healer!' cried another. His heart went out to them. He had helped so many people yesterday and he dearly wanted to help all the people who were in the foyer, but that was no longer possible. He was on a different path now and he didn't have a clue where it was leading. Eventually they reached the bottom of the staircase, which was a bit of a relief because there was no crowd on the staircase and therefore, they were no longer being jostled from side to side. However, just as they were about to take their first steps up the staircase, he suddenly saw a couple of familiar faces in the crowd. It was Jeff and Sharon, little Tommy's mum and dad. They had heard about everything that had gone on yesterday and last night and they were now desperate to get to him. As soon as they saw where he was and as soon as he saw them, their faces lit up with desperate hope. They were shouting his name and Jeff was using his sizeable frame to move through the crowd. Eventually, they got to the other side of the wall at the side of the staircase and Jeff reached out to him.

'Ben! We need you to help little Tommy! Ben, he's dying! Please, Ben! Please, Ben!' As he looked at them and saw their desperation and the tears running down their cheeks, he could feel his heart breaking. Of all the people he could have healed, it was this little boy that he wanted to heal the most. He felt the tears filling his eyes. He was becoming as desperate as they were to help their son who still lay desperately ill in ICU.

'I will help him! I will help him!' he shouted, trying to fight back his tears. It was a promise that he had no idea he could keep, but he had to say something to them as he moved up the stairs. Jeff kept on reaching out towards him and his wife Sharon was now shouting hysterically behind him. It was as if they were losing their son there and then as he moved up the stairs. It was a gut-wrenching experience and it made him sick to his stomach. There was no justice in what was happening and it was making him angry. He was angry with the hospital, he was angry with the police, but now he was also angry with the Sender. There were all these people in the hospital who needed healed and the Sender was allowing him to be taken away from them. The Sender was allowing the patients to be frustrated and his friends to be hurt. He simply could not understand it!

By the time they got to the top of the staircase, he could feel his blood boiling with anger. He wanted to break away from the police and run to ICU, but the route to the ICU was also blocked with crowds of people. The corridor that led to that part of the hospital was barricaded by security guards who were lined along the balcony corridor. This gave the police a fairly clear route to the door to the car park which was a little way down the balcony corridor to the left of the staircase. Seeing that the way was clear, Sergeant Stokes paused before making his way to the door for the carpark.

He pressed on his radio, 'This is Sergeant Stokes, be advised, we are about to enter the adjoining carpark at level one. Repeat, we are entering the carpark now!' He could not have been more wrong. The first clue as to what was about to happen was when all six of them found themselves walking on something like grit that crunched beneath their feet. Then, no sooner had they noticed this fine debris on the floor than there was a loud crunching and snapping noise from the ceiling. Instinctively, Eddie stopped and pulled him back a little and all the other officers with him. It was a good thing that he did because in the next second, an entire section of the roof came crashing down on the balcony floor in front of them. It was one of the glass pyramid shaped sections of the roof and when it hit the floor there was a huge noise of shattering glass and steel frame slamming against marble floor. Everyone on the balcony and in the foyer below flinched at the sound of the crash and there were gasps of shock all around. For a brief moment, a hush descended on the hospital, but then as people began to look towards the big hole in the ceiling, a man suddenly jumped down from the roof and landed on the floor with a thud that seemed to reverberate around the whole foyer.

As soon as he landed, he straightened himself up and stepped to one side. As soon as he did so, another man jumped down from the roof and landed with similar impact. The second man also stood up straight and moved to the other side of the balcony corridor that overlooked the foyer. Both men took a moment to survey their surroundings. Both of them were about six feet tall and looked like fitness instructors. They both wore blue jeans, hiking boots and neat fitting jackets; one khaki green and the other black. Neither of them looked the least bit nervous as they scanned the hundreds of people who were looking at them. They were cool and calm and projected complete control of the situation. Then the man in the green jacket spoke to the crowd on the balcony.

'We're here for the healer!' He said in a deep authoritative voice that was made all the more demanding by the Northern Irish accent that came with it. It was then that Sergeant Stokes decided to step forward.

'The healer stays with us!' he shouted as aggressively as he could as he walked towards the man in the green jacket. Sergeant Stokes had his baton held out in front of him in a threatening manner, but there wasn't a hint of concern in the Northern Irish man's face. Instead, he kept a steely stare on the man who was approaching him.

'Wrong answer!' he growled as he suddenly took a step towards Sergeant Stokes. Before Sergeant Stokes even knew what was happening, the man in the green jacket had closed down the distance between them, to the point that he was able to grab the baton out of his hand and throw it to the ground. It was almost in the same action that the assailant then grabbed Sergeant Stokes by the stab vest and threw him across the corridor and up against the wall. Stokes hit the wall with a thud and a groan, but the green jacket wasn't finished. No sooner had the Sergeant bounced off the wall than the Northern Irish man stepped towards him with a lightning-fast right arm that flashed out in front of him. The punch caught Sergeant Stokes full on the nose and immediately threw his head back towards the wall again. He sunk to the ground with blood streaming down his face and a look in his eyes which indicated that he didn't know what day it was.

Without a hint of emotion in his face, the man in the green jacket stepped back from the Sergeant on the ground and looked up at the remaining three officers who now looked a lot more nervous. The other officer who was standing in front of him and Eddie pulled out his baton and flicked it out to the side to extend it. While keeping his other hand firmly on his shoulder, he held the baton out in front of him in a desperate attempt to slow the inevitable. The man in the black jacket looked at the officer with a disapproving shake of the head.

'Don't even think about it, cub!' he said with real menace in his voice. The officer with the baton looked nervously at Sergeant Stokes who was gradually coming back to his senses and trying to sit upright. Very slowly, the man in the green jacket began walking towards the group of police officers who were still holding on to their two captives. Without looking away from them, he shouted to his colleagues who were still on the roof.

'Area secure! One more soldier!' Immediately another man who was dressed in a similar style jumped down from the roof. The impact of the third man landing on the balcony floor seemed to alarm Sergeant Stokes so much that he scrambled to his feet and stumbled back towards the top of the staircase. He took one look at his fellow officers who were standing in front of him and then started walking unsteadily down the staircase; leaving his fellow officers to take their stand alone. The other officers looked over their shoulders to see where he was going and one of them even called after him.

'Sarge!' he shouted after his senior officer, but it was no use, Stokes was gone.

Both he and Eddie could now sense that the three officers were all very nervous. Their breathing was speeding up and their grip on their two captives was loosening as they now turned their focus to the man in the green jacket who was getting closer and closer. He stopped about one pace away from them and leaned forward to inspect his quarry.

'So, you're the healer,' he said, looking straight at him. For a moment, he studied him up and down as if there was no-one else there. It was almost as if he was looking right inside his mind to see if he was genuine or not. Coming from any other man this behaviour might have seemed rather strange, but this man had the air of someone who had a long history of judging what sort of people he was dealing with. Having apparently made up his mind, the man in the green jacket then turned his head slightly and barked out another order.

'We have the healer! Lower the patient!' Having given the order, the boss of this crew turned his head back to face him, but the attention of everyone else was now on the hole in the roof.

After a few grunts and groans coming from the roof, a pair of legs appeared, dangling down through the ceiling. These legs then shuffled further over the hole and it became apparent that these legs being supported by a pair of ropes that were slung underneath them. For a couple of seconds, this man in the ropes was suspended over the hole. At this point, the two other men on the balcony stood under the hole in the ceiling to guide the man down from the roof.

'OK, let him down!' shouted one of the men underneath the hole. With a few more grunts and growls of someone taking the strain, the man in the ropes was gradually lowered down from the roof. For a moment, he swung unsteadily from side to side as the men on the roof loosened and tightened their grips on the ropes, but before long the men below him had caught him and they steadied his descent. In the next few seconds, the man was on the floor and the ropes were removed from him by his friends. Without waiting, the two friends then lifted him by the arms and carried him over to the balcony wall where they set him down. It was very noticeable that as they lifted him, his legs dragged behind him. He was clearly paralysed from the waist down. No sooner had he been set down against the balcony wall than the two men from the roof now jumped down to join the rest of the team. They were both black and had arms that were so big that it was no surprise that they had been given the job of holding the ropes. As soon as they landed on the floor, they started walking over to where the man in the green jacket was standing. The leader of this team was still looking at him intensely as the two black team members came to a standstill on either side of him.

'Area secured, boss! Ready to proceed!' one of them barked while standing ramrod straight and keeping his face forward.

Now faced with three huge men standing in front of them, he could feel the remaining police officers shrinking in confidence. Their grip on himself and Eddie now disappeared altogether. It was pretty clear to all who was in charge now! The man who was referred to as 'boss' now took a step back and to the side and stretched his arm out in the direction of his paralysed friend. He looked at the boss's face who now raised his eyebrows slightly as if to emphasize the invitation for him to get moving. Following this cue, he silently started moving forwards. Eddie was still close behind him and kept one arm on his shoulder. Thankfully the 'boss' had no objections and they both started walking towards the man who was seated on the floor. As soon as they started walking, the man in the green jacket started walking behind them, leaving his two colleagues to keep an eye on the remaining police officers. He approached the man on the floor whose legs were stretched out in front of him. Two of the team members were standing beside him and they watched Ben carefully as he approached.

The man on the ground looked up at him with a smile. He had short untidy fair hair and he was clean shaven.

'So, you're the guy!' he said with his eyes glistening. Ben paused before answering. There was strong emotion in the man's voice which made him feel a little nervous.

'Yes,' he said, 'I am.' There was another second of them looking at each other and then he instinctively knelt down in front of him. The man's eyes filled up with tears and his breathing became heavier.

'Can you help me?' he said abruptly, while trying to fight back the tears.

'Yes, I can!' Ben replied with as much confidence as he could muster. This was no time to allow self-doubt to re-emerge. He had healed dozens of people now and this would be no different.

'OK! Thank you!' said the man in front of him; and he then put his head back and closed his eyes. There was no need for further invitation; he shuffled forward on his knees and leaned over the man who was keeping his eyes firmly shut. It was as if he couldn't bear to look in case of disappointment. He looked at the man's face for a second and then put his hands out over both thighs. Gently he lowered his hands down and pressed them on the man's legs. For a terrible moment nothing happened, but then suddenly the heat rushed through his arms and the pins and needles sensation surged through his hands and down his fingers. The paralysed man suddenly gasped and arched his back. His eyes popped wide open with shock and the muscles in his legs started to twitch erratically. Underneath his hands he could feel a flurry of muscular movement. The paralysed man leaned forward with a look of shock still on his face. He looked at Ben and then looked at his feet. They were moving! Now was the time to let go and he removed his hands from the man's legs and leaned back. The paralysed man started to move his feet more deliberately and more often. The two friends who were standing either side of him began to laugh as they saw these feet moving vigorously. They were clearly overjoyed for their friend and they put their hands on his shoulders. But this wasn't the end of the restoration because as the feet began to move more, so did the rest of the legs. The knees began to bend and before long both legs were pushing up and down as if he was on an exercise bike.

With a look of pure childish excitement, the paralysed man grabbed the arms of the two friends who were on either side of him. Automatically, they grabbed his arms in response and they quickly pulled him up to a standing position. For a moment, his friends suspended him a little off the ground but as he continued to pound the floor with the full strength of his legs, they gradually reduced their support and as soon as they did, the man who was paralysed just moments ago was now jumping around the balcony like a five-year-old!

'I can walk! I can walk!' he shouted with his eyes full of joy. All of his friends were laughing and as they watched, the man in the green jacket put his hand on Ben's shoulder.

'Thank you,' he said as he turned to look at him. 'This man lost his ability to walk while serving his country and you have given that back to him. Thank you.' He patted his shoulder again and then they both turned to enjoy the celebrations of their friend.

The celebrations were just beginning to die down, partly due to the fact that the man was getting out of breath, when there was a call from the other end of the balcony. 'Hey boss, we've got company!' Everyone looked around in the direction of the voice to where the police officers had been standing. The two black team members were now slowly walking backwards because Sergeant Stokes had returned with reinforcements. He had gathered together about thirty security guards and a few other police officers and was leading them up the stairs and onto the balcony.

'Right! All of you are under arrest! Get down on the ground, now!' he shouted with as much aggression as possible. The officers who had been on the balcony the whole time quickly fell in behind them and this time, they all had their batons drawn. There was no way that the man in the green jacket and the rest of his team would be able to stop this crowd of police officers and security guards. The whole team of men from the roof instinctively turned to face the oncoming crowd, but before they could get into any kind of formation, Sergeant Stokes gave the order to charge. Like a rugby team chasing a ball, this crowd of police and security guards came rushing in their direction. The two black team members were the first to face the attack and they did so with gusto. They changed from retreat into a charge of their own and immediately floored two of the officers with knockout punches. But it wasn't long before their arms were weighed down by a couple of people on either side. Their legs were beaten with batons and eventually they were on the floor and restrained. Seeing that their friends were down, the others quickly rallied to their aid. Chief amongst them was the man who had been paralysed. With his newfound vigour, he rushed at the people who were surrounding his friends and leapt on top of them; sending at least two of them reeling backwards. The rest of the friends waded into the fight; however, they were quickly out flanked by greater numbers and before long he and Eddie found themselves pinned against the balcony wall by a team of about six or seven security guards. Eddie put his big arms around him once again and held him tight while the security guards started to bundle them back towards the police near the stairs.

The whole of the balcony area was in complete chaos. He and Eddie were surrounded by a dozen arms that were pushing and pulling them in various directions with no clear route in mind. When they tried to go in one direction, they were bumped and jostled in another direction. It seemed that the team of men from the roof were putting up a lot more resistance than Officer Stokes had anticipated. There were the sounds of some furious scuffles going on with plenty of people crying out as the team members fought back to try and regain control of the balcony. Then, just as they seemed to be getting back to the stairs, a familiar face appeared in front of them; it was Sergeant Stokes. His face was still bloodied from the first confrontation, but he seemed to be enjoying this second one.

'Well, well, look what we have here!' he announced with an obnoxious smile.

'You are in some serious trouble! Both of you! I am going to make sure that you do some serious time!' Having made his threats, he turned his head to see which direction he wanted to go in, but as soon as he did, he took another punch straight to the nose. Blood splattered all over his face once again and he dropped to the ground, out of sight. In his place, the man in the green jacket quickly appeared and began to give the security officers who surrounded them the same treatment. They tried to resist, but then the two black team members appeared alongside their leader. They put their massive arms around the heads of the security guards and quickly pulled them away. Having freed Eddie and Ben, the man in the green jacket took them both away from the stairs along the balcony wall. The other team members then rallied around them. They were able to hold the crowd off for a while, but they were being quickly over run on every side. Bravely Eddie joined in the defence, even with the injuries that he had already sustained in the staff room. Before long, they found themselves at the end of the corridor and pressed up against the security door that led into the first-floor car park.

In front of him, there was furious fighting. Punches were being thrown both ways and many of the faces were bloodied and bruised. Then suddenly, Eddie fell down. He had been hit by a police baton on the head and it had stunned him; making him fall backwards. He managed to catch his friend and lower him to the ground. The team of men were getting pushed backwards and there was very little room left. Ben looked up at the man in the green jacket who was severely bruised around his left eye.

'Right, mate! This is it! We can't hold them off much longer. You have to go now!' He looked at Eddie who was slowly coming around from his fall and then he froze. Seeing that Ben wasn't moving, the man in the green jacket decided to take action. He broke away from the fighting and with one hand holding off a security guard, he lifted him onto his feet by his collar and bundled him through the door to the car park and then pulled the door closed behind him.

Chapter 27
Lights Out

Such was the force with which he was pushed with that he couldn't help but fall backward onto the cold concrete floor of the carpark as the door in front of him slammed shut. He gave himself a few seconds to lie on his back and gather his senses. He could still hear the rumbling of noise from the other side of the door, but now that he was in the carpark, there was an eerie sense of calm. The air was much cooler in the carpark and despite the noise from the other side of the door, there was a strange silence. He was about to get up when he could hear footsteps coming towards him. He immediately got up to see who it was, but as soon as he got to his feet, he found himself lying on the ground again in a bit of a daze. Initially he thought that he had tried to get up too quickly and lost his balance. The thought of such a clumsy action actually made him smile to himself, but the smile quickly disappeared. As he looked at the ceiling from where he was lying, a face suddenly appeared standing over him; it was Sister Montgomery! It was then that he realised why he had fallen over a second time. It wasn't anything to do with a loss of balance at all, but more to do with the fact that Sister Montgomery was holding a fire extinguisher in her hand. As she stood over him, looking down at him, his first instinct was to get up and run away, but for some reason he wasn't able to move his legs. It was then that he could also feel a warm sensation around the back of his head. There was nothing he could do and he began to feel afraid.

'So, you thought you could just run away, did you!' said Sister Montgomery in a low but menacing voice. For some reason, she kept the fire extinguisher in her hands as she stood over him.

'You thought you could just come into my hospital and cause mayhem and just walk away!' Her voice got a little louder now and she began to pace a little; up and down from the spot where he was lying.

'I have worked here for twenty years! Twenty Years! And I have done my duty and I have done my exams and I have got to this position and you just think that you can walk in here and act like God! You're just a porter! She was getting more and more worked up and was almost screaming. At the same time, he was feeling more and more helpless. He couldn't move and he could feel himself getting colder. If there was ever a time when he needed his friends, this was it! But for now, he was at the mercy of Sister Montgomery and she was not there to help him.

'Do you know what your problem is, Mr Archer? You have no respect!' she continued with real anger in her voice.

'You come into this hospital and everything is working great! The doctors and nurses are working together; the professionals are working together; and you have no respect for that! No respect!' She was shouting again and it was making him more afraid. He could sense that he was in serious trouble if he didn't get medical help quickly. Where was the Sender? Why was he not helping? He needed someone to protect him against this rampant hatred, but there was no stopping it! Sister Montgomery continued to pace up and down and was getting increasingly agitated.

'You've brought ruin on this hospital!' she screamed! This was a respectable hospital before you came along! And now it's a circus!' she screamed again; but this time with a notable rasp in her breathing. 'You're a disgrace! You're a disgrace!' She kept on shouting, but the breathing was becoming more and more laboured. She took one hand off the fire extinguisher to get her inhaler from her pocket and quickly put it too her mouth. She inhaled from it vigorously, but it was no use, she was going into a full asthma attack. In a fit of rage, she threw the inhaler away and began swinging the fire extinguisher in his direction. He put his arms up to defend himself and managed to protect himself from the first couple of blows. He should have been even more afraid at this point, but there was also confusion in his mind. He simply did not understand where all this hatred was coming from. This woman was in need of help herself, but rather than get help she was determined to keep on hurting him.

However, her ability to keep up this attack was quickly waning. The breathing was becoming more and more laboured, to the point that she was reduced to a wheeze. The fire extinguisher was dropped to the ground and now she was leaning on it as a support. He looked at her as she fell to her knees. She looked at where he was lying and her face was filled with fear. Gone was the anger and the bitterness that had filled her whole being just a moment ago. Instead, she was now reaching out to the person that she had just been attacking. Her breathing had almost stopped now and her whole chest was convulsing in a desperate attempt to get air into her lungs. She was now completely slumped over the fire extinguisher. Eventually, even it gave way and she landed with some force on her front with her face on the ground and arms outstretched. After all the fury of the last few minutes, both on this side of the door and the other, there they both lay at the edge of life; both looking at each other and both helpless. Whatever their differences were in the past, they were now irrelevant. They were both watching each other die; both facing the same fate. He could feel himself getting colder and colder and he could see Sister Montgomery's face becoming blue with lack of oxygen. There was a slight noise coming from her mouth that suggested her lungs were still vainly trying to work, but her full consciousness was gone.

For a period of time, it seemed like he was floating in and out consciousness, but then suddenly something changed. He could feel his body getting warmer and for a moment he could actually feel the sensation that he got when he was healing other people. There was that pins and needles feeling all over his body and he could feel all his fear disappearing. It was the most wonderful feeling of indescribable peace that he had ever experienced. And yet, at the same time, he could actually see his own blood flowing away from his body along the ground. If the Sender was going to save him, then this flow of blood was going to have to be stopped! But it didn't stop! In fact, it kept on flowing; and as it slowly trickled along the ground, it got closer and closer to the outstretched and motionless hand of Sister Montgomery. His whole attention was now on this flow of his own blood towards this dying woman. It was almost as if he was right there at the forefront of where his blood was going. And then there was contact! His blood touched the tips of her fingers and as it touched them, he felt another surge of warmth and tingling through his body. He felt even better than before but his body still didn't move. However, the body of the Sister did! Within a few seconds of his blood touching her, her eyes suddenly opened wide and she took an enormous gasp of air. Her eyes automatically filled with tears and her breathing became frantic, as if she was in a panic. She was obviously confused and disorientated, but she still didn't move. Perhaps she was still too weak from the lack of oxygen. He looked at her and she looked and him. Neither of them was able to speak and even if they could, he wasn't sure that they would know what to say. But before any conversation could develop, something happened that would separate them forever.

It started as a bit of a blur in his vision and both of them blinked as if to clear their eyes. But then the mist began to thicken in front of them and before long, there was a definite gathering of smoke or cloud that filled the carpark. The Sender was here! Suddenly the smoke was so thick that he couldn't see anything. He could hear Sister Montgomery's breathing getting louder, but this was soon overtaken by a whole variety of other noises. The first noise that came clearly through the smoke was the fire alarm going off throughout the whole building. It was a piercing alarm that was accompanied by flashing red lights that appeared at various points around the carpark. This noise was then added to by the pounding of fists on the door into the carpark from the hospital. Having seen the smoke coming from under the door to the carpark, Eddie was desperate to get to his friend. This was made easier to hear by the fact that all the other noise from behind the door had suddenly disappeared. The fire alarm and the sight of smoke had clearly started an evacuation of the building in the other direction. But like a true friend, Eddie was not going to give up that easily. He was determined to get into the carpark and was bashing against the door with all his might. He thought about how wonderful it would be to see Eddie and all his other friends after this incredible day was over. But just as he was thinking that, it felt like someone else had got to him first. There was the feeling of someone putting their arms around his back and his legs and lifting him up. His first thought was that it must be a fire man who had arrived on the scene without him seeing. But as he looked around, there was no fireman to be seen. Whatever it was that was lifting him was invisible. And it wasn't just lifting him up to chest height, it was lifting him much higher.

He was still trying to figure out the reason behind his elevation when suddenly the door to the hospital burst open wide and Eddie rushed in. The smoke began to clear a little now and not far behind Eddie, all his other friends appeared. Dr Kanu and Enid followed closely behind Eddie and hobbling in behind them was Mark who had the injured Mo's arm hanging over his shoulder for support. All of them had ignored the fire alarm so that they could be with their friend. It was the greatest expression of love that he had ever seen! Immediately he wanted to go to them and speak to them, but he couldn't; all he could do was watch them. As soon as Eddie saw Sister Montgomery lying on the ground next to a pool of blood, he rushed over to her and knelt down beside her.

As soon as she saw him, she flinched, as if startled by an attacker. Her eyes were wide with fear and she bolted herself upright and immediately shuffled backwards to sit against the nearby wall. She put her bloodstained hands to her mouth in horror and looked straight ahead with a dead stare.

'Sister Montgomery! What happened? Where's Ben?' Eddie said in a sympathetic yet clear voice. There was no answer from the Sister. Dr Kanu and Enid then rushed over to give Sister Montgomery some medical care. Dr Kanu quickly lifted out her eye torch and shone it in the Sister's eyes. 'Sister Montgomery, can you hear me? Sister Montgomery! Do you know where you are?' All three of them were kneeling down around the Sister and were looking at her face that was staring straight ahead; still with her hands fastened to her mouth in shock.

'Ah, guys, I think you need to look at this!' said Mo in a rather confused tone. He and Mark were standing a few feet away from where the others were crouched around Sister Montgomery and while Mark was observing what was going on in front of him, Mo was looking in the other direction. He was looking at the opposing wall that Sister Montgomery had been staring at since she sat up. Immediately they all looked to see what Mo was drawing their attention to. Suddenly they could see why Sister Montgomery had such a horrified look on her face. There was something written on the wall in front of her. And it wasn't like any writing that they had ever seen. It was as if the writing had been burned onto the wall with a blow torch, but the writing was plain to read.

'I will send another,' whispered Enid.

'I will send another,' repeated Mark in a louder voice.

For a moment, they all stayed where they were and just looked at the writing. Some repeated it to themselves and others remained silent. 'What does it mean?' Mo asked; turning to Eddie. 'Where is Ben?' he asked with tears in his eyes; sensing the worst.

'I think he's gone!' said Eddie; choking with the emotion of this admission. Eddie slumped down against the wall beside Sister Montgomery. 'I should have stayed with him!' he mumbled, shaking his head.

'No, Eddie! You did all that you could!' said Dr Kanu as she leaned over and put her hand on Eddie's shoulder.

'He really is gone, isn't he!' said Mo to those who were now all sitting on the ground. Eddie lifted his head,

'Yes, he is! The Sender has taken him away.' Eddie announced with some certainty.

'But where?' Mark interjected. Eddie took a deep breath; 'I guess we just have to wait and see, mate!' he sighed. Suddenly Eddie got to his feet. 'We just have to wait for the next one to be sent!' Eddie declared, this time with even more certainty.

At this point, the fire fighters arrived. A team of about four were led by a man with a broad moustache and short brown hair. 'Hey, guys, why did you not leave the building? Did you not hear the alarms going off?' Mark was the first to come up with an answer.

'Oh yes, we did, but we had to find our friends. Then the firefighter saw the large pool of blood on the floor and Sister Montgomery with the blood on her hands.

'Oh my!' he exclaimed. 'What happened here? Is she alright?' he said as he looked towards Dr Kanu.

'Oh yes! She's fine! Just in shock.' explained Dr Kanu, calmly. The fire fighter shook his head in confusion.

'Well, I'll tell ya; this is one strange case! You wanna hear all the stories that are going around amongst the crowd outside! Talk about people being healed, paralysed people walking and even sick kids making miraculous recoveries! I've never heard anything like it in all my life! And then this fire that doesn't seem to have any source at all! I tell ya, I can't wait to see how all of this gets explained!'

'Yeah, you and me both!' piped up Mo with a smile.

'But we have hope!' added Enid to everyone's surprise.

'Yes! Hope!' echoed Dr Kanu; getting to her feet and helping Enid up as well.

'We will hope and we will wait!' declared Eddie; summing up the feeling in the group. Mo laughed, with a little more cheer now in his face!

'And who knows who we will meet along the way!'

The End